# Paris for One and
# Other Stories

# Paris for One and Other Stories

JOJO MOYES

PENGUIN BOOKS

PENGUIN BOOKS

UK | USA | Canada | Ireland | Australia
India | New Zealand | South Africa

Penguin Books is part of the Penguin Random House group of companies
whose addresses can be found at global.penguinrandomhouse.com.

'Paris for One' was first published in Penguin Books, 2015; 'Between the Tweets' was
first broadcast on Radio 4, 2011; 'Love in the Afternoon' was first broadcast on
Radio 4, 2010; 'A Bird in the Hand' was first published in *Woman & Home*, 2009;
'Crocodile Shoes' was first published in *Woman & Home*, 2011; 'Holdups' was first broadcast
on Radio 4, 2014; 'Honeymoon in Paris' was first published in digital in Penguin Books, 2012;
'Last Year's Coat' was first published in *The Coffee Shop Book Club* by Orion, 2013; 'Thirteen
Days with John C' was first published in *The Book Lovers' Appreciation Society* by Orion, 2009;
'Margot' was first published in *Stylist,* 2014; 'The Christmas List' was first
published in digital by Bragelonne, 2014

First published in 2016
First published in Great Britain in this edition 2017
Published in Penguin Books 2017
001

Copyright © Jojo's Mojo Ltd, 2016

The moral right of the author has been asserted

Set in 11.21/13.10 pt Garamond MT Std
Typeset by Jouve (UK), Milton Keynes
Printed in Great Britain by Clays Ltd, St Ives plc

A CIP catalogue record for this book is available from the British Library

B FORMAT ISBN: 978–1–405–92816–8
OM PAPERBACK ISBN: 978–0–718–18974–7

www.greenpenguin.co.uk

For my mother, Lizzie Sanders

# Contents

# Paris for One

# I

Nell shifts her bag along the plastic seating in the station and checks the clock on the wall for the eighty-ninth time. Her gaze flicks back as the door from Security slides open. Another family – clearly Disney bound – walks through into the departure lounge, with baby stroller, screaming children, and parents who have been awake way too long.

For the last half hour, her heart has been thumping, a sick feeling high in her chest.

'He will come. He will still come. He can still make it,' she mutters under her breath.

'Train 9051 to Paris will be leaving from Platform Two in ten minutes. Please make your way to the platform. Remember to take all luggage with you.'

She chews her lip, then texts him again – the fifth time.

Where are you? Train about to leave!

She had texted him twice as she set off, checking that they were still meeting at the station. When he didn't answer, she told herself it was because she had been on the Underground. Or he had. She sends a third text, and a fourth. And then, as she stands there, her

3

phone vibrates in her hand and she almost buckles with relief.

Sorry, babe. Stuck at work. Not going to make it.

As if they had planned to catch up over a quick drink. She stares at the phone in disbelief.

Not going to make this train? Shall I wait?

And, seconds later, the reply:

No, you go. Will try for later train.

She is too shocked to be angry. She stands still as people get to their feet around her, pulling on coats, and punches out a reply.

But where will we meet?

He doesn't answer. *Stuck at work*. It's a surf- and scuba-wear shop. In November. How stuck can he be?

She gazes around her, as if this might still be a joke. As if he will, even now, burst through the doors with his broad smile, telling her that he was teasing her (he is a bit too fond of teasing her). And he will take her arm, kiss her cheek with wind-chilled lips, and say something like, 'You didn't think I'd miss this, did you? Your first trip to Paris?'

But the glass doors stay firmly shut.

'Madam? You need to go to the platform.' The Euro-star guard reaches for her ticket. And for a second she hesitates – *will he come?* – and then she is in the crowd, her

4

little wheeled case trailing behind her. She stops and types:

Meet me at the hotel, then.

She heads down the escalator as the huge train roars into the station.

'What do you mean, you're not coming? We've planned this for ages.' It is the annual Girls' Trip to Brighton. They have travelled there, on the first weekend of November, every year for six years – Nell, Magda, Trish and Sue – piled into Sue's old four-wheel drive or Magda's company car. They would escape their daily lives for two nights of drinking, hanging out with the lads from stag weekends, and nursing hangovers over cooked breakfasts in a tatty hotel called Brightsea Lodge, its outside cracked and faded, the scent of its interior suffused with decades of drink and cheap aftershave.

The annual trip has survived two babies, one divorce, and a case of shingles (they spent the first night partying in Magda's hotel room instead). Nobody has ever missed one.

'Well, Pete's invited me to go to Paris.'

'Pete is taking you to Paris?' Magda had stared at her as if she'd announced she was learning to speak Russian. '*Pete* Pete?'

'He says he can't believe I've never been.'

'I went to Paris once, on a school trip. I got lost in the Louvre, and someone put my sneaker down a toilet in the youth hostel,' said Trish.

'I snogged a French boy because he looked like that bloke who goes out with Halle Berry. Turned out he was actually German.'

'*Pete-with-the-hair* Pete? *Your* Pete? I'm not trying to be mean. I just thought he was a bit of a . . .'

'Loser,' said Sue helpfully.

'Knob.'

'Prat.'

'Obviously we're wrong. Turns out he's the kind of bloke who takes Nell on romantic weekends to Paris. Which is . . . you know. Great. I just wish it wasn't the same long weekend as *our* long weekend.'

'Well, once we'd got the tickets . . . it was difficult . . .' Nell mumbled with a wave of her hand, hoping nobody would ask who had actually purchased these tickets. (It had been the only weekend left before Christmas when the discount had applied.)

She had planned the trip as carefully as she organized her office paperwork. She had searched the Internet for the best places to go, scanning TripAdvisor for the best budget hotels, cross-checking each one on Google, and entering the results on a spreadsheet.

She had settled on a place behind the rue de Rivoli – 'clean, friendly, very romantic' – and booked an 'executive double room' for two nights. She pictured herself and Pete tangled up in a French hotel bed, gazing out the window at the Eiffel Tower, holding hands over croissants and coffee in some street café. She was only really going on pictures: she didn't have much idea what you did on a weekend in Paris, apart from the obvious.

At the age of twenty-six, Nell Simmons had never been away for a weekend with a boyfriend, unless you counted that time she went rock-climbing with Andrew Dinsmore. He had made them sleep in his Mini, and she woke up so cold that she couldn't move her neck for six hours.

Nell's mother, Lilian, was fond of telling anyone who would listen that Nell was 'not the adventurous type'. She was also 'not the type to travel', 'not the kind of girl who can rely on her looks', and now, occasionally, if her mother thought Nell was out of earshot, 'no spring chicken'.

That was the thing about growing up in a small town – everyone thought they knew exactly what you were. Nell was the sensible one. The quiet one. The one who would carefully research any plan and who could be trusted to water your plants, mind your kids, and not run off with anyone's husband.

No, Mother. What I really am, Nell thought as she printed off the tickets, gazing at them, then tucking them into a folder with all the important information, is the kind of girl who goes to Paris for the weekend.

As the big day grew nearer, she started to enjoy dropping it into conversation. 'Got to make sure my passport is up-to-date,' she said when she left her mother after Sunday lunch. She bought new underwear, shaved her legs, painted her toenails a vivid shade of red (she usually went for clear). 'Don't forget I'm leaving early on Friday,' she said at work. 'You know. For Paris.'

'Oh, you're so lucky,' chorused the girls in Accounts.

'I'm well jell,' said Trish, who disliked Pete slightly less than everyone else.

Nell climbs on to the train and stows her bag, wondering how 'jell' Trish would be if she could see her now: a girl beside an empty seat going to Paris with no idea whether her boyfriend was even going to turn up.

# 2

The Gare du Nord in Paris is teeming. She emerges through the platform gates and is frozen to the spot, standing in the middle of crowds of people, all pushing and shoving, wheeled cases crashing into her shins. Groups of youths in tracksuit tops stare sullenly from the sidelines, and she remembers suddenly that the Gare du Nord is the pickpocketing epicenter of France. Her handbag clamped to her side, she walks tentatively in one direction and then the other, temporarily lost among the glass kiosks and escalators that seem to lead nowhere.

A three-note chime sounds on the loudspeaker, and the station announcer says something in French that Nell can't understand. Everyone else is walking briskly, as if they know where they're going. It is dark outside, and she feels panic rising like a bubble in her chest. *I'm in a strange city, and I don't even speak the language.* And then she sees the suspended sign: TAXIS.

The queue is fifty people long, but she doesn't care. She scrabbles in her bag for the hotel printout, and when she finally reaches the front of the queue, she holds it out. 'Hôtel Bonne Ville,' she says. 'Um . . . *s'il vous plaît.*'

The driver looks back at her as if he cannot understand what she says.

'Hôtel Bonne Ville,' she says, trying to sound French (she had practised at home in front of the mirror). She tries again. *'Bonne Ville.'*

He looks blank and snatches the piece of paper from her. He stares at it for a moment.

'Ah! Hôtel Bonne Ville!' he says, lifting his eyes to heaven. He thrusts the piece of paper back at her and pulls into the heavy traffic.

Nell sits back in the seat and lets out a long breath.

*And . . . welcome to Paris.*

The journey, hobbled by traffic, takes twenty long, expensive minutes. She gazes out the window at the busy streets, the hairdressers and nail bars, repeating the French road signs under her breath. The elegant grey buildings rise high into the city sky, and the coffee shops glow in the winter night. Paris, she thinks, and with a sudden, unexpected surge of excitement, she feels suddenly that it will be okay. Pete will come later. She will be waiting for him at the hotel, and tomorrow they will laugh at how worried she was about travelling alone. He always said she was too much of a worrier.

*Chill out, babe*, he will say. Pete never got stressed about anything. He'd travelled the world with his backpack and still carried his passport in his pocket – 'just in case.' When he'd been held up at gunpoint in Laos, he said, he'd just chilled. 'No point getting stressed about it. Either they were going to shoot me or they weren't. Nothing I could do about it.' Then he nodded. 'We ended up going for a beer with those guys.'

Or there was the time when he was on a small ferry in Kenya, which overturned, mid-river. 'We just cut the tires off the sides of the boat and hung on till help came. I was pretty chill about that, too – till they told me there were crocodiles in the water.'

She sometimes wondered why Pete, with his tanned features and his endless life experiences (even if the girls sniffed at them), had chosen her. She wasn't flashy or wild. In fact, she had barely been beyond her own post-code. He once told her he liked her because she didn't give him a hard time. 'Other girlfriends are like this in my ear.' He mimed a yapping motion with his hand. 'You . . . well, you're relaxing to be with.'

Nell occasionally wondered if this made her sound a bit like a Furniture Warehouse sofa, but it was probably best not to question these things too hard.

*Paris.*

She winds down the window, taking in the sounds of the busy streets, the scent of perfume, coffee and smoke, the breeze catching and lifting her hair. It is just as she'd pictured it. The buildings are tall, with long windows and little balconies – there are no office blocks. Every street corner seems to have a café with round tables and chairs outside. And as the taxi heads further into the city, the women look more stylish and people are greeting each other with kisses as they stop on the pavement.

I'm actually here, she thinks. And suddenly she is

grateful that she has a couple of hours to freshen up before Pete arrives. For once she does not want to be the wide-eyed innocent.

I'm going to be *Parisian*, she tells herself, and sinks back in her seat.

The hotel is in a narrow street off a main boulevard. She counts out the euros according to the sum on the taxi's meter and hands them to the driver. But instead of taking the money, the driver acts as if she has insulted him, waving towards her suitcase in the boot, grimacing and gesticulating.

'I'm sorry. I don't understand,' she says.

'*La valise!*' he yells. And follows up with something else in rapid-fire French that she cannot understand.

'The guide said this journey should be thirty euros max. I looked it up.'

More yelling and gesticulating. After a pause she nods, as if she has understood, then anxiously thrusts another ten euros at him. He takes the money, shakes his head, then dumps her suitcase on the pavement. She stands there as he drives off and wonders if she has just been ripped off.

But the hotel looks nice. And she's here! In Paris! She decides that she will not let anything upset her. She walks in and finds herself in a narrow lobby infused with the scents of beeswax and something else that she decides is indefinably French. The walls are panelled wood, the armchairs old but elegant. All the door handles are brass.

Already she's wondering what Pete will think of it. *Not bad,* he will say, nodding. *Not bad, babe.*

'Hello,' she says, nervous, and then, because she has no idea how to say it in French, *'Parlez anglais?* I have booked a room.'

Another woman has arrived behind her, huffing and puffing as she scrabbles in her bag for her own paperwork.

'Yeah. I have a room booked, too.' She slaps her own paperwork on the desk beside Nell's. Nell shifts to the side and tries not to feel crowded.

'Ugh. I have had a *nightmare* getting here. *A nightmare.*' The woman is American. 'Paris traffic is the *pits.*'

The receptionist is in her forties, with short, well-cut black hair in a Louise Brooks bob. She glances up at the two women with a frown. 'You both have bookings?'

She leans forward and examines the bits of paper. Then she pushes each one towards its owner. 'But I have only one room left. We are fully booked.'

'That's impossible. You confirmed the booking.' The American woman pushes the paper back at her. 'I booked it last week.'

'So did I,' says Nell. 'I booked mine two weeks ago. Look, you can see on my printout.'

The two women stare at each other, suddenly aware that they are in competition.

'I am sorry. I do not know how you each have this booking. We only have one room.' The Frenchwoman manages to make it sound as if it is their fault.

'Well, you will have to find us another room,' says the woman. 'You must honour the bookings. Look, there they are in black and white.'

The Frenchwoman lifts a perfectly plucked eyebrow. 'Madame. I cannot give you what I do not have. There is one room, with twin beds. I can offer one of you a refund, but I do not have two rooms.'

'But I can't go anywhere else. I'm meant to be meeting someone,' says Nell. 'He won't know where I am.'

'I'm not moving,' says the American, folding her arms. 'I have just flown six thousand miles, and I have a dinner to go to. I have no time to find somewhere else.'

'Then you may share the room. I can offer each of you a discount of fifty per cent.'

'Share a room with a stranger? You have got to be kidding me,' says the American.

'Then I suggest you find another hotel,' says the receptionist coolly, and she turns to answer a telephone.

Nell and the American woman stare at each other. The American woman says, 'I have just got off a flight from Chicago.'

Nell says, 'I've never been to Paris before. I don't know where I would find another hotel.'

Neither of them moves. Nell says finally, 'Look – my boyfriend is going to be meeting me here. We could both take our cases up for now, and when he arrives, I'll see if he can find us another hotel. He knows Paris better than I do.'

The American woman looks her up and down slowly, as if working out whether to trust her. 'I'm not sharing with two of you.'

Nell holds her gaze. 'Believe me, that is not my idea of a fun weekend away either.'

'I don't suppose we have a lot of choice,' the woman says. 'I can't believe this is happening.'

They inform the receptionist of their plan, the American woman with disproportionate irritation, Nell thinks, considering that Nell has basically just given her the room. 'And when this lady leaves, I still want my fifty per cent discount,' the woman is saying. 'This whole thing is shameful. You would never get away with service like this where I come from.'

Nell wonders if she has ever been more uncomfortable, trapped between the Frenchwoman's lack of interest and the American's boiling resentment. She tries to imagine what Pete would do. He would laugh, take it all in his stride. His ability to laugh at life is one of the things she finds attractive about him. It's fine, she tells herself. They will joke about this later.

They take the key and share a tiny lift up to the third floor. Nell walks behind. The door opens on to an attic room with two beds.

'Oh,' says the American. 'No bath. I hate that there's no bath. And it's so *small*.'

Nell drops her bag. She sits on the end of the bed and texts Pete to tell him what's happened and ask if he can find another hotel.

I'll wait here for you. Can you let me know whether you'll arrive in time for supper? Am quite hungry.

It is already eight o'clock.

He doesn't respond. She wonders if he is in the Channel tunnel: if he is, he is at least an hour and a half away. She sits in silence as the American woman huffs and puffs and opens her suitcase on the bed, taking all the hangers as she hangs up her clothes.

'Are you here on business?' says Nell when the silence becomes too heavy.

'Two meetings. One tonight and then a day off. I haven't had a day off this whole month.' The American says this as if it is Nell's fault. 'And tomorrow I have to be on the other side of Paris. Right. I've got to go out now. I'm going to trust that you won't touch my stuff.'

Nell fixes her with a look. 'I'm not going to touch your stuff.'

'I don't mean to be rude. It's just I'm not in the habit of sharing rooms with total strangers. When your boyfriend arrives, I'd be glad if you could hand in your key downstairs.'

Nell tries not to show her anger. 'I'll do that,' she says, and picks up her book, pretending to read as, with a backward glance, the American leaves the room. And it is just at this moment that her phone beeps. Nell snatches it up.

Sorry, babe. Not going to get there. Have a great trip.

# 3

Fabien sits on the rooftop, pulls his wool hat further down over his eyes, and lights another cigarette. It is the spot where he always used to smoke when there was a chance that Sandrine would come home unexpectedly. She hadn't liked the smell, and if he smoked inside, she used to screw up her nose and say that the studio apartment smelled disgusting.

It is a narrow ledge, but big enough for a tall man and a mug of coffee and 332 pages of handwritten manuscript. In summer he sometimes naps out here, and he waves daily to the teenage twins across the square. They sit on their own flat roof to listen to music and smoke, away from the gaze of their parents.

Central Paris is full of such spaces. If you don't have a garden or a tiny balcony, you find your outside space where you can.

Fabien picks up his pencil and starts crossing out words. He has been editing this manuscript for six months, and the lines of writing are thick with pencil marks. Every time he reads his novel, he sees more faults.

The characters are flat, their voices fake. Philippe, his friend, says he has to get a move on, get it typed and give it to the agent who is interested. But every time he looks at it, he sees more reasons he cannot show anyone his book.

It is not ready.

Sandrine said he didn't want to hand it over because until he did, he could still tell himself he had hope. It was one of the less cruel things she'd said.

He checks his watch, knowing he has only an hour before he has to start his shift. And then he hears his mobile phone ringing from inside. Damn! He curses himself for forgetting to tuck it into his pocket before coming out on to the roof. He balances his mug on the pile of pages, to stop them from blowing away, and turns to clamber back in through the window.

Afterwards he is not sure quite what happened. His right foot slips on the desk that he uses to climb back in, and his left foot shoots backward as he tries to keep himself from falling. And his foot – his great clumsy foot, as Sandrine would call it – kicks the mug and the pages off the ledge. He turns in time to hear the mug smash on the cobbles below and to watch 332 carefully edited white pages fly out into the darkening skies.

He watches as his pages catch the wind and, like white doves, float into the streets of Paris.

# 4

Nell has spent an hour lying on the bed, and she still cannot work out what to do. Pete is not coming to Paris. He is actually not coming. She has travelled all the way to the capital of France, with new underwear and painted red toenails, and Pete has stood her up.

For the first ten minutes, she had stared at the message – its cheery 'Have a great trip' – and waited for more. But there is no more.

She lies on the bed, her phone still in her hand, staring at the wall. She realizes that some part of her has always known this might happen. She peers at the phone, flicks the screen on and off, just to make sure she is not dreaming.

But she knows. She probably knew it last night, when he didn't respond to her calls. She might even have known it last week, when all her ideas for what they might do in Paris were met with, 'Yeah, whatever' or 'I don't know.'

It was not just that Pete was an unreliable boyfriend – in fact, he quite frequently disappeared without telling her where he was going. If she was honest with herself, he hadn't actually invited her to Paris at all. They had been talking about places they'd been, and she had admitted that she'd never been to Paris, and he'd said, vaguely, 'Really? Oh, Paris is awesome. You'd love it.'

Two days later she had emerged from her monthly risk-assessment presentation to potential graduates ('Risk assessment plays a vital role in helping organizations understand and manage risk, in order to avoid problems and capitalize on opportunities! Enjoy your tour around the factory floor – and be careful near that machinery!') and found the sandwich trolley outside in the hallway. It had arrived at least ten minutes early. She had gazed at the selection, mentally totting up the pros and cons, and then eventually settled on a salmon and cream cheese, even though it was a Tuesday, and she never bought salmon and cream cheese on a Tuesday.

'What the heck. We got a bonus this week, right? Let's push the boat out,' she had said cheerily to Carla, who pushed the trolley. And then she'd walked to the office kitchen, stopping outside to get some water from the dispenser, and as she paused to fill her cup, she'd found herself listening in on a conversation between two of her co-workers on the other side of the wall.

'I'm going to spend mine on a trip to Barcelona. I've been promising to take my wife since we got married.' It sounded like Jim from Logistics.

'Shari's buying one of them fancy handbags. That girl will blow her bonus in two days.'

'Lesley's putting hers towards a car. Nell?'

'Nell ain't going to Barcelona.'

They had both laughed. Nell, her plastic cup half raised to her lips, had frozen.

'Nell will put it in a savings account. Maybe after doing a spreadsheet. It takes that girl half an hour to choose between types of sandwich.'

'"Should I go for the ham on rye? But it's Tuesday, and I usually have ham on rye on Friday. Maybe I'll go for the cream cheese. I usually have cream cheese on a Monday. But heck, let's push the boat out!"' They had laughed again at the crude imitation of her voice. Nell looked down at her sandwich.

'Man, that girl has never had a wild moment in her life.'

She only ate half her sandwich, even though she loved salmon and cream cheese. It had tasted oddly gummy in her mouth.

That night she went to her mother's. After years of pre-varication, Lilian had finally admitted that the house was too big for one person and had agreed to move, but pry-ing her from the place where she'd lived for twenty-five years was a little like prying a snail from its shell. Twice a week Nell would arrive to go through the boxes of memorabilia or clothes or paperwork piled high on shelves around the old house and try to persuade her mother to let at least some of them go. Mostly she would spend an hour convincing her mother that she didn't need a straw donkey from a Majorcan holiday in 1983, then emerge from the bathroom at the end of the night to find that her mother had snuck it back into her spare room. It was going to be a lengthy process. Tonight it was postcards and baby clothes. Lost in memories, Lilian held up each one, wondering aloud whether they 'might find another use someday'.

'Oh, you did look lovely in this little dress. Even with your knees. That reminds me – you know Donna Jackson from the nail bar? Her daughter Cheryl went on one of those Internet dating things. Well, she went out with this man, and when she went back to his apartment, his shelves were full of books about serial killers.'

'And was he?' said Nell, trying to shove some moth-eaten wool baby cardigans into a bag while her mother was distracted.

'Was he what?'

'A serial killer.'

'Well, how would I know?'

'Mum, did Cheryl come home again?'

Lilian folded the dress and put it to one side on her 'keep' pile.

'Oh, sure. She told Donna he wanted her to wear a mask or a furry tail or something, so she blew him.'

'She blew him off, Mum. Off.'

'Oh, what's the difference? Anyway, I'm glad you're a sensible girl and don't take risks. Oh, did I tell you, Mrs Hogan asked would you feed her cat when she goes away?'

'Okay.'

'Because I'll have moved by then. And she said she needs someone completely reliable.'

Nell had stared at the little pair of shorts in her hands for a long time before shoving them into the bin bag with unnecessary savagery.

The next morning she was walking across the concourse to work when she'd paused outside the travel agent's. A sign in the window said ONE DAY ONLY, SPECIAL DEAL – 2 FOR ONE – THREE NIGHTS IN PARIS – CITY OF LIGHTS. Almost before she knew what she was doing, she had walked in and bought two tickets. She had presented Pete with them, glowing half with embarrassment, half with pleasure, the next night when they'd gone back to his place.

'You did what?' He'd been drunk, she remembered now, and had blinked slowly, as if in disbelief. 'You bought me a ticket to Paris?'

'Us,' she'd said as he fumbled with the buttons of her dress. 'A long weekend in Paris. I thought it would be . . . fun. We should, you know, go crazy!'

*That girl has never had a wild moment in her life.*

'I checked out hotels, and I've found one just behind rue de Rivoli. It's three-star, but it has a ninety-four-per cent satisfaction rating, and it's a low-crime area – I mean, the only thing they say to worry about is bag snatchers, so I'll get one of those bu—'

'You bought me a ticket to Paris!' He'd shaken his head, his hair flopping over one eye. And then he said, 'Sure, babe. Why not? Nice one.' She couldn't remember what else he'd said, as at that point they'd collapsed on to his bed.

Now she would have to go back to England and tell

Magda, Trish and Sue that they were right. That Pete was exactly who they said he was. That she'd been a fool and wasted her money. She had blown off the Girls' Trip to Brighton for nothing.

She screws her eyes shut until she is sure that she will not cry, then pushes herself upright. She looks at her suitcase. She wonders where to find a taxi and whether her ticket can be changed. What if she gets to the station and they won't let her on the train? She wonders whether to ask the receptionist downstairs if she will ring Eurostar for her, but she is afraid of the woman's icy gaze. She has no idea what to do. Paris suddenly feels huge and unknown and unfriendly and a million miles from home.

Her phone beeps again. She snatches it up, her heart suddenly racing. He is coming after all! It will be all right! But it's Magda.

Having fun, you filthy mare?

She blinks at it and suddenly feels horribly homesick. She wishes she were there, in Magda's hotel room, a plastic cup of cheap fizz on the bathroom sink as they fight for mirror space to put on their makeup. England is an hour behind. They will still be getting ready, their suitcases spilling new outfits on to the carpet, the music turned up loud enough to cause complaints.

She thinks, briefly, that she has never felt so lonely in her life.

All great, thanks. Have fun!

She types slowly and presses SEND, waiting for the whooshing sound that tells her it has flown across the English Channel. And then she turns off her phone so that she won't have to lie anymore.

Nell examines the Eurostar timetable, pulls her notebook from her bag, and writes a list, working out her options. It is a quarter to nine. Even if she makes it to the station, she is unlikely to get a train that will take her back to England early enough for her to get home. She will have to stay here tonight.

In the harsh light of the bathroom mirror, she looks tired and fed up, her mascara blurred with tears. She looks exactly like the kind of girl who has just travelled all the way to Paris to be stood up by her unreliable boyfriend. She rests her hands on the sink, takes a long, shaky breath, and tries to think clearly.

She will find something to eat, get some sleep, and then she will feel better. Tomorrow she will catch the early train home. It is not what she'd hoped, but it is a plan, and Nell always feels better with a plan.

She shuts the door, locks it, and goes downstairs. She tries to look carefree and confident, like a woman who often finds herself alone in strange cities.

'Um. Do you have a room-service menu? I couldn't find one in my room,' she asks the receptionist.

'Room service? Mademoiselle, you are in the gastronomic capital of the world. We do not do room service here.'

'Okay, well, then do you know anywhere nice I could get a bite to eat?'

The woman looks at her. 'You want a restaurant?'

'Or café. Anything. Somewhere I could walk to. Oh, and . . . um . . . if the other lady comes back, will you tell her I'll be staying this evening?'

The Frenchwoman raises an eyebrow a fraction, and Nell imagines her thinking, So your boyfriend never turned up, mousy English girl? That's no surprise. 'There is Café des Bastides,' she says, handing over a small tourist map. 'You turn right outside, and it's two streets down on the left. It's very nice. Fine to' – she pauses – 'eat alone.'

'Thank you.'

'I will call Michel and make sure he has a table for you. Name?'

'Nell.'

'*Nell.*' The woman pronounces it as if it is an affliction.

Her cheeks flaming, Nell grabs the map, slides it into her handbag, and walks briskly from the hotel lobby.

The café is busy, the tiny round tables outside bulging with couples or groups sitting shoulder to shoulder in thick coats, smoking, drinking, chatting as they look out over the busy street. Nell hesitates and glances up, checking the name on the billboard, and wonders briefly if she can really face sitting in here alone. Perhaps she could just nip into a supermarket and buy a sandwich. Yes, that would probably be the safer option. A huge man with a beard stands in the doorway, and his gaze lands on her. 'The Englishwoman? Yes?' his voice booms out over the tables.

Nell flinches. 'You are NELL? Table for one?' A handful of heads swivel to look at her. Nell ponders whether it is possible to die spontaneously of embarrassment.

'Um. Yes,' she mutters into her chest. He gestures her inside, finds her a small table and chair in a corner by the window, and she slides in. There is a steamy fug on the inside of the windows, and around her the tables hum with well-dressed women in their fifties exclaiming in words she cannot understand, young couples gazing at each other over glasses of wine. She feels self-conscious, as if she is wearing a sign that says PITY ME. I HAVE NOBODY TO EAT WITH. She gazes up at the blackboard, repeating the unfamiliar words in her head several times before she has to speak them aloud.

'*Bonsoir.*' The waiter, who has a shaven head and wears a long white apron, puts a jug of water in front of her. '*Qu'est-ce –*'

'*Je voudrais le steak frites, s'il vous plaît,*' she says in a rush. The meal – steak and chips – is expensive, but it is the only thing she thinks she can pronounce.

The waiter gives a small nod and glances behind him, as if distracted. 'The steak? And to drink, mam'selle?' he says in perfect English. 'Some wine?'

She was going to have Coke. But she whispers, 'Yes, please.'

'*Bon*,' he says. In minutes he is back with a basket of bread and a jug of wine. He puts them down as if it is absolutely normal for a woman to be sitting there on a Friday evening by herself, and then he is gone.

Nell doesn't think she has ever seen a woman sitting alone in a restaurant, apart from that time when she went on a sales trip to Corby and that woman sat alone with her book by the Ladies and ate two desserts instead of a main course. Where Nell lives, girls eat out in groups, mostly curry at the end of a long night's drinking. Older women might go alone to bingo or to a family event. But women don't just go out and eat by themselves.

But as she looks around her now and chews a piece of crusty French bread, she sees that she is not the only single diner. There is a woman on the other side of the window, a jug of red wine on her table, smoking a cigarette as she watches the people of Paris bustle by. There is a man in the corner reading his paper, spooning forkfuls of something into his mouth. Another woman, long hair, a gap in her teeth, is chatting to a waiter, her collar high around her neck. Nobody is paying them any attention. Nell relaxes a little, unwinding her scarf.

The wine is good. She takes a sip and feels the tension of the day start to ooze away. She has another sip. The steak arrives, seared brown and steaming, but when she cuts into it, it is bloody inside. She wonders whether to send it back, but she doesn't want to make a fuss, especially not when it might involve speaking in French.

Besides, it tastes good. The chips are crisp and golden and hot, and the green salad is delicious. She eats it all, surprising herself with her appetite. The waiter, when he returns, smiles at her evident pleasure, as if noticing her for the first time. 'Is good, uh?'

'Delicious,' she says. 'Thank – er, *merci.*' He nods and refills her glass. She feels a brief, unlikely moment of pleasure. But as she reaches for it, she somehow misjudges and knocks half a glass of red wine on to the waiter's apron and shoes. She peers over the table, at the deep red stains.

'I'm so sorry!' Her hands fly to her mouth.

He sighs wearily as he mops at himself with a cloth. 'Really. It's of no matter.'

'I'm sorry. Oh, I –'

'Really. No matter. It has been this kind of a day.'

He gives her a vague smile, as if to say he understands, and disappears.

She feels her cheeks burning red and pulls her notebook from her bag, to give herself something to do. She flicks quickly past her list for sightseeing in Paris and stares at an empty page until she is sure nobody is looking.

'*Live in the moment*,' she writes on the clean page, and underlines it twice. It is something she once saw in a magazine.

She looks up at the clock. It is nine forty-five. Only about 39,600 more ruddy moments, she thinks, and then she can get back on the train and pretend this trip never happened.

The Frenchwoman is still behind the reception desk when Nell returns to the hotel. Of course she is. She slides the key across the counter towards Nell. 'The other lady is not back yet,' the woman says. She pronounces it *ze uzzer.* 'If she returns before I finish, I will let her know you are in the room.'

Nell mutters a thank-you and heads upstairs.

She runs a shower and steps under it, trying to wash away the disappointment of the day. Finally, at half past ten, she climbs into bed and reads one of the French magazines from the bedside table. She doesn't understand most of the words, but she hasn't brought a book. She hadn't expected to spend any time reading.

Finally, at eleven, she turns off the light and lies in the dark, listening to the sound of mopeds whizzing down the narrow streets and to the chatter and bursts of laughter of French people making their way home. She feels as if she has been locked out of a giant party.

Her eyes fill with tears, and she wonders whether to call the girls and tell them what has happened. But she is not ready for their sympathy. She does not let herself think about Pete, and about the fact that she has effectively been dumped. She tries not to imagine her mother's face when she has to tell her the truth about this romantic weekend away.

And then the door opens. The light flicks on.

'I don't believe it.' The American woman stands there, her face flushed with drink, a large purple scarf draped around her shoulders. 'I thought you would be gone.'

'So did I,' said Nell, pulling the covers over her head. 'Would you mind turning down the light, please?'

'They never said you were still here.'

'Well, I am.'

She hears the clunk of a handbag on the table, the rattle of hangers in the wardrobe. 'I do not feel comfortable spending the night with somebody I don't know in the room.'

'Believe me, you were not my first choice for tonight's sleeping companion either.'

Nell stays under the covers while the woman fusses about and goes in and out of the bathroom. Nell hears her scrubbing her teeth, gargling, the flush of a loo through walls that are far too thin. She tries to imagine she is somewhere else. In Brighton, maybe, with one of the girls, drunkenly making her way to bed.

'I might as well tell you, I am not happy,' the woman says.

'Well, sleep somewhere else,' snaps Nell. 'Because I have just as much right to this room as you. More, if you look at the dates on our bookings.'

'There's no need to be snippy,' said the woman.

'Well, there's no need to make me feel worse than I already bloody do.'

'Honey, it's not my fault your boyfriend didn't turn up.'

'And it's not *my* fault the hotel double-booked us.'

There is a long silence. Nell considers that maybe she has been too harsh. It is daft, after all, two women fighting in such a small space. We're in the same boat, she thinks. She tries to come up with something friendly to say.

And then the woman's voice cuts across the dark. 'Well, just so as you know, I'm putting my valuables in the safe. And I am trained in self-defense.'

'And my name is Georges Pompidou,' Nell mutters. She raises her eyes to heaven in the dark and waits for the click that tells her the light has gone out.

'Just for the record,' comes a voice in the darkness. 'That is a really weird name.'

Even though Nell is exhausted and a bit sad, sleep remains annoyingly elusive, approaching and then skittering away like a bashful lover. She tries to relax, to calm her thoughts, but around midnight a voice in her mind says firmly, *Nope. No sleep for you, lady.*

Instead her brain spins and churns like a washing machine, throwing up black thoughts like so much dirty laundry. Had she been too keen with Pete? Was she not cool enough? Was it because of her handwritten list of French art galleries, with their pros and cons (length of journey time versus possible size of queue)?

Was she just too boring for any man to love?

The night drags and sags. She lies in the dark, trying to block her ears against the sound of the stranger snoring in the next bed. She tries stretching, yawning, changing her position. She tries deep breathing, relaxing bits of her body, and imagining her darker thoughts locked in a box and herself throwing away the key.

At around three in the morning, she accepts that she will probably be awake until dawn. She gets up and pads silently over to the window, pulling the curtain a few inches away from the glass.

The rooftops glow under the streetlamps. A light drizzle falls silently on to the pavement. A couple, their heads tilted close, make their way slowly home, murmuring to each other.

This should have been so wonderful, she thinks.

The American woman's snoring grows louder. She snorts, emits a guttural choking sound, and then, after a brief, tantalizing silence, snores again. Nell reaches into her suitcase for earplugs (she's brought two pairs, just in case) and climbs back into bed. I will be home in a little over eight hours, she thinks, and with that comforting thought she finally drifts off to sleep.

## 5

At the café Fabien sits by the kitchen hatch, watching as Émile scrubs at the huge steel pans, with René, a sous-chef, working silently beside him. He is sipping a large coffee, and his shoulders slump. The clock says a quarter to one.

'You'll write another one. It will be better,' says Émile.

'I put everything I had into that book. And now it's all gone.'

'Come on. You say you are a writer. You must have more than one book in your head. If not, you will be a very hungry writer. And maybe next time, do the edits on a computer, yes? Then you can just print out another copy.'

Fabien has found 183 pages of the 300-plus that had blown away. Some of them were blurred with dirt and rainwater, stamped with footprints. Others had disappeared into the Paris evening. As he walked the streets around his home, he spotted the odd page flying into the air or sodden in a gutter, ignored by passersby. Seeing his words out there, his innermost thoughts exposed to view, made him feel as if he were standing in the street stark naked.

'I'm such a fool, Émile. Sandrine told me so many times not to take my work out on the roof . . .'

'Oh, no. Not a Sandrine story. Please!' Émile empties the sink of greasy water and refills it. 'I need some brandy if we are going to have a Sandrine story.'

'You drank all the brandy already,' says René.

'What am I going to do?'

'What your great hero, the writer Samuel Beckett, tells you to do: "Try again. Fail again. Fail better." '

Émile looks up, his brown skin glistening with sweat and steam. 'And I'm not just talking about the book. You need to get out there again. Meet some women. Drink a little, dance a little . . . Find some material for another book!'

'I would read that book,' says René.

'There,' says Émile. 'René will read your book. And he only reads pornography!'

'I don't read the words,' says René.

'We know that, René,' says Émile.

'I don't know. I'm not really in the mood,' Fabien says.

'Then put yourself in the mood!' Émile is like a radiator, always making you feel warmer. 'At least you have a reason to get out of that apartment now, eh? Go and live. Think about something else.'

He finishes the last pan. He stacks it with the others, then flicks the tea towel over his shoulder.

'Okay. Olivier is working his shift tomorrow night, yes? So you and me. Out for some beers. What do you say?'

'I don't know . . .'

'Well, what else are you going to do? Spend the night

35

in your tiny apartment? Monsieur Hollande, our president, on the television will tell you there is no money. Your empty home will tell you there is no woman.'

'You're not making things sound any better, Émile.'

'I am! I am your friend! I am giving you a million reasons to go out with me. Come on, we'll have some laughs. Pick up some bad women. Get arrested.'

Fabien finishes his coffee and hands the cup to Émile, who puts it in the sink.

'Come on. You have to live so that you have something to write about.'

'Maybe,' he says. 'I'll think about it.'

Émile shakes his head as Fabien salutes them and leaves.

# 6

It is the knocking that wakes her. It comes to her at first from a distance, then grows louder, so that she pulls the pillow over her ears. Then she hears a voice. 'Housekeeping.'

*Housekeeping.*

Nell pushes herself upright, blinking, a faint ringing in her ears, and for a moment she has no idea where she is. She stares at the strange bed, then at the wallpaper. There is a muffled rapping sound. She reaches up to her ears and pulls out the plugs. Suddenly the sound is deafening.

She walks over to the door and opens it, rubbing her eyes. 'Hello?'

The woman – in a maid's uniform – apologizes, steps back. *'Ah. Je reviendrai.'*

But Nell has no idea what she has just said. So she nods and lets the door close. She feels like she has been run over. She glances across at the American woman, but there is only an empty bed, the cover ruffled and the wardrobe door hanging open to reveal a row of empty hangers. Panicky, she scans the room for her suitcase, but it is still there.

She hadn't realized that the woman was going to leave

so early, but Nell is relieved not to have to face that cross red face again. Now she can shower in peace and –

She glances down at her phone. It is a quarter past eleven.

It can't be.

She flicks on the television, skipping through until she hits a news channel.

It really is a quarter past eleven.

Suddenly awake, she begins to gather up her things, dumping them into her suitcase, and pulls on her clothes. Then, grabbing the key and her tickets, she runs downstairs. The Frenchwoman is behind the desk, as immaculate as she had been last night. Nell wishes suddenly that she had paused to brush her hair.

'Good morning, Mademoiselle.'

'Good morning. I wondered if you could . . . if . . . Well, I need to change my Eurostar ticket.'

'You would like me to call Eurostar?'

'Please. I need to get home today. A . . . family emergency.'

The woman's face does not flicker. 'Of course.'

She takes the ticket and dials, then speaks in rapid French. Nell runs her fingers through her hair, rubs sleep from her eyes.

'They have nothing until five o'clock. Will this suit you?'

'Nothing at all?'

'There were some spaces on the early trains this morning, but nothing now until five.'

Nell curses herself for sleeping late. 'That's fine.'

'And you will have to buy a new ticket.'

Nell stares at her ticket, which the woman is holding towards her. And there it is in black and white: NON-TRANSFERABLE. 'A new ticket? How much will that be?'

The woman says something, then puts her hand over the receiver. 'One hundred and seventy-eight euros. You want to book it?'

*A hundred and seventy-eight euros. About a hundred and forty pounds.* 'Uh . . . um . . . You know what? I . . . I just have to work something out.'

She dares not look at the woman's face as she takes the ticket back from her. She feels like a fool. Of course a cheap ticket would be nontransferable. 'Thank you so much.' She bolts for the safety of her room, ignoring the woman, who is calling after her.

Nell sits on the end of the bed and swears softly to herself. So she can either pay half a week's wages to get home or carry on alone with the World's Worst Romantic Weekend for one more night. She can hide in this attic room with its French television that she can't understand. She can sit by herself in cafés, trying not to look at all the happy couples.

She decides to make herself a coffee, but there is no kettle in the room.

'Oh, for God's sake,' she says aloud. She decides she hates Paris.

And it is then that she sees a half-open envelope on

the floor, partway under the bed, with something sticking out from it. She bends down and picks it up. It is two tickets to a show by an artist she has vaguely heard of. She turns them over. They must have belonged to the American woman. She puts them down. She'll decide what to do with them later. For now she needs to put on some makeup, brush her hair, and then she really needs to get a coffee.

Outside in the daylight, she feels better. She walks until she sees a café she likes the look of and orders a café au lait and a croissant. She sits out on the street, huddled against the cold, beside several other people who are doing the same thing. She pets the small dog of an elderly woman who sits nearby, her scarf knotted with the precision of Japanese origami. She takes a couple of pictures. A Frenchman tips his hat to her, and she can't help but smile.

The coffee is good and the croissant is delicious. She makes a note of the café's name in her book, in case she wants to come back. She leaves a tip and walks slowly back to the hotel, thinking, Well, I've had worse breakfasts. Across the road there is a handbag shop, and she gazes through the window at the elegant, precision-cut leatherwork, the gorgeous pastel colours. The shop looks like a film set. She stops at the sound of cello music, looking up until she locates the sound, coming through a partially open balcony window. She listens, then sits briefly on the step. It is the most beautiful thing she has ever heard. When the music stops, a girl emerges on to the balcony holding the cello and looks down. Nell stands, suddenly a little embarrassed, and she walks on, deep in thought.

She cannot work out what to do. She walks slowly, debating with herself, scribbling her reasons for and against taking the five-o'clock train into her little notebook. If she got that train, she could actually make the late train down to Brighton and surprise the girls. She could rescue this weekend. She could get blind drunk and confess all, and they would look after her. That was what girlfriends were for.

But the thought of spending another hundred and fifty pounds on an already disastrous weekend makes her heart sink. And she does not want her first trip to Paris to end with her running away, tail between her legs. She does not want to remember the first time she went to Paris as the time she got dumped and ran home without even seeing the Eiffel Tower.

She is still thinking when she arrives at the hotel, so she almost forgets until she reaches into her pocket for the key. And pulls out the American woman's tickets.

'Oh. Excuse me?' she says to the receptionist. 'Do you know what happened to the woman who was sharing my room? Room Forty-two?'

The woman flicks through a sheaf of papers. 'She checked out first thing this morning. A . . . family emergency, I believe.' Her face reveals nothing. 'There seem to be many such emergencies this weekend.'

'She left some tickets in the room. For an artist's show. I was wondering what to do with them.' She holds them out, and the receptionist studies them.

'She went straight to the airport . . . Oh. This is a very popular show, I think. It was on the news last night. People are queuing for many hours to see it.'

Nell looks at the tickets again.

'I would go to this exhibition, Mademoiselle.' The woman smiles at her. 'If you can . . . if your family emergency can wait.'

Nell gazes at the tickets. 'Maybe I will.'

'Mademoiselle?'

Nell turns back to her.

'We will not be charging you for the room if you choose to stay. To make up for the inconvenience.' She smiles again, in apology.

'Oh. Thank you,' Nell says, surprised.

And she decides. It's not that much longer, after all.

# 7

Fabien sits on his rooftop in his T-shirt and pyjama bottoms, thinking, his empty coffee cup beside him. He looks at the little photograph of Sandrine that he has been holding in his hand. And then, when the air grows too chill for him to stay out there any longer, he climbs back in – carefully this time – and gazes around him at the apartment. She was right. It is a mess. He grabs a bin bag and begins to tidy.

An hour later the little apartment is at least partially transformed: the dirty clothes confined to the laundry basket, the old newspapers by the door for recycling, the washing-up done and stacked neatly in the drainer. Everything is ordered, contained. He is washed, shaved and dressed. There is nothing now stopping him from writing. He places the remaining pages, precisely sorted into numbered order, beside his laptop and straightens the top page. He gazes at it.

Time passes. He rereads some of his pages and then sets them down. He picks up one page and studies it for a while, then places his fingers on the keys. He checks his phone. He gazes out the window at the grey rooftops. He goes to the bathroom. He stares back at his keyboard. Finally he checks his watch, stands, and grabs his jacket.

There is nobody waiting outside the little kiosk that faces Notre-Dame. Fabien stops his moped, pulls off his helmet, and gazes at the Seine for a moment, watching the mammoth tourist boat glide past, with its hordes of sightseeing passengers, all exclaiming and taking photographs through the huge windows. The little *Rose de Paris* with its handful of wooden seats sits patiently against the dock, uninhabited. He removes a package from the back of the moped and walks down to the kiosk, where his father is sitting on his stool reading the newspaper.

'Salmon,' he says, handing his father the package. 'Émile said it wouldn't keep.'

Clément kisses his son on both cheeks, then unwraps it and takes a bite, chewing appreciatively.

'Not bad. Tell him less dill next time. We are not Russians. The pastry is good, though.'

'Nothing doing?'

'It's that new big boat. It takes all the tourist trade.'

They gaze at the water for a while. A couple walk down to the riverside and hesitate a few feet from the kiosk before apparently changing their minds and walking away. Fabien scratches his ankle.

'If you don't need me, I might go to see the Kahlo exhibition.'

'In case you see Sandrine there?'

Fabien shakes his head. 'No! I like Frida Kahlo.'

'Sure you do,' says Clément, gazing out at the water. 'You rarely talk of anything else.'

'She said I never do anything with my life. I just . . . want to show her. I can do culture. I can change. Oh, and I tidied my apartment.'

There is a short silence. Fabien glances over quizzically as his father slaps at his pockets, as if searching for something.

'I was trying to find you a medal,' Clément says.

Fabien stands, smiling wryly. 'I'll come back at four, Papa. In case you need help then.'

Clément finishes the last of the salmon. He folds the paper carefully into a small square and wipes his mouth. He pats his son on his arm with his free hand.

'Son,' he says as Fabien turns to leave. 'Let her go. Don't take it all so seriously, eh?'


Sandrine always said he got up too late. Now, standing near the end of a queue that is marked with signs saying ONE HOUR FROM THIS POINT, TWO HOURS FROM THIS POINT, Fabien kicks himself for not getting there early, as he had originally planned.

He had joined the end cheerfully some forty-five minutes ago, thinking the queue would move quickly. But he has crept forward just some ten feet. It is a cold, clear afternoon, and he is starting to feel the chill. He pulls his wool beanie further down over his head and kicks the ground with the toes of his boots.

He could just quit the queue, head off, and go back to help his father as he'd said he would. He could go home and finish tidying up the apartment. He could put more oil in his moped and check the tires. He could do the paperwork he'd put off doing for months. But nobody else has ducked out of the queue, and neither does he.

Somehow, he thinks, adjusting his hat over his ears, he might feel better if he stays. He will have achieved something today. He will not have given up, like Sandrine says he always does.

It is, of course, nothing to do with the fact that Frida Kahlo is Sandrine's favourite artist. He turns up his collar, picturing himself bumping into her at the bar. 'Oh, yes,' he would say casually. 'I just went to see the Diego Rivera and Frida Kahlo exhibition.' She would look surprised, maybe even pleased. Perhaps he will buy the catalogue and give it to her.

Even as he thinks about it, he knows it is a stupid idea. Sandrine is not going to be anywhere near the bar where he works. She has avoided it since they split up. What is he doing here anyway?

He looks up to see a girl walking slowly towards the end of the long line of people, her navy hat set low over her fringe. Her face wears the look of dismay he sees on everyone else's when they see how long the queue is.

She stops near a woman a few people down from him. In her hand she holds two slips of paper. 'Excuse me? Do you speak English? Is this the queue for the Kahlo exhibition?'

46

She is not the first to ask. The woman shrugs and says something in Spanish. Fabien sees what she is holding and steps forward. 'But you have tickets,' he says. 'You do not need to queue here.' He points towards the front of the queue. 'Look – if you have tickets, the queue is there.'

'Oh.' She smiles. 'Thank you. That's a relief!'

And then he recognizes her. 'You were at Café des Bastides last night?'

She looks a little startled. Then her hand goes to her mouth. 'Oh. The waiter. I spilled wine all over you. I'm so sorry.'

'*De rien,*' he says. 'It's nothing.'

'Sorry, anyway. And . . . thanks.'

She makes as if to walk away, then turns and gazes at him and then at the people on each side of him. She seems to be thinking. 'You're waiting for someone?' she asks Fabien.

'No.'

'Would you . . . would you like my other ticket? I have two.'

'You don't need it?'

'They were . . . a gift. I don't need the other one.'

He stares at the girl, waiting for her to explain, but she says no more. He holds out a hand and takes the offered ticket. 'Thank you!'

'It's the least I can do.'

They walk beside each other to the small queue at the front, where tickets are being checked. He can't stop

47

grinning at this unexpected turn of events. Her gaze slides towards him, and she smiles. He notices her ears have gone pink.

'So,' he says. 'You are here for a holiday?'

'Just the weekend,' she says. 'Just – you know – fancied a trip.'

He tilts his head sideways. 'It's good. To just go. Very . . .' he searches for the word ' . . . *impulsif*.'

She shakes her head. 'You . . . work in the restaurant every day?'

'Most days. I want to be a writer.' He looks down and kicks at a pebble. 'But I think maybe I will always be a waiter.'

'Oh, no,' she says, her voice suddenly clear and strong. 'I'm sure you'll get there. You have all that going on in front of you. People's lives, I mean. In the restaurant. I'm sure you must be full of ideas.'

He shrugs. 'It's . . . a dream. I'm not sure it's a good one.'

And then they are at the front, and the security guard steers her towards the counter to have her bag searched. Fabien sees she feels awkward and does not know if he should wait.

But as he stands there, she lifts a hand as if to say good-bye. 'Well,' she says. 'I hope you enjoy the exhibition.'

He pushes his hands deeper into his pockets, and nods. 'Good-bye.'

She has slightly red hair and a smattering of freckles.

She smiles again, and her eyes crinkle, as if she is predisposed to seeing jokes where other people might not. He realizes he doesn't even know her name. And then, before he can ask, she heads down the stairs and disappears into the crowd.

For months Fabien has been stuck in a groove, unable to think of anything but Sandrine. Every bar he has been to reminds him of somewhere they've been. Every song he hears reminds him of her, of the shape of her top lip, the scent of her hair. It has been like living with a ghost.

But now, inside the gallery, something happens to him. He finds his emotions gripped by the paintings, the huge, colourful canvases by Diego Rivera, the tiny, agonized self-portraits by Frida Kahlo, the woman Rivera loved. Fabien barely notices the crowds that cluster in front of the pictures.

He stops before a perfect little painting in which she has pictured her spine as a cracked column. There is something about the grief in her eyes that won't let him look away. *That* is suffering, he thinks. He thinks about how long he's been moping about Sandrine, and it makes him feel embarrassed, self-indulgent. Theirs, he suspects, was not an epic love story like Diego and Frida's.

He finds himself coming back again and again to stand in front of the same pictures, reading about the couple's life, the passion they shared for their art, for workers' rights, for each other. He feels an appetite growing within him for something bigger, better, more meaningful. He wants to live like these people. He has to make his writing better, to keep going. He has to.

He is filled with an urge to go home and write something that is fresh and new and has in it the honesty of these pictures. Most of all he just wants to write. But what?

And then he sees her, standing in front of the girl with the broken column for a spine, her eyes locked on the girl in the painting, her eyes wide and sad. Her navy hat is clutched in her right hand. As he watches, a tear slides down her cheek. Her left hand lifts and, still gazing at the picture, she wipes it away with her palm. She looks over suddenly, perhaps feeling his gaze on her, and their eyes meet. Almost before he knows what he is doing, Fabien steps forward.

'I never . . . I never got a chance to ask you,' he says. 'Would you like to go for a coffee?'

# 8

The Café Cheval Bleu is packed at four o'clock in the afternoon, but the waitress finds Fabien a table inside. Nell has the feeling he is one of those men who always get a good table inside. He orders a tiny black coffee, and she says, 'For me, too,' because she does not want him to hear her terrible French accent.

There is a short, awkward silence.

'It was a good exhibition, yes?'

'I don't normally cry at pictures,' she says. 'I feel a bit silly now that I'm out here.'

'No. No, it was very moving. And the crowds, and the people, and the photographs . . .'

He starts to talk about the exhibition. He says he has known about the artist's work but did not realize that he would be so moved by it. 'I feel it here, you know?' he says, thumping his chest. 'So . . . powerful.'

'Yes,' she says.

Nobody she knows talks like this, she tells him. They talk about what Tessa wore to work, or *Coronation Street*, or who fell over blind drunk last weekend.

'We talk about these things too. But . . . I don't know . . . I think . . . it inspired me. I want to write like they paint. Does that make sense? I want someone to read and feel it like . . . *bouf!*'

She can't help smiling.

'You think it's funny?' He looks hurt.

'Oh, no. It was the way you said *bouf.*'

'*Bouf?*'

'It's not a word we have in England. It just . . . I . . .' She shakes her head. 'It's just a funny word. *Bouf.*'

He stares at her for a minute, then lets out a great laugh. '*Bouf!*'

And the ice is broken. The coffee arrives, and she stirs two sugars into it so that she will not make a face drinking it.

Fabien swallows his in two gulps. 'So how do you find Paris, Nell-from-England? This is your first trip?'

'I like it. What I've seen. But I haven't been to any of the sights. I haven't seen the Eiffel Tower or Notre-Dame or that bridge where all the lovers attach little padlocks. I don't think I'll really have time now.'

'You will come back. People always do. What are you going to do this evening?'

'I don't know. Maybe find another place to eat. Maybe just flop at the hotel.' She laughs. 'Are you working at the restaurant?'

'No. Not tonight.'

She tries not to look disappointed.

He glances down at his watch. '*Merde!* I promised my father I would help him with something. I have to go.' He looks up. 'But I am meeting some friends at a bar later this evening. You would be welcome to join us, if you like.'

'Oh. You're very kind, but –'

'But what?' His face is cheerful, open. 'You cannot spend your evening in Paris in your hotel room.'

'Really. I'll be fine.'

She hears her mother's voice: *You don't just go out with strange men.* He could be anyone. He has a shaven head.

'Nell. Please let me buy you one drink. Just to say thank you for the ticket.'

'I don't know . . .'

'Think of it as Parisian custom.'

He has the most amazing grin. She feels herself wobble. 'Is it far?'

'Nowhere is far.' He laughs. 'You are in Paris!'

'Okay. Where shall we meet?'

'I'll pick you up. Where is your hotel?'

She tells him and says, 'So where are we going?'

'Where the night takes us. You are the Impulsive Girl from England, after all!' He salutes, and then he is gone, kick-starting his moped and roaring away down the road.

Nell lets herself back into her room, her mind still buzzing with the afternoon's events. She sees the paintings in the gallery, Fabien's large hands around the little coffee cup, the sad eyes of the tiny woman in the painting. She sees the gardens beside the Seine, wide and open, and the river flowing beyond them. She hears the hiss of the doors opening and closing on the Métro. She feels as if every bit of her is fizzing. She feels like someone out of a book.

She has a shower and washes her hair. She sorts through the few clothes she brought with her – Pete is not a great one for dressing up – and wonders whether any of them is Parisian enough. Everyone here is so stylish. They do not dress like each other. They do not dress like English girls, for sure.

She heads down to reception. The receptionist is studying some figures and looks up, her hair swinging glossy as a show pony's tail.

'Excuse me? Do you know where I could get a nice outfit? Like, sort of French-looking?'

The receptionist waits just a second before she answers.

'French-looking?'

'I may be going out with some people tonight, and I would like to look a little more . . . French.'

The receptionist puts down her pen.

'You want to look French.'

'Or just maybe not stand out?'

'Why would you not want to stand out?'

Nell takes a breath, lowers her voice. 'I just . . . Look, my clothes are all wrong, okay? And you have no idea what it is like to be a not-Frenchwoman surrounded by very chic Frenchwomen. In Paris.'

The receptionist considers this for a moment, then leans over the desk and looks at what Nell is wearing. Then she rights herself, scribbles a few words on a piece of paper, and hands it to her.

'It's a short walk down rue des Archives. Tell her Marianne sent you.'

Nell gazes at it. 'Oh, thank you. Are you Marianne?'

The receptionist raises an eyebrow.

Nell turns to the door. Lifts a hand. 'Oooo-kay! Thank you . . . Marianne.'

Twenty minutes later Nell stands in front of a mirror in a loose sweater and some black lightweight drainpipe jeans. The assistant – a woman with artfully tousled hair and an armful of clattering bangles – drapes a scarf around Nell's neck, fixing it in a way that seems to Nell to be indefinably French. The shop smells of figs and sandalwood.

'*Très chic, Mademoiselle,*' she says.

'Do I look . . . Parisian?'

'Straight out of Montmartre, Mademoiselle,' the woman says with a suspiciously straight face. Nell would suspect that the woman was laughing at her, except she doesn't think these women actually do humour. It probably gives one wrinkles.

Nell takes a deep breath. 'Well, I guess it's all stuff I'll wear again.' She gives a little shiver of excitement. 'I could wear the top to work . . . Okay, I'll take it!'

While she is standing at the counter, paying and trying not to think too hard about how much, her eyes are drawn to the dress in the window, a 1950s-cut summer frock, a ridiculous emerald green with pineapples. She saw it when she walked past that morning, its shantung silk shimmering subtly in the watery Parisian sunshine. It made her think of old Hollywood film stars.

'I love that dress,' she says.

'It would look very nice with your colouring. You want to try it?'

'Oh, no,' says Nell. It's not really my –'

Five minutes later Nell is standing in front of the mirror in the green dress. She barely recognizes herself. The dress transforms her: heightens the colour of her hair, pulls her in at the waist. It turns her into a more sophisticated version of herself.

The shop assistant arranges the hem, stands, and pulls her mouth down at the corners in a Gallic expression of approval. 'It fits you perfectly. *Magnifique!*'

Nell stares at this new Nell in the mirror. She even seems to stand differently.

'You would like it? It is the last one – maybe I can do something with the price . . .'

Nell looks at the label and comes to.

'Oh, I'd never wear it. I like to buy things on a cost-per-wear basis. This dress would probably work out at like . . . thirty pounds a wear. No. I couldn't.'

'You don't ever do something just because it makes you feel good?' The assistant shrugs. 'Mademoiselle, you need to spend more time in Paris.'

Twenty minutes later Nell is back in her hotel room, with a shopping bag. She puts on the tight black jeans and pumps and the loose sweater. She eyes the French magazine on the bed, and after flicking through its pages she props up a picture against the mirror and does her hair and her eye makeup like the French model's. Then she stares at her reflection and smiles, giddy.

She is in Paris, in Parisian clothes, getting ready to go out with a Frenchman she picked up in an art gallery!

She puts on her lipstick, sits down on the bed, and laughs.

Twenty minutes later she is still sitting on the bed, staring into space.

*She is in Paris, in Parisian clothes, getting ready to go out with a Frenchman she has picked up in an art gallery.*

She must be insane.

This is the stupidest thing she has ever done in her life.

This is even stupider than buying a ticket to Paris for a man who had once told her he couldn't decide if her face looked more like a horse or a currant bun.

She will be in a newspaper headline or, worse, in one of those tiny news stories that aren't important enough to be a headline.

### GIRL FOUND DEAD IN PARIS AFTER BOYFRIEND FAILS TO SHOW UP

'I told her not to go out with strange men,' says mother.

She gazes at herself in the mirror. What has she done? Nell grabs her key, slips into her shoes, and runs down the narrow staircase to Reception. Marianne is there, and Nell waits for her to come off the phone before she leans over and says quietly, 'If a man comes for me, will you tell him I am ill?'

The woman frowns. 'Not a family emergency?'

'No. I . . . er . . . I have a stomach ache.'

'A stomach ache. I'm so sorry, Mademoiselle. And what does this man look like?'

'Very short hair. Rides a moped. Obviously not in here. I – He's tall. Nice eyes.'

'Nice eyes.'

'Look, he's the only man likely to come in here asking for me.'

The receptionist nods as if this is a fair point.

'I – He wants me to go out this evening, and . . . it's not a good idea.'

'So . . . you don't like him?'

'Oh, no, he's lovely. It's just, well . . . I don't really know him.'

'But . . . how will you know him if you don't go out with him?'

'I don't know him well enough to go out in a strange city to a place I don't know. Possibly with other people I don't know.'

'That's a lot of don't-knows.'

'Exactly.'

'So you will be staying in your room tonight.'

'Yes. No. I don't know.' She stands there, hearing how silly she sounds.

Marianne looks her slowly up and down. 'It's a very nice outfit.'

'Oh. Thank you.'

'What a pity. Your stomach ache. Still.' She smiles, turns back to her paperwork. 'Maybe some other time.'

Nell sits in her room watching French television. A man is talking to another man. One of them shakes his head so hard his chins wobble in slow motion. She looks at the clock often as it ticks slowly around to eight o'clock. Her stomach rumbles. She remembers Fabien saying something about a little falafel stall in the Jewish quarter. She wonders what it would have felt like on the back of that moped.

She pulls out her notebook and grabs the hotel pen from the bedside table. She writes:

REASONS I AM RIGHT TO STAY IN TONIGHT

1. He might be an axe murderer.
2. He will probably want sex.
3. Perhaps both 1 and 2.
4. I may end up in a part of Paris I don't know.
5. I may have to talk to taxi drivers.
6. I may have problems getting back into the hotel late at night.
7. My outfit is silly.
8. I will have to pretend to be impulsive.

9. I will have to speak French and eat French food in front of French people.
10. If I go to bed early, I will be up nice and early for the train home.

She sits there, staring at her neat list for some time. Then on the other side of the page she writes:

1. I am in Paris.

She stares at it a bit longer. Then, as the clock strikes eight, she shoves the notebook back into her bag, grabs her coat, and runs down the narrow staircase towards Reception.

He is there, leaning on the desk and talking to the receptionist, and at the sight of him she feels the colour flood her cheeks. As she walks towards them, her heart beating fast, she is trying to work out how to explain herself. Whatever she says will sound stupid. It will be clear that she was afraid of going out with him.

'Ah, Mademoiselle. I was just telling your friend here that I thought you might take a few minutes,' Marianne says.

'You are ready to go?' Fabien is smiling. She cannot remember the last time someone looked so pleased to see her – except perhaps her cousin's dog when he tried to do something quite rude to her leg.

'If you return after midnight, Mademoiselle, you will need to use this code at the main door.' The receptionist hands her a small card. As Nell takes it, Marianne adds quietly, 'I am so glad your stomach ache is better.'

\*

'You're not well?' Fabien says as he hands her a spare helmet.

The Paris evening is crisp and cold. She has never been on a bike before. She remembers reading about how many people die while riding bikes. But the helmet is already on her head, and he is shifting forward on his seat, motioning for her to get on behind.

'I'm fine now,' she says.

Please don't let me die, she thinks.

'Good! First we will drink, and then maybe we eat, but first we show you some of Paris, yes?' As she wraps her arms around his waist, the little moped leaps forward into the night. And with a squeal they are off.

# 9

Fabien whizzes down the rue de Rivoli, dipping in and out of the traffic, feeling the girl's hands tighten around his waist whenever he speeds up. At the traffic lights, he stops and asks, 'You okay?' His voice is muffled through his helmet.

She is smiling, her nose tipped red. 'Yes!' she says, and he finds he is grinning, too. Sandrine always looked blankly at him on the moped, as if she were barely able to hide her thoughts about the way he drove. The English girl squeals and laughs, and her hair flies up, and sometimes, when he swerves to avoid a car that pulls out of a side street, she yells, 'Oh my God, oh my God, oh my God!'

He takes her down crowded avenues, through back streets, whizzing over Pont de la Tournelle, then over the Île Saint-Louis, so that she can see the river glittering beneath them. They ride around the back of Pont de l'Archevêché, so she can see the cathedral of Notre-Dame lit up in the darkness, its gargoyles gazing down with shadowed faces from its Gothic towers.

Then, before she can breathe, they are on the road again, riding along the Champs-Élysées, weaving through the cars, beeping at pedestrians who step out into the road. At one point he slows and points upward, so that she can see the Arc de Triomphe. He feels her lean back a little as they drive past. He puts his thumb up, and she puts her own up in response.

He speeds over a bridge and turns along the river. He dodges the buses and taxis and ignores the horns of drivers, until he sees the spot he wants. He slows and cuts the engine by the main path. Tourist boats float along the river with their bright lights, and there are stalls selling Eiffel Tower key rings and cotton candy. Then there it is. The tower soars above them, a million pieces of iron pointing into the infinite sky.

She releases her grip on his jacket and gets off the bike carefully, as if during the journey her legs have become shaky. She pulls off her helmet. He notices that she does not bother to fix her hair, as Sandrine would have done. She is too busy gazing upward, her mouth an O of surprise.

He pulls off his own helmet, leans forward over the handlebars.

'There! Now you can say you have seen all of Paris's finest sights – and in . . . uh . . . twenty-two minutes.'

She turns and looks at him, her eyes glittering. 'That,' she says, 'was the most bloody terrifying and absolutely best thing I have ever done in my entire life.'

He laughs.

'It's the Eiffel Tower!'

'You want to go up? We will probably have to queue.'

She thinks for a moment. 'I think we've done enough

queuing for today. What I would really like is a stiff drink.'

'A what drink?'

'Wine!' she says, and climbs back on to the moped. 'A glass of wine!'

He feels her hands slide around his waist as he starts the engine up again and drives back into the night.

The Lanes of Brighton are heaving, thick with catcalling hen parties, groups of highly groomed young men who eye them speculatively, having not yet toppled over into drunken incoherence. Magda, Trish and Sue are walking together in a row, even though it forces people off the pavement, trying to work out the location of the bar that Magda heard does happy hour if you are girls visiting alone.

'Oh, heck,' says Magda, reaching into her purse. 'I've forgotten my phone.'

'It's probably safer at the hotel,' says Trish. 'You'll only get drunk and lose it again.'

'But what if I meet someone? How will I get his number?'

'You can get him to write it on your – Pete?'

'My what?'

'Pete? Pete Welsh?'

The three women stop and stare at the disheveled figure hanging out of the Mermaid's Arms bar. He blinks at them.

Magda marches up to him, confused. 'What are you . . . ? Aren't you meant to be in Paris?'

Pete rubs at the top of his head. The amount of alcohol he has consumed may be slowing his Rolodex of excuses.

'Oh. That. Yeah. Well. It was kind of tricky getting away from work.'

The women stare at one another as they register the surroundings.

'And where's Nell?' says Sue. 'Oh my God. Where's Nell?'

Nell is squashed into the end booth at the Bar Noir, in some unspecified part of central Paris; she has long since stopped trying to guess where. There was a mention of food sometime ago, but it seems to have been forgotten. She has relaxed in here, with Émile and René and that friend of Émile's with the red hair whose name Fabien never can remember. She has taken off her hat and her coat, and her hair swings around her face as she laughs. Everyone speaks in English for her, but Émile is trying to teach her to swear in French. There are many bottles on the table, and the music is so loud that they all have to shout.

'*Merde!*' Émile is saying. 'But you have to pull the face, too. *Merde!*'

'*Merde!*' She throws up her hands like Émile, then bursts out laughing again. 'I can't do the accent.'

'*Sheet.*'

'*Sheet,*' she says, copying his deep voice. 'I can do that one.'

'But you don't swear like you mean it. I thought all English girls cursed like sailors, no?'

'*Bouf!*' she says, and swings around to look at Fabien.

'*Bouf?*' says Émile.

'*Bouf,*' says René.

'More drinks!' says Émile.

Fabien finds he keeps watching her. Not beautiful, not in the way Sandrine was beautiful. But there is something about her face that keeps you looking: the way she screws up her nose when she laughs. The way she looks a little guilty when she does it, as if she is doing something she shouldn't. Her smile, wide, with tiny white child's teeth.

They lock eyes for a moment, and he sees a question and an answer between them. Émile is fun, the look says, but we both know that this is about us. When he looks away, he feels a little knot of something in his belly. He goes up to the bar, orders another round of drinks.

'You finally moved on, eh?' says Fred, behind the bar.

'She's just a friend. Visiting from England.'

'If you say so,' Fred says, lining up the drinks. He doesn't need to ask what they want. It's Saturday night. 'I saw her, by the way.'

'Sandrine?'

'Yes. She said she has a new job. Something to do with a design studio.'

He feels a brief pang that something so major has happened in her life without him knowing.

'It's good,' Fred says, not meeting his eye, 'that you are moving on.'

And in that one sentence, Fabien realizes that Sandrine has someone else. *It's good that you are moving on.*

As he carries the drinks towards the table, it hits him. It's a pang of discomfort but not of pain. It doesn't matter. It's time to let her go.

'I thought you were getting wine,' Nell says, her eyes widening as he arrives with the drinks.

'It's time for tequila,' he says. 'Just one. Just . . . because.'

'Because you are in Paris and it's Saturday night,' says Émile. 'And who needs an excuse for tequila?'

He sees a flash of doubt on her face. But then she lifts her chin. 'Let's do it,' she says. She sucks the lime, then downs the contents of the little glass, screwing her eyes shut with a shudder. 'Oh, my God.'

'Now we *know* it's Saturday night,' says Émile. 'Let's party! Are we going on later?'

Fabien wants to. He feels alive and reckless. He wants to see Nell laughing until the small hours. He wants to go to a club and dance with her, one hand on her sweaty back, her eyes locked on his. He wants to be awake in the early hours for the right reasons, alive with the drink and the fun and the streets of Paris. He wants to bathe in the sense of hope that comes with someone new, someone who sees in you only the best of everything, not the worst. 'Sure. If Nell wants to.'

'Nell,' says René. 'What kind of name is this? It's a normal English name?'

'It's the worst name ever,' she says. 'My mother named me after someone in one of Charles Dickens's books.'

'It could have been worse. You could have been – what is her name? – Miss Havisham.'

'Mercy Pecksniff.'

'Fanny Dorrit.' They are all laughing.

She claps a hand over her mouth, giggling. 'How do you all know so much about Dickens?'

'We studied together. English literature. Fabien reads all the time. It's terrible. We have to fight to get him to come out.' Émile lifts a glass. 'He is like a . . . a . . . how do you say it? A hermit. He is a hermit. I have no idea how you got him out tonight, but I am very happy. *Salut!*'

'*Salut!*' she says, and then she reaches into her pocket for her phone and stares at it. She looks shocked and peers closer, as if checking she has read correctly.

**Are you OK?????**

It is from Trish.

'Everything is okay?' Fabien says when she says nothing.

'Fine,' she says. 'Just my friends being weird. So . . . where are we going?'

It is two thirty in the morning. Fabien has drunk more than he has drunk in weeks. His sides hurt from laughing. The Wildcat is packed. One of Fabien's favourite tracks comes on, which he always played in the restaurant during cleanup time until the boss banned it. Émile, who is in crazy party mode, leaps on to the bar and starts dancing, pointing at his chest and grinning at the people below him. A cheer goes up.

Fabien feels Nell's fingers resting on his arm and takes her hand. She is laughing, her hair sweaty, with strands stuck to her face. She took off her coat sometime ago, and he suspects they may not find it again. They have been dancing for hours.

The redheaded girl gets up on the bar beside Émile, helped by a sea of hands, and starts dancing. They shimmy together, swigging from bottles of beer. The barmen stand back, watching and occasionally moving a glass out of the way of a stray foot. It is not the first time the bar of the Wildcat has become a dance floor, and it will not be the last.

Nell is trying to say something to him.

He stoops lower to hear her, catching a faint trace of her scent.

'I've never danced on a bar,' she says.

'No? Do it!' he says.

She laughs, shakes her head, and he holds her gaze. And it is as if she remembers something. She reaches a hand to his shoulder, and he helps her up, and there she is, above him, righting herself and then, suddenly, dancing. Émile lifts a bottle in salute, and she is off, locked into the rhythm, her eyes closed, hair swinging. She wipes sweat from her face and swigs from a bottle. Two, then three more people join them up there.

Fabien is not tempted. He just wants to stand here,

feeling the music vibrate through him, part of the crowd, watching her, enjoying her pleasure, knowing he is part of it.

She opens her eyes then, searching him out among the sea of faces. She spots him and smiles, and Fabien realizes he is feeling something he thought he had forgotten how to feel.

He is happy.

It is 4 a.m. Or maybe 5 a.m. She has long since stopped caring. She and Fabien are walking side by side down a silent street, her feet uneven on the cobbles, her calves aching from the dancing. She gives a small shiver, and Fabien slows, removing his jacket and placing it over her shoulders.

'I will call the Wildcat tomorrow,' Fabien says, 'and ask if anyone found your coat.'

'Oh, don't worry,' says Nell, enjoying the weight of his jacket, the faint male scent it gives off as she moves. 'It was an old coat. Oh – damn. It had the code in it.'

'Code?'

'To the hotel. I won't be able to get in.'

Fabien doesn't look at her as he speaks. 'Well . . . you could . . . stay . . . at my apartment.' He says it casually, like it's no big deal.

'Oh. No,' says Nell quickly. 'You're very sweet, but –'

'But –'

'I don't know you. Thank you, though.'

Fabien looks at his watch. 'Well . . . the hotel doors

will open in an hour and forty minutes. We can look for an all-night café. Or we can walk. Or . . .'

Nell waits as he thinks. Fabien smiles suddenly, holds out his arm, and after the smallest hesitation she links hers through it and they set off down the street.

There is a moment, just as Fabien starts heading down the slope that leads to the quayside, when Nell's courage briefly fails her. There is no way she cannot end up as a cautionary headline, surely, she thinks as she gazes at the inky black of the river, the shadows of the trees, and the utter emptiness of the quay below. And yet something – perhaps an English predisposition not to appear rude, not to make a fuss, even if it does end up in your untimely murder – propels her forward. Fabien walks ahead with the easy stride of someone who has been here a million times before. Not a serial killer's walk, she thinks as she picks her way down. Not that she has a clear idea of how a serial killer walks. Just not like that. He turns and motions to her to follow and then stops beside a small wooden boat lined with bench seats and tethered to a huge iron ring. Nell slows and stares at it.

'Whose is this?'

'My father's. He takes tourists along the river.'

He holds out his hand, and she takes it, climbing aboard. Fabien motions to the bench beside him, then reaches into a chest, from which he hauls a wool blanket. He hands it to Nell, waiting as she adjusts it over her lap, and then he starts the boat and they're off, chugging gently against the tide into the center.

Nell looks up as they head into the dark waters, gazing out at the silent Parisian streets, the glitter of streetlamps on the water, and thinks she must now be in a dream. This cannot be her, drifting along in the Parisian waters with a stranger in the middle of the night. But she no longer feels afraid. She feels elated, giddy. Fabien looks back at her, perhaps seeing her smile, and motions to her to stand. He hands her the tiller, and she takes it, feeling the little boat break the waters beneath her.

'Where are we going?' she says, and realizes she doesn't entirely care.

'Just keep steering,' says Fabien. 'I have something to show you.'

They chug quietly upstream. Paris is illuminated around them, its sounds distant and beautiful, as if they are alone here in its epicenter, a dark, glittering bubble.

'So,' says Fabien. 'We have two hours to find out everything. Ask me anything. Anything you like.'

'Oh, God. I'm hopeless at this. So . . . what did you love most as a child?'

'A child? Football. I could recite all the players in Paris Saint-Germain: *Casagrande, Algerino, Cissé, Anelka . . .*'

'Okay,' says Nell, who feels suddenly that the Premier Division may slightly kill her romantic Parisian vibe. 'Then . . . who was the first girl you ever fell in love with?'

'Easy,' says Fabien firmly. 'Nancy Delevigne.'

'Great name. What did she look like?'

'Long dark hair, all ringlets. *Comme ça.*' He twists his fingers near his face as if to suggest curls. 'Big, dark eyes. A beautiful laugh. She went off with my friend Gérard. It was to be expected,' he says, when he sees her face fall. 'He had a better –'

He mimes bouncing up and down. Nell's eyes widen briefly.

'How you say . . . trampoline? We were seven. Here, steer this way a little. There is a strong current in this part.'

He places his hand over hers on the tiller as they pass under a bridge. She registers the warmth of it, tries not to reveal the flush of colour that travels to her cheeks.

'Nobody more recently?' says Nell.

'Yes. I lived with Sandrine for two years. Until three months ago.'

'What happened?'

Fabien shrugs. 'What didn't happen? I didn't get a better job. I didn't finish my book and become the next Sartre. I didn't grow, change, fulfill my potential . . .'

'Yet!' says Nell before she can stop herself. As Fabien turns, she says: 'Why does there have to be some kind of time frame on these things? I mean, you have a nice job, with people you like. You're writing a book. Hey, you're a man who goes to art exhibitions by himself! It's not like you're lying in bed in your boxers.'

'There may have been some lying in bed in my boxers.'

Nell shrugs. 'Well. That's basically Rule One in the Breakup Rulebook: *Lie around in your boxers feeling sorry for yourself.*'

'And Rule Two?' says Fabien, grinning.

'Oh, humiliate yourself a little, then Rule Three, maybe have a night with someone completely unsuitable, then Four, realize you're enjoying life again, and then Five, just as you've decided you don't need to be in a relationship after all, boom! There you go. Miss Perfect will turn up.'

Fabien leans forward on the tiller. 'Interesting. And I really have to go through all these stages?'

'I think so,' says Nell. 'Well, maybe you could skip one or two.'

'Well, I have already humiliated myself.' He grins, unwilling to say more.

'Come on,' says Nell. 'You can tell me. I live in another country. We are never going to see each other again.'

Fabien screws up his face. 'Okay . . . well, for weeks after Sandrine left, I would hang around her office, my face like this –'

He pulls what Nell can only describe as a Gallic Sadface.

'– thinking that if she saw me, she would fall in love with me again.'

Nell is trying not to laugh. 'Yup. That face'll do it for a girl every time. I'm sorry. I'm really not laughing.'

'You're right to laugh,' says Fabien. 'I suspect that it was a kind of madness.'

'A romantic madness. If you're French, you can get away with that kind of thing, I bet.' She thinks. 'Well, as long as you didn't also put a tracking device on her car or something.'

'So, Nell, now I ask you something.'

Nell waits. He has moved his hand away, and she feels the absence of it.

'Not relationships,' she says. 'There's a reason I'm an expert on Breakups 101.'

'Okay, then . . . tell me . . . the best thing that has ever happened to you.'

'The best? Oh, I'm kind of hoping it hasn't happened yet.'

'Then tell me the worst thing.'

And there it is. Nell feels the sudden chill in the air.

'Oh, you don't want to know that.'

'You don't want to say?'

She can feel him looking at her, but she keeps her eyes straight ahead, her hand clasping the tiller.

'It's kind of . . . oh, I don't know. Okay. The day Dad died. Hit-and-run. I was twelve.'

She is so good at saying it now, as if it happened to someone else entirely. Her voice even, light, as if it were the most insubstantial of facts. As if it hadn't smashed their existence into a million pieces, a falling meteor, radioactive for years afterwards, scorching the earth. She rarely tells anyone these days. There is no point – it skews the direction of travel, changes the way people react to her. She realizes, dimly, that she has never told Pete.

'He was out running – he used to run three times a week, and on the Friday he would go to the café on the corner for a big breakfast afterwards, which my Mum always said kind of missed the point. Anyway, he crossed the road, and a man in a pickup truck shot the lights and broke his spine in three places. It was his forty-second birthday. Me and Mum were waiting for him at the café as a surprise. I can still remember it. Sitting in that booth, so hungry, trying not to look at the menu, not understanding why he wasn't there yet.'

Please don't say something stupid, she wills him silently. Please don't do the head tilt or tell me something inspirational that happened to a neighbour of yours.

But there is silence, and then Fabien's voice falls silently into the water. 'That's bad. I'm sorry.'

'My mum was kind of messed up by it. She doesn't go out much anymore. I'm trying to get her to move, because that house is way too big for her, but she's sort of stuck.'

'But you went the other way.'

Nell turns to face him. 'I'm sorry?'

'You decided to . . . what is the saying . . . take life by the horns?'

She swallows. 'Oh. Yeah. Fabien, I should really –'

But his attention is drawn to something up ahead. 'Hold on. We need to slow down.'

Before she can speak again, he has slowed the boat

and points. Nell is briefly diverted, following the direction of his arm.

'What's that?'

'The Pont des Arts. You can see the gold? That's the love locks. You remember?'

Nell stares up at the tiny padlocks, bunched so tightly that the sides of the bridge have become bulbous and glittering. All that love. All those dreams. She wonders briefly how many of those couples are still together. How many are happy, or broken, or dead. She can feel Fabien watching her. Her heart feels suddenly heavy.

'I had a plan to add one. It was going to be one of my things. While we – I was here.'

She feels the weight of it in her bag suddenly. She reaches in to find it. She then sets it on the bench beside her and stares at it for a moment. 'But you know what? It's a stupid idea. I read a thing on the train over about how so many people do it that the whole damn bridge is collapsing. Which kind of misses the point, right? I mean, it's an idiotic thing to do.' Her voice lifts angrily, surprising herself. 'You just destroy the thing you love. By weighing it down. Right? People who do it are just *stupid*.'

Fabien stares up as they float gently underneath. Then he points again.

'I think mine is around ... there.' Fabien shrugs. 'You're right. It's just a stupid piece of metal. It means nothing.' He glances down at his watch. '*Alors* ... it's almost six o'clock. We should head back.'

\*

Half an hour later, they are outside the hotel. They stand there in the chill dawn, both somehow a little awkward in the light.

Nell shrugs her way out of his jacket, missing the warmth of it already. 'The whole padlock thing,' she says, handing it over. 'It's a long story. But I never meant that you were –'

Fabien cuts her off. '*De rien*. My girlfriend used to tell me my head was full of dreams. She was right.'

'Your girlfriend?'

'Ex-girlfriend.'

Nell can't help but smile. 'Well, my head is totally full of dreams right now. I feel like . . . I feel like I just fell into someone else's life. Thank you, Fabien. I had the best night. And morning.'

'It was my pleasure, Nell.'

He has taken a step closer. They are facing each other, inches apart. Then the porter appears, hooking open the doors noisily and dragging a door stand across the pavement.

'*Bonjour, Mademoiselle!*'

Nell's phone vibrates. She looks down.

Call me.

It is from Magda.

'Everything okay?' says Fabien.

Nell shoves her phone into her back pocket. 'It's . . . uh, fine.'

The spell is broken. Nell glances behind her. Some

distant part of her brain is wondering why Magda is calling her at this hour.

'You had better get some sleep,' says Fabien gently. There is stubble greying his chin, but he looks cheerful. She wonders if she looks like a sad horse and rubs self-consciously at her nose.

'Nell?'

'Yes?'

'Would you like ... I mean ... For your Parisian experience, would you like to come to dinner tonight?'

Nell smiles. 'I would like that very much.'

'Then I will pick you up at seven.'

Nell watches as he climbs aboard his moped. And she heads in through the open door of the hotel, still smiling.

Pete has now been wedged between Trish and Sue in Magda's backseat for a full forty-five minutes. He is almost completely sober, having been frog-marched from the pub to Magda's car, a twenty-minute walk up the seafront, silenced by the collective wrath of three too-sober women.

'I have never heard anything like it. And believe me, I have had a lot of crappy boyfriends. I am basically the queen of crappy boyfriends.' Magda whacks her steering wheel for emphasis, unwittingly veering into the middle lane.

'You know Nell gets anxious about stuff. She doesn't even get the late train unless she's checked to see exactly where it's stopping.'

Magda turns in her seat to look behind her. 'You left her to go all the way to Paris by herself? What were you even thinking!'

'I didn't ask to go to Paris,' Pete says.

'Then you just say no!' says Sue on his left. 'You just say, "No, Nell, I do not want to go to Paris with you." It's really simple.'

Pete peers to the side. 'Where are you guys taking me?'

'Shut up, Pete,' says Trish. 'You don't get the right to talk.'

'I'm not a bad guy.' His voice emerges as a whine.

'Ugh,' says Trish. 'The old "I'm not a bad guy" talk. I hate the "I'm not a bad guy" talk. It makes me really stabby. How many times have you heard the "I'm not a bad guy" talk, Sue?'

'About a billion times,' says Sue, her arms folded. 'Usually after they've slept with someone I know. Or nicked my German sausage.'

'I've never nicked anyone's German sausage,' mutters Pete.

'Your girlfriend bought you tickets to go to Paris. You failed to go. You went drinking in Brighton with the lads instead. What exactly would you have to do in *your* book to be a bad guy, Pete?'

'Like, kill a kitten or something?' Pete says hopefully.

Magda purses her lips and swerves into the slow lane. 'Kitten killing is way down the list on this one, Pete.'

'Below German sausage even,' says Sue.

Pete sees the sign to Gatwick. 'So . . . uh . . . where are we actually going?'

In the mirror Magda and Sue exchange a look.

Nell wakes up at a quarter past one. Actual lunchtime. She blinks blearily and stretches luxuriously when she realizes where she is. The little hotel room on the top floor feels curiously homey now, her new Parisian purchases hung neatly in the wardrobe, her makeup scattered all over the shelf from the previous night. She climbs slowly out of bed, hearing the unfamiliar street sounds of the city below, and despite her lack of sleep feels suddenly elated, as if something magical has happened. A quarter past one, she thinks, and shrugs in what she fancies is Gallic fashion. She has a few hours to herself to enjoy Paris. And then she will meet Fabien for her last night. She sings when she climbs into the shower and laughs when the water runs briefly cold.

Nell walks what feels like the length of Paris. She walks through the numbered arrondissements, meandering through a food market, gazing at the glossy produce, both familiar and not at the same time, accepting a plum at a stallholder's urging and then buying a small bag in lieu of breakfast and lunch. She sits on a bench by the Seine, watching the tourist boats go by, and eats three of the plums, thinking of how it felt to hold the tiller, to gaze on to the moonlit waters. She tucks the bag under her arm as if she does this all the time and takes the

Métro to a *brocante* recommended in one of her guide-books, allowing herself an hour to float amongst the stalls, picking up little objects that someone once loved, mentally calculating the English prices, and putting them down again. And as she walks, in a city of strangers, her nostrils filled with the scent of street food, her ears filled with an unfamiliar language, she feels something unexpected wash through her. She feels connected, alive.

When she walks back to her hotel, the girl is playing the cello again, a low sound, resonant and beautiful. Nell pauses underneath the open window and then sits down on the curb to listen, heedless of the curious looks of passersby. This time when the music stops, she cannot help herself and stands and applauds, clapping into the echoing street. The girl emerges on to the balcony and looks down, surprised, and Nell smiles up at her. After a moment the girl smiles back and then takes a small bow. Nell hears the music in her ears the whole way back to the hotel.

The woman at the airline desk is staring at the three women who surround the disheveled man.

Magda smiles reassuringly. 'This gentleman would like a ticket to Paris. On the next possible flight, please.'

The woman checks her screen. 'Certainly, sir. We have . . . a seat on a British Airways flight that leaves for Charles de Gaulle in an hour and ten minutes.'

'He'll take it,' says Magda quickly. 'How much is the ticket, please?'

'One way? That will be . . . one hundred and forty-eight pounds.'

'You're kidding me,' says Pete, who hasn't spoken since they entered the airport terminal.

'Open your wallet, Pete,' says Magda, in a voice that suggests it is not a good idea for him to disagree.

The airline woman has started to look properly concerned now. Magda opens Pete's wallet and starts counting money on to the desk beside his passport.

'A hundred and ten pounds. That's all my money for the weekend,' Pete protests. Magda reaches into her bag.

'Here. I have twenty. And he'll need cash to get into Paris. Girls?'

She waits as the others pull notes from their bag, counting them out carefully until they have enough. The woman slides the money towards her slowly, all the while watching Pete.

'Sir,' she says, 'are you . . . happy to take this flight?'

'Yes he is,' says Magda.

'This is nuts,' says Pete. He stands there, looking sullen and awkward.

The airline woman appears to have had enough. 'You know, I'm not sure I can issue this ticket if the gentleman here is not travelling voluntarily.'

There is a short silence. The girls exchange glances. A queue has started to build behind them.

'Oh, explain it to her, Mags,' says Sue.

Magda leans forward. 'Miss Airline lady. Our best friend, Nell, is a nervous traveller.'

'She's a nervous everything,' says Trish.

'So she gets anxious about all sorts of stuff,' says Magda. 'New places, the possibility of foreign invasion, objects falling off tall buildings, that kind of thing. Well, she and this gentleman here were due to go on a romantic trip to Paris this weekend. A big step for her. *Huge.* Except this gentleman here decided not to turn up and went drinking with his low-life mates in Brighton instead. So now our very nice friend is all alone in a strange city. Probably too afraid to leave her hotel room, given that she doesn't speak a word of French, and feeling like the biggest idiot in the world.

'Therefore we think it would be a good idea if Pete here got on your flight and gave his girlfriend a romantic twenty-four hours in Paris. So there may be a little coercion involved, yes, but it is done with good intentions.' She steps back. 'It is done with *love.*'

There is a short silence. The check-in woman stares at the four of them. 'Okay,' she says finally. 'I'm calling security.'

'Oh, come *on*!' exclaims Magda, throwing up her hands. 'Seriously?'

Pete looks briefly smug.

The woman has a phone to her ear and dials a number. She looks up at Pete. 'Yes. I think it would be sensible if your friend here had an escort to make sure he makes it on to that plane.' She then speaks into the phone. 'Desk Eleven. Can I have a security officer over here, please?'

She fills out the last of the ticket and hands it to Pete with his passport. An unsmiling security guard approaches.

'We need to make sure this gentleman gets to Gate Fifty-six safely. There you go, sir. Your boarding pass.'

As Pete turns away, she mutters 'Douchebag.'

The smell of chopped herbs seeps through the window of the tiny kitchen. As Fabien and Clément stand side by side preparing food, Émile is carting a table and chairs through the French windows that open on to a tiny cobbled square.

'Not those chairs, Émile. Haven't you got any more comfortable ones?' Fabien is uncharacteristically stressed, his skin pink with effort.

'These will be fine,' says Émile.

'And the duck. Papa – you didn't forget the marinade, yes?'

Émile and Clément exchange looks.

Clément walks to the fridge. 'And now my son thinks he can tell me how to cook duck. Yes, I have prepared the marinade.'

'I just want it to be special,' says Fabien, opening a drawer and rifling through it. 'A perfect traditional French meal. Shall we put some little lights in the tree? Émile? Do you still have those Christmas lights? The white ones. No colours.'

'The box under the stairs,' says Émile. As they watch, Fabien disappears. He reappears minutes later with a

PARIS FOR ONE AND OTHER STORIES

tangled string of lights, a man possessed. He walks outside and starts stringing them in the branches that hang over the table, standing on the tabletop to get to the high point. Then he starts rearranging the table and chairs, examining them from different views until he is satisfied. And then moving them again just in case.

Clément watches him steadily. 'All this for a woman he has met twice,' he murmurs.

'Don't knock it, Clément,' says Émile, handing him some garlic. 'You know what this means . . .'

They turn to face each other. 'No more Sandrine!' Clément considers this, then abruptly pulls off his apron. 'Actually, I'll pop down to the *poissonnerie* and buy some oysters.'

Émile is chopping with renewed vigour. 'Good idea. I'll make my tarte tatin with calvados.'


The door of the boutique jingles merrily as Nell opens it.

'*Bonjour!*' she says. 'I need that dress. The pineapple dress.'

The shop assistant remembers her immediately. 'Mademoiselle,' she says, slowly, 'the price is the same. It will be – how you say? – thirty pounds a wear!'

Nell closes the door behind her. She is glowing, and she still has the taste of ripe plums in her mouth. 'Well, I've been thinking about what you said. Sometimes you just have to do what feels good, right?'

The assistant is out from behind the counter before Nell has barely taken another step. 'Then, mam'selle, you must have the lingerie to go with it . . .'

An hour and a bit later, Nell walks down the wooden staircase of the Hôtel Bonne Ville, enjoying the way the skirt of the green pineapple dress billows slightly with each step. She pauses at the bottom to check that she has everything in her purse and looks up to see Marianne watching her. The receptionist lifts her chin and nods approvingly.

'You look very nice, Mademoiselle.'

Nell walks over to her and leans across the counter, conspiratorially. 'I got the lingerie, too. I think I'm basically living on bread and cheese for the next two months.'

Marianne straightens her paperwork and smiles. 'Then you are now an honorary Parisienne. Congratulations.'

She steps outside just as Fabien pulls up on his moped. He stops and gazes at her for a moment, and she lets him, conscious of the impression she is making. He holds out her coat, which he has retrieved, and she takes it. Then she glances down and sees his shoes – dark blue suede and somehow indefinably French.

'I love your shoes!'

'I just bought them.'

'Today?'

'I couldn't wear my work shoes.'

She pulls a face. 'Because I drenched them in wine?'

Fabien looks at her as if she has not understood anything he's been saying. 'No! Because I am going out to dinner with an Englishwoman in Paris.'

He gazes at her until she smiles back, and then he climbs off his bike, secures it, and holds out his arm.

'Tonight we walk. It's not far. Okay?'

Paris buzzes gently in the autumn evening. Nell carries her coat, even though it is just a degree colder than is comfortable, because she is enjoying wearing the pineapple dress so much and because she suspects it's what a Parisienne would do. They walk slowly, as if they have all the time in the world, pausing to look in shop windows or to point out particularly beautiful masonry carvings above their heads. Nell wishes briefly that she could bottle this evening, this feeling.

'You know,' says Nell, 'I was thinking about last night.'

'Me also,' says Fabien.

Nell looks at him.

Fabien reaches into his pocket and pulls out a little padlock. 'You left this. On the boat.'

Nell glances at it and then shrugs. 'Oh, throw it away. It's kind of meaningless now, right?'

As she stoops to stroke a passing dog, she does not see Fabien slide it into his pocket. 'So what were you thinking about?' he says.

'About your dad and his boat.' She straightens up. 'I was thinking he shouldn't try to compete with those big tourist boats. He should do something different. You and he. Like, individual tours of Paris, for lovers. You could advertise online, show people all those things you showed me, talk about the history. Maybe offer a hamper with lovely food and champagne? It would be heaven. Even just you and me last night . . . it was all very . . .' Her voice tails away.

'You thought it was romantic?'

She feels suddenly foolish. 'Oh, I didn't mean –'

They walk on without looking at each other, both feeling strangely awkward again.

'It's a good idea, Nell,' Fabien says, perhaps to break the silence. 'I'll tell my father. Maybe we can set something up with the restaurant.'

'And you must get a really good website. So people can book directly from other countries. Paris is the city of romance, right? And you could make it all sound beautiful.' She finds herself uncharacteristically voluble, her voice lifting, her hands waving as they walk.

'A boutique tour,' he says, mulling it over. 'I like it. Nell, you . . . you make everything sound possible. Oh. We're here! Okay, so now you must close your eyes. Hold my arm –'

He stops at the corner of a little cobbled square. Nell closes her eyes and then opens them abruptly as her purse starts to buzz. She tries to ignore it, but Fabien gestures at it, signaling to go ahead. He does not want this moment to be interrupted. She smiles apologetically and pulls out her phone.

And stares at it in shock.

'Everything is okay?' says Fabien after a moment.

'Fine,' she says, then lifts a hand to her face. 'Actually ...' she says. 'No. I think I need to go. I'm really sorry.'

'Go?' says Fabien. 'You cannot go, Nell! The night is just beginning!'

She looks stunned. 'I'm ... I'm really sorry. Something has ...'

She is reaching for her bag and coat. 'I'm sorry. Something has ... someone has turned up to see me. I have to –'

He looks down at her, and he can see it on her face. 'You have a boyfriend.'

'Sort of. Yes.' She bites her lip.

He is shocked by how disappointed he feels.

'He has turned up at the hotel.'

'You want me to take you?'

'Oh, no. I think I can walk it from here.'

They stand for a moment, paralysed. Then he lifts his arm and points 'Okay. You walk down to the church there, then turn left, and you are on the road of your hotel.'

She cannot meet his eye. Finally she looks up. 'I'm really sorry,' she says. 'I had such a great time. Thank you.'

He shrugs. '*De rien.*'

'It was nothing,' she translates.

But it was something. He realizes he cannot ask for her number. Not now. He raises a hand. She looks at him once more. Then, almost reluctantly, she turns away, and she is off, half walking, half running down the street towards the church, her bag flying out behind her.

Fabien watches her, then turns and walks around the corner. In the tiny courtyard, Émile stands in full waiter's uniform by the little table, set with two places. A bottle of champagne sits on ice. Above it fairy lights twinkle in a tree.

'Ta-daa!' says Émile. 'I was beginning to think you would never get here! Quick! The duck is going to dry out.' He peers around Fabien. 'What? Where is she?'

'She had to go.'

'But . . . where? Did you tell her we did all this –'

Fabien sits heavily on one of the chairs. After a moment he leans forward and blows out the candle on the table. Émile watches his friend, then throws his tea towel over his shoulder and pulls out the other chair.

'Okay. You. Me. We're going clubbing.'

'I'm not in the mood.'

'Then you can drink and I will dance. And then you can go home and write something incandescent and rage-filled about the fickle nature of Englishwomen.'

Fabien looks over at him. He sighs, beaten. Émile holds up a finger.

'But first let me put this food back in the fridge. We can eat it later. C'mon, don't look at me like that! Duck is six euro fifty a kilo!' He lifts the chair to take it back inside. 'Besides, I hate to say it, but your papa's marinade is really good.'

He is waiting in Reception. He sits, legs apart, arms wide along the back of the sofa, and doesn't get up when he sees her. 'Babe!'

She is frozen. She glances at Marianne, who is looking very hard at some paperwork.

'Surprise!'

'What are you doing here?'

'I thought we could turn your weekend in Paris into one night in Paris. Still counts, right?'

She stands in the middle of the reception area. 'But you said you weren't coming.'

'You know me. Full of surprises. And I couldn't leave you here alone with the cheese-eating surrender monkeys!'

It's like she is looking at a stranger. His hair is too long, and his faded jeans and T-shirt, which she had thought were so cool, just look tacky and tired in the elegant confines of the hotel.

Stop it, she tells herself. He has come all this way. He has done the very thing she wanted him to do. That must count for something.

'You look great. Cute dress! Do I get a welcome?'

She steps forward, kisses him. He tastes of tobacco. 'Sorry. I . . . I'm just a bit shocked.'

'I like to keep you on your toes, eh? So, shall we dump my stuff and get a drink? Or we could spend the evening upstairs with a bit of room service?' He grins and lifts an eyebrow. Nell sees the receptionist out of the corner of her eye. She is looking at him the way she would look at something nasty a guest had trodden into her hallway.

He hasn't shaved, she thinks. He hasn't even shaved.

'They don't do room service here. Only breakfast.'

'What?'

'They don't do room service. At this hotel.'

'Everywhere does room service,' says Pete. 'What kind of hotel is this?'

Nell doesn't dare look at Marianne's face.

'Well, they don't here. Because . . . because why would you eat in when you're in Paris?'

He shrugs and rises from his seat. 'Okay. Whatever.'

It is then that she notices his feet.

'What?' he says, catching her staring.

'You didn't change your shoes.' As he frowns, she says, 'You came for a romantic weekend to Paris. In your flip-flops.'

He sounds irritable now. 'What, are you going to tell me some fancy French restaurant won't serve me because I'm wearing flip-flops?'

Nell tries to stop looking at his feet.

'What's the matter, Nell? Jeez. This isn't the welcome I was expecting.'

She tries to pull herself together. She takes a breath and raises a small smile. 'Okay,' she says, trying to sound conciliatory. 'You're right. It's good that you came. Let's go upstairs.'

They begin to make their way across the reception area. Then Nell stops, thinking. Pete turns around, now properly irritated.

'One thing, though,' she says. 'I just . . . I just want to know – how did you end up coming after all? You said you weren't going to make it. That's what the text said. Very clearly.'

'Well . . . I didn't like to leave you here alone. I know how anxious you get about stuff. Especially when plans change and that.'

'But you were fine leaving me alone on Friday night. And last night.'

He looks awkward. 'Yes. Well.'

There is a long silence.

'Well . . . what?'

He scratches his head, smiles his charming smile. 'Look, do we have to go into this now? I've just got off a flight. Let's go upstairs, hit the sack, then go hit the Paris hot spots. Yes? C'mon, babe. This ticket cost a small fortune. Let's just have a good time.'

Nell stares at him as he holds out his hand. Almost reluctantly she passes him the room key, and he turns and begins to walk up the wooden stairs, his holdall slung over his back.

'Mademoiselle.'

Nell turns, in a daze. She has forgotten that the receptionist is there.

95

'Your friend left a message.'

'Fabien?' She fails to keep the eagerness from her voice.

'No. A woman. While you were out.' She hands over a piece of hotel-headed paper.

> PETE IS ON HIS WAY. HAVE KICKED
> HIS ARSE. SORRY, WE HAD NO IDEA.
> HOPE REST OF WEEKEND WORKS
> OUT OK. TRISH XXX

Nell stares at the note, gazes towards the stairwell, and then she turns back to the receptionist. She thinks for a moment as she hears Pete's feet echo in the staircase, and then suddenly she stuffs the piece of paper deep into her pocket.

'Marianne? Could you tell me the best place to get a taxi?' she says.

'With pleasure,' says the receptionist.

She has forty euros in her pocket, and she throws twenty at the driver, then leaps out, not caring about the change.

The bar is a dark mass of bodies, bottles and low lights. She pushes her way through, scanning the faces for someone she knows, her nostrils filled with the smells of sweat and perfume. The table they sat at is filled with people she does not recognize. He is nowhere to be seen.

She goes upstairs, where it is quieter and people sit

chatting on sofas, but he is not there either. She fights her way back down the stairs to the bar where she was served.

'Excuse me!' She has to wait to get the attention of the barman. 'Hello! My friend who was here. Have you seen him?'

The barman squints, then nods as if he remembers. 'Fabien?'

'Yes. Yes!' Of course they all knew him.

'He is gone.'

She feels her stomach drop. She has missed him. That's it. The barman leans across to pour someone a drink.

'*Merde*,' she says softly. She feels hollow with disappointment.

The barman appears beside her, a drink in his hand. 'You could try the Wildcat. That's where he and Émile usually end up.'

'The Wildcat? Where is that?'

'Rue des Gentilshommes des –' His voice is drowned in a burst of laughter, and he turns away, leaning across to hear someone else's order.

Nell runs out on to the street. She stops a taxi.

'Emergency!' she says.

The driver, an Asian man, looks up into his mirror, waiting.

'Wildcat,' she says. 'Rue des Gentilshommes something. Please tell me you know it.'

He turns in his seat. '*Quoi?*'

'Wildcat. Bar. Club. Wild. Cat.'

Her voice lifts. He shakes his head. Nell puts her face into her hands, thinking. Then she winds down her window and yells at two young men on the pavement outside the bar. 'Excuse me! You know the Wildcat? Wildcat Bar?'

One nods, lifts his chin. 'You want to take us?'

She scans their faces – drunk, cheerful, open – and she makes a judgment.

'Sure, if you know it. Where is it?'

'We show you!'

The young men jump in, all drunken smiles and handshakes. She declines the offer to sit on the lap of the short one and accepts a mint from the other. She is squashed between them, breathing in the smell of alcohol and cigarette smoke.

'It's a good club. You know it?' The man who first spoke to her leans across and shakes her hand cheerfully.

'No,' she says. And as he tells the taxi driver where to go, she leans back in a car of strangers and waits to see where she will end up next.

# 11

'One more drink. Ah, come on. It's just getting good.'
Émile claps a hand on Fabien's shoulder.

'I'm not really in the mood.'

'So she had a boyfriend. It happens! C'mon, you can't
let it get you down. You only knew her two days.'

'You hardly knew her at all,' adds René.

Fabien says nothing but swigs back his beer.

'You take it all too seriously, you know? But look – it
means you are over Sandrine. So that's good! And you
are a handsome man –'

'Very handsome,' adds René.

Fabien raises an eyebrow.

'What?' Émile protests. 'I cannot appreciate the male
form? Fabien! My friend! If I were a woman, I would be
climbing all over you! I would be swimming in the still
waters of Fabien. I would be climbing the Fabien tree.
What?'

'Too much,' says René.

'Okay. So, luckily for womankind, I am other ways
inclined. But c'mon! Let's go find other women! At least
now we have more than one name to avoid.'

'Thanks, Émile, but I'll finish this beer and go. Work
tomorrow. You know.'

Émile shrugs, lifts his own bottle, then turns back to the girl he's been talking to.

It was bound to happen. Fabien watches Émile laughing with the redhead. Émile has liked her for ages, but he is not sure how much she likes him back. Émile is not unhappy, though. He just bounces on to the next thing, like a puppy. *Hey! Let's have fun!*

Don't knock it, Fabien scolds himself. Better than being a loser like you.

He feels a faint dread at what will come next. The long evenings at his flat. The work on the book that he is no longer sure is worth working on. The disappointment because Nell simply disappeared. The way he will kick himself for thinking it was going to be something more. He can't blame her – he never even asked if she had a boyfriend. Of course a girl like her would have a boyfriend.

He feels his mood sinking further and knows it is time to go home. He does not want to depress anyone else. He claps Émile on the shoulder, nods goodbye to the others, and pulls his hat lower over his ears. Outside, he climbs on to his moped, wondering if he should even be driving after all he's had to drink.

He kick-starts the little bike and pulls out on to the street.

He has stopped at the end of the road to adjust his jacket when he hears the clunking sound. He looks down and sees that Nell's little padlock has fallen out of his pocket.

He picks it up from the ground and gazes at it, rubbing dirt from the brass surface. There is a public bin over by the railings, and he considers whether to throw it in. It is then that he hears the whistle.

Another whistle.

He turns. Émile is standing on the pavement beside a crowd of people. He is pointing at someone and waving for Fabien to come back.

Fabien recognizes the tilt of her head, the way she stands, one heel lifted, the flash of a green dress beside Émile. He sits for a moment. Then, a smile breaking over his face, he turns his bike and rides back to her.

'So,' says Émile as the two of them gaze at each other. 'Does this mean I don't get to eat the duck?'

# 12

They are walking arm in arm through the deserted streets, past art galleries and huge old buildings. It is a quarter to four in the morning. Her legs ache from the dancing, her ears are still ringing, and she thinks she has never felt less tired in her life.

When they left the Wildcat, they had swayed a little, drunk on the evening, beer, tequila and life, but somehow in the last half hour she has sobered.

'Nell, I have no idea where we are going.'

She doesn't care. She could walk like this for ever. 'Well, I can't go back to the hotel. Pete might still be there.'

He nudges her. 'You shared with the American woman. Maybe he's not so bad.'

'I'd rather share with the American. Even with the snoring.'

She has told him the whole story. At first Fabien looked like he wanted to hit Pete. She realized, with shame, that she quite liked that.

'Now I feel a little bit sorry for Pete,' says Fabien. 'He comes all the way to Paris to find you, and you run away with a Cheese-Eating Surrender Monkey.'

Nell grins. 'I don't feel bad about it. Isn't that awful?'

'You are clearly a very cruel woman.'

She huddles closer to him. 'Oh. Horrible.'

He puts his arm around her. 'You know, Nell, I'm sure you will probably say no, but I just wanted to tell you again – you can stay with me. If you like.'

She hears her mother suddenly. *You'd go back to a strange man's house? In Paris?*

'That would be lovely. But I'm not going to sleep with you. I mean, I think you're wonderful, but –'

Her words hang in the night air.

'But you don't know me. And we are both at the wrong stage of your breakup chart.'

Her hand closes around the little piece of paper with the code in her pocket. 'So is it okay? For me to come back with you?'

'It's your Paris weekend, Nell.'

His flat is ten minutes' walk away, he says. She has no idea what will happen next.

It is absolutely thrilling.

Fabien lives at the top of a narrow block that looks over a courtyard. The stairs are lined with cream stone, and they smell of old wood and polish. They walk up in silence. He has warned her that elderly women live in the other apartments. If he makes any noise after 10 p.m. they will rap on his door early in the morning to complain. He does not mind, though, he tells her. His apartment is cheap because the owner is too lazy to update it. Sandrine hated it, he tells her.

As they reach the top of the stairs, she steels herself.

'Fabien?' she says with a grin, 'You don't have any books about serial killers, do you?'

He opens the door and ushers her in. She stops on the threshold and stares.

Fabien's flat is one big room, with one large window looking out over the rooftops. A desk is covered with piles of paper, and over it hangs an antique mirror. The floor is wood. It might have been painted a long time ago, but is now pale and colourless. There is a large bed at one end, a small sofa against a wall, and the third wall is covered with pictures cut from magazines.

'Oh,' he says, when he sees her looking. 'I did that when I was a student. I am too lazy to take them down.'

Everything – the desk, the chairs, the pictures – is strange and interesting. She walks around, gazing at a stuffed crow on a shelf, the workshop light that hangs from the ceiling, the collection of pebbles by the bathroom door. The television is a tiny box that looks twenty years old. There are six glasses and a stack of mismatched plates on the mantelpiece.

He runs his hand over his head. 'It's still a mess. I was not expecting –'

'It's beautiful. It's . . . it's magical.'

'Magical?'

'I just . . . like it. How you put things together. Everything looks like it's a story.'

He blinks at her, as if he is seeing his home through different eyes.

'Excuse me for a moment,' he says. 'I just need . . .' He motions to the bathroom.

It is probably a good thing. She feels reckless, like someone she doesn't know. She peels off her jacket, straightening her dress, and walks slowly around the room until she is gazing out of the window. The rooftops of Paris, dark and moonlit, are like a promise.

She looks down at the pile of pages with scribbling covering the typescript. Some are dirty, marked with the tread of people's shoes. She picks one up and starts to scan it for words she knows.

When he finally comes out of the bathroom, she is holding her fourth page and sorting through the pile for the fifth.

'Translate it for me,' she says.

'No. It's no good. I don't want to read this –'

'Just these pages. Please. So I can say, "When I was in Paris, a real writer read to me from his own work." It's part of my Paris adventure.'

He looks at her as if he cannot say no to her. She puts on her best pleading face.

'I have not shown it to anyone.'

She pats the sofa next to her. 'Maybe it's time.'

Fabien walks over to the window and opens it. 'Come on, then. Your Paris adventure needs a Paris rooftop.'

'You want me to sit on a rooftop!' Nell peers out, but he is already climbing through. 'Okay!'

Nell and Fabien sit on the ledge. A half-drunk bottle of wine sits beside them. He is reading to her, his voice halting as he translates into English. Her head rests on his shoulder.

'"Because she knew already that this would be the thing that would end them. And that in the deepest part of her, she had known it from the beginning, like someone stubbornly ignoring a weed growing until it blocked out the light."'

'You can't stop,' says Nell when he does.

'The other pages are missing. Anyway – like I said, it's no good.'

'But you can't stop. You have to remember what you wrote, all the changes you lost, and send it off to a publisher. It's really good. You have to be a writer. Well, you *are* a writer. Just not a published one yet.'

He shakes his head.

'You *are*. It's . . . it's lovely. I think it's . . . The way you write about the woman. About how she feels, the way she sees things. I saw myself in her. She's . . .'

He looks at her, surprised. Almost without knowing what she is doing, she leans forward, takes his face in her hands, and kisses him. She is in Paris, in the apartment of a man she does not know, and she has never done anything that felt less risky in her life. His arms close around her, and she feels herself being pulled into him.

'You are . . . *magnifique*, Nell.'

'And everything you say sounds better because it's in French. I might just have to speak in a fake French accent for the rest of my life.'

He pours them each a glass of wine, and they sit, gaze at each other, and grin. They talk about work and their parents, their knees touching, leaning against each other. He tells her that this evening has released him from Sandrine. She talks about Pete and giggles when she thinks about him reaching the room and turning back to find she is not there. They imagine the American woman turning up at the room now, when Pete is there, and giggle some more.

'You know . . . I thought after Sandrine left that I was doomed. Last night, when we were dancing, I realized I was just confused. I had mistaken feeling for feeling unhappy.'

Nell winds her fingers through his. 'Well, when Pete didn't turn up this weekend, I wanted to die. I thought everyone would laugh at me till next Christmas. Nell, the girl who got stood up in the City of Lights.'

'And now?' says Fabien softly.

'I feel . . .' says Nell, tracing his palm with her finger, 'I feel like I fell in love with an entire city.'

At some point he helps her back through the window. She walks to the loo and stares at herself in the mirror. She is grey with tiredness. Her hair is all over the place, her eye makeup has rubbed off. And yet she glows; she looks full of mischief and joy.

When she comes back, he is reading her book. Her bag is on the floor.

She stops. 'What are you doing?'

'What is this?' He holds out the list.

REASONS I AM RIGHT TO STAY IN TONIGHT.

'I am an axe murderer? I might want to have sex with you?'

He is laughing, but he is a little shocked, too.

'Oh, God. I didn't mean for you to see that.'

She has blushed to her ears.

'It fell out of your bag. I was just putting it back in. "I will have to pretend to be impulsive."' He looks up at her, surprised.

She is filled with shame. 'Okay. I'm not the person you think I am. Or at least I wasn't. I'm not impulsive. I nearly didn't come tonight, because even the thought of taxi drivers scared me. I let you think I was a different kind of person. I'm . . . I'm sorry.'

He studies the list, and then he looks up again. He is half laughing. 'Who says you are a different kind of person?'

She waits.

'Was it somebody else dancing on that bar? Chasing me around Paris in a taxi with strange men? Leaving her boyfriend in a hotel room without even telling him she was going?'

'*Ex*-boyfriend,' says Nell.

He reaches out a hand, and she takes it. She lets him pull her to him. She sits astride his lap and studies his lovely, kind face.

'I think you are exactly this woman, Nell-from-England. You are whoever you choose to be.'

It is getting light outside. They kiss again, for perhaps for ever, she is not sure how long. She realizes she is still quite drunk after all. She sits with her lips almost on his and traces the shape of his face with her fingertips.

'This has been the best night of my life,' she says softly. 'I feel . . . I feel like I just woke up.'

'Me also.'

They kiss again.

'But I think we should stop now,' he says. 'I am trying to be a gentleman and remember what you said. And I don't want you thinking I am an axe murderer or a sex maniac. Or . . .'

Nell entwines her fingers with his. 'Too late,' she says, and pulls him from the sofa.

# 13

Even before his eyes are fully open, Fabien knows that something is different. Something has shifted, a weight no longer pressing down on him from the moment he comes awake. He blinks, his mouth dry, and pushes himself up on to his elbow. Nothing in the room is different, but he definitely has a hangover. He tries to clear the fog in his head, and then he hears the sound of a shower.

Then the previous night filters back to him.

He lies back on the pillow for a minute, letting the events arrange themselves in his head. He remembers a girl dancing on a bar, a long walk through Paris, dawn spent in her arms. He remembers laughing, a book of lists, her sweet smile, her leg over his.

He pushes himself upright, pulls on his jeans and the nearest sweater. He walks to the cafetière and refills it, then runs down the stairs to the bakery to grab a bag of croissants. As he returns, he opens the front door just as Nell emerges from the bathroom wearing the green dress from last night, her hair wet around her shoulders. They stand still for a moment.

'Good morning,' he says.

'*Bonjour,*' she responds.

She seems to be watching him to see how he reacts. When he smiles, her smile is just as wide.

'I have to go back to the hotel and catch my train. It's . . . quite late.'

He checks his watch.

'It is. And I have to go to work. But you have time for coffee? I have croissants. You cannot leave Paris without coffee and croissants.'

'I have time if you have.'

They are a little awkward with each other now, the ease of last night fading. They climb back on to the bed, sitting on top of the covers, both dressed, close enough to be friendly but not enough to suggest anything else. She sips the coffee and closes her eyes.

'Oh, that's good,' she says.

'I think everything tastes good this morning,' he says, and they exchange a look. He eats swiftly, more hungry than he has felt for ages, until he sees he has eaten more than his share and slows down, offering her a croissant, which she waves away. Outside, church bells are chiming and a small dog yaps.

'I have been thinking,' he says, still chewing. 'I have an idea for a new story. It is about a girl who makes lists for everything.'

'Oh, I wouldn't write that,' she says, giving him a sideways look. 'Who would believe it?'

'It's a good story. She's an amazing character. But she is a little too careful. She has to weigh up everything. The . . .'

'Pros and cons. For and against.'

'Pros and cons. I like this phrase.'

'And what happens to her?'

'I don't know yet. Something knocks her out of her habits.'

'*Bouf!*' she exclaims.

He grins, licks crumbs from his fingers. 'Yes. *Bouf!*'

'You'll have to make her very beautiful.'

'I don't need to make her beautiful. She *is* beautiful.'

'And incredibly sexy.'

'You only have to see her dance on a bar to know it.'

He reaches across and feeds her a piece of croissant, and after a moment they kiss. And then they kiss some more. And suddenly the croissants, the work and the train are forgotten.

Sometime later Fabien pulls up in front of the hotel behind the rue de Rivoli. The roads are surprisingly quiet. A few tourists stroll by, looking up to take pictures of the buildings. He is late for work, but the restaurant will have only a few customers on a Monday morning, regulars who come to sit with a dog and a newspaper, or tourists killing time until they are due to go home. But it will fill up later, and by four o'clock it will be packed.

Behind him he feels Nell release her arms from around his waist. She climbs off the seat and stands beside the bike. She pulls off the helmet and hands it to him, then ruffles her hair, which has been flattened by the helmet, so that she is standing there in her coat and her crumpled green dress.

She looks tired and untidy, and he wants to put his arms around her.

'You sure you don't want me to take you to the station? You will be okay getting there? You remember what I told you about the Métro station?'

'You're already late for work. I'll find it.'

They gaze at each other. She shifts her weight from one foot to the other, her handbag dangling in front of her. Fabien finds he no longer knows what he wants to say. He takes off his helmet and rubs at his hair.

'Well,' she says.

He waits.

'I'd better get my suitcase. If it's still there.' She twists her hands around the handbag strap.

'You will be okay? With this Pete? You don't want me to go in with you?'

'Oh, I can deal with *him*.' She screws up her nose as if Pete is of no importance. Fabien wants to kiss it.

And he cannot help himself. 'So ... Nell-from-England. Will we ... speak again?'

'I don't know, Fabien-from-Paris. We don't really know anything about each other. We might have nothing in common. And we live in different countries.'

'This is true.'

'Plus, we had one perfect night in Paris. It might be a shame to spoil it.'

'This is also true.'

'Besides, you are a busy man. You have a job and a whole book to write. And you do have to write it, you know. Quite quickly. I'm anxious to hear what happens to this girl.'

Something has happened to her face, some subtle change. She looks relaxed, happy, confident. He wonders how this could have happened in forty-eight hours. He wishes he knew what to say to her. He kicks at the pavement, wondering how a man who prides himself on being good with words can find himself without a single one. She glances behind her at the hotel.

'Oh.' She reaches into her bag and pulls out her notebook, handing it to him. 'Here. For your research. I don't think I need it anymore.'

He looks at it, then tucks it carefully inside his jacket. She leans forward and kisses him again, one hand on his cheek.

'Good-bye, Fabien,' she says as she steps back.

'Good-bye, then, Nell.'

They face each other on the empty pavement, and then, finally, when they can stand there no longer, he pulls on his helmet. With a roar of his engine and a wave of his hand, he rides off towards rue de Rivoli.

# 14

Nell is still smiling as she walks into the hotel. The receptionist is still behind her shiny desk. Nell wonders if the woman has a home or just sleeps there, on her feet, behind the desk, like giraffes do. She realizes she should be embarrassed, turning up in last night's dress, but finds she cannot do anything except smile.

'Good morning, Mademoiselle.'

'Good morning.'

'I trust you had a good evening?'

'Oh, I did,' she says. 'Thank you. Paris is . . . so much more fun than I could ever have imagined.'

The woman nods to herself and gives Nell a small grin. 'I am very happy to hear that.'

Nell takes a deep breath and looks over towards the stairs. This is the bit she is dreading. For all her brave words to Fabien, she is not looking forward to Pete's accusations or to his fury. She has wondered, privately, whether he will have done something horrible to her suitcase. He didn't seem like the kind of man to do such a thing, but you never knew. She stands there, bracing herself to go up to Room 42.

'Can I help you with anything, Mademoiselle?'

She turns her head and smiles. 'Oh. No. I'm . . . I just

have to go up and speak to my friend. He may . . . be a little cross that I did not include him in last night's plans.'

'Then I am very sorry to tell you he is not here.'

'No?'

'A rule of the hotel. I realized after you left that we cannot have someone using the room who is not the person who booked it. And the room was in your name. So Louis had to ask him to leave.'

'Louis?'

She nods towards the porter, a man the size of two back-to-back sofas standing upright. He is pushing a small trolley loaded with suitcases. As he hears his name, he gives a small salute.

'So my friend did not stay in my room?'

'No. We directed him to the youth hostel near Bastille. I'm afraid he was not very happy.'

'Oh!' Nell's hand has clapped over her mouth. She is trying not to laugh.

'I apologize, Mademoiselle, if this causes you any inconvenience. But he was not on the original booking, and he did not arrive with you, so once you were gone . . . It was a matter of security.' Nell notices that the receptionist's mouth is also twitching. 'A rule of the hotel.'

'A rule of the hotel. Quite. It's very important to stick to hotel rules,' says Nell. 'Well. Um. Thank you very much.'

'Your key.' The receptionist hands it to her.

'Thank you.'

'I hope you enjoyed your stay with us.'

'Oh, I did.' Nell stands in front of her and has to fight the urge to hug the woman. 'Thank you so much. I will remember it . . . always.'

'That is very good to hear, Mademoiselle,' says the receptionist, and finally she turns back to her papers.

Nell is walking up the stairs slowly. She has just turned on her phone, and the text messages are pinging through, one by one, the later ones with lots of capital letters and exclamation marks. Most she barely reads before she deletes them. There is no point in spoiling her good mood.

But the last one arrived at ten o'clock that morning, from Magda.

Are you okay? We are all desperate for news. Pete sent Trish a really weird text last night, and we can't work out what's going on.

Nell pauses outside Room 42, her key in her hand, listening to the bells pealing across Paris and the sound of French people talking in the reception area below. She breathes in the smell of polish and coffee and the scent of her own slightly stale clothes. She stands for a moment and remembers, and a smile breaks over her face. She types a text:

I had the best weekend away EVER.

# Six Months Later

Lilian is wearing her new fuchsia-coloured sports leggings, her second-favourite pair. She walks down the path like a slightly plump flamingo, a great smile on her face. She has a whole selection of sportswear now, ever since she began attending the gym on the corner by the new house. Nell picks her up on her way to work and takes her three times a week – once for aqua aerobics, once for Stretch'n'Calm, and once for boxing.

She reaches Nell's car and holds up a hand bearing a plastic canister. 'Sorry – I forgot my drink holder. You know we're doing kickboxing today?'

'Okay!' says Nell, who is still reconciling herself to this new version of her mother.

'Who knew I'd be so good at hitting things?' Lilian says, pulling the seat belt across her chest. 'Luka says that if I get any better, he's going to start me on Thai boxing. That sucker really hurts.' She turns to face her daughter. 'Now. Did you book your Paris trip?'

'No. Hey, did I tell you I got an interview for that promotion?' Nell pulls the car on to the main road. 'Keep your fingers crossed.' She starts to list the benefits of the new job, but Lilian isn't listening.

'I don't understand why you won't just go back,' her mother says, shaking her head. 'You only live once.'

'Says the woman who used to have palpitations when I rode my bike to the post office.'

Lilian pulls down the passenger mirror and purses her lips at her reflection. 'Sweetheart, there is a big difference between wanting someone to be safe and wanting them not to do anything at all.'

Nell signals and takes a left. 'Well, I do plenty of things. And I think sometimes it's nice just to remember something for what it was. Three perfect days in Paris. Three perfect, romantic days. Going back would be –'

'Well, that's hardly going to get you laid.'

Nell hits the brakes. She turns her face to stare at her mother.

'What?' says Lilian. 'Your generation didn't invent sex, you know. You're young! Nothing wobbles! You can still wear teeny tiny underwear! And Mr Frenchie sounded perfectly lovely. Better than that waste-of-skin Pete Welsh anyhow.' She thinks for a minute. 'Mind you, one of Cheryl's serial-killer loonies sounded better than Pete Welsh. Look, you're holding up traffic. You need to keep moving.'

When they reach the gym, Nell pulls into a parking spot near the door and waits for her mother to pull her gym bag from the footwell.

'I'll call you tonight,' says Nell.

'Think about what I said.'

Lilian climbs out of the car. She leans in through the open door, her expression suddenly soft and serious.

'Nell – I'm going to tell you something. After your dad died, I know I went into hibernation. I was just . . . I don't know, stuck . . . and then before you know it, being stuck becomes a habit. You came back from Paris all those months ago, and you were so different, so glowing and alive, and I thought, *My God. You get one chance at this stuff.* One chance! So don't be like me, sweetheart. Don't waste ten years of your life worrying about what might happen. None of us can afford to lose time . . .'

As Nell's eyes fill unexpectedly with tears, Lilian adds, 'Also, your ovaries aren't going to stay useful for ever. It's like buying those supermarket peaches that are meant to ripen at home. One minute they're hard, and the next minute they're all wrinkled and only fit for the trash. You might want to factor that into your thinking –'

'I'm going now, Mum,' says Nell.

'Think about it, sweetheart!' Lilian calls, closing the passenger door. 'I love you!'

On Tuesdays, Nell meets the girls for lunch in the park. It's a bit bracing, given they are barely into April, but they like to sit at one of the communal tables and encourage the onset of spring by eating their sandwiches outside.

'Are we still going to the Texas Grill tonight?' says Magda. She has a hangover and has pushed her egg sandwich to one side, and she is eyeing a muscular young dog walker speculatively.

'I don't know,' says Nell. 'I was thinking maybe we could do something else.'

'But it's Tuesday,' says Magda.

'So? You know there's a free concert at the bullring?'

'A concert?'

'Some orchestra from Austria. They're doing it for nothing. We could go there first and get a beer afterwards? It would be nice to do something different. Widen our horizons a little!'

Magda and Sue exchange a look.

'Uh . . . okay,' says Magda, pulling up her collar.

'But it's Two-for-One Ribs at the Texas Grill on Tuesdays,' says Sue.

'Ooh. And they do that great barbecue sauce,' says Trish.

'Shoot,' says Magda, looking behind her to see if the coffee-shop queue has died down yet. 'Let's do the concert thing some other time.'

That afternoon Nell is standing by the photocopier preparing handouts for the afternoon's presentation when her boss walks past. He slows, dips his head towards hers. 'I can't say anything formally yet, Nell. But we should be able to announce something by Friday.' He taps his nose. 'Every organization needs a balance, and we all agree you'd be the safe pair of hands that we need to offset the more . . . unpredictable elements in our organization, eh?'

'Thank you, sir,' says Nell.

'It's a big responsibility,' he says, straightening up. 'I suspect you'll need some time to weigh up the pros and cons.'

The words are like a bolt through her. Nell stares at him. He extends his hand for her to shake it, and after she does, he turns and walks away.

Nell stands, her head suddenly buzzing, holding the handouts limply in her other hand.

Minutes later she is at her desk. She glances behind her, a little furtively, then opens her browser and types in 'PARIS BOAT TOURS'. She skims through the list until she finds what she is looking for: 'LA ROSE DE PARIS BOAT TOURS'. She leans forward, clicks, and gazes at the images that appear in front of her.

*'Make your trip to the City of Lights a symbol of your love. Enjoy an intimate tour-for-two around the most romantic river on earth. We bring a cordon bleu picnic and champagne and our knowledge of Paris's most beautiful sites – you just bring each other!'* runs the text, against a simple black-and-white backdrop. The picture accompanying it shows Fabien with his arm around his smiling father. Nell smiles and gazes wistfully at it for a moment.

*'BOOKING NOW FOR SEPTEMBER! RESERVATIONS STRICTLY LIMITED due to POPULAR DEMAND.'* She jumps as Mr Nilson's secretary appears behind her.

'They're ready for you, Nell,' she says. 'That looks nice. Planning a holiday?'

\*

Nell stands before a PowerPoint presentation, closing her speech. In front of her are twenty-two graduates, mostly watching her intently, and only occasionally checking their phones. 'So, to summarize,' she says, her hands clasped, 'risk assessment plays a vital role in helping organizations understand and manage risk, in order to avoid problems and capitalize on opportunities . . . Thank you for your time. And enjoy your tour of the factory floor!'

Her smile fixed, she stands as if about to leave. But there is something about their expectant faces, their dewy complexions, the way she has delivered this speech once a month for the past four and a half years. She holds up a finger.

'Actually, I'd like to rephrase that. Sure, enjoy the factory if that's your thing. But, you know, you guys are young. You should think really seriously about whether this is the right path for you. There are a lot of alternatives. Like, so many. Do you really want to be clambering on to the corporate ladder at . . . what, twenty-one, twenty-two? Here at eight thirty a.m. on the dot and having to leave your jacket on your chair when you run out for a coffee and eating the *same damn sandwiches* every day? Ham on rye! Cream cheese! When you don't even really like cream cheese? Shouldn't you be dancing on bars, and wearing unsuitable shoes in new places, and eating food that frightens you?' She scans the room. 'Who here has danced on a bar, huh?'

The graduates' heads swivel. Two hands rise tentatively.

'There you go!' Nell applauds them. 'So think – do you really want to spend the best years of your life ticking boxes on a bunch of industry-approved plastics? Really?'

She looks out at the stunned faces. Then she turns and sees Mr Nilson, whose mouth is hanging slightly open, and collects herself.

'If you do, then great! Fill out an application form on your way out! . . . And . . . um . . . don't forget to wear your safety helmets!'

Nell rushes out of the room, her mind racing. Beside her cubicle are two of her colleagues. They stop talking as she approaches.

'So I heard you got that promotion, Nell. Congratulations.'

'I did,' says Nell, gathering her belongings from her desk. 'But I'm not going to take it.'

'Why?' says Rob. 'Doesn't have "Health and Safety" in the title?'

'No. She needs to think about it really carefully.'

The two men laugh, as if this is the funniest thing they have ever heard. Nell stands and waits for them to stop.

'Actually,' she says, 'I've decided to run off to Paris and have hot monkey sex with a random waiter I picked up. Like I did the last time I went. Have a nice day, gentlemen!'

She smiles sweetly, gathers the box of her belongings to her chest, and half runs towards the exit, her phone pressed to her chin.

'Mum?' she says. 'Meet me at the travel agent's when you get this. The one opposite my office.'

Clément and Fabien carry the hamper from the back of Fabien's bike down to the boat and load it carefully into the front. It is a clear, crisp day, and the light glints off the water, as if in apology for having been absent for the long winter months.

'Did you get the roses?' Fabien asks his father.

'I got them,' says Clément, checking the life jackets. 'But I don't know whether we should put roses out today.'

'Why? Oh, these tartines smell good. Nice job, Papa.'

'They are Émile's. And I think it's lesbians today. I thought roses might be too traditional. Maybe they want something more . . . modern.'

'Lesbian roses?' Fabien ducks as his father swings a life jacket at his head.

'You can mock, Fabien,' Clément says. 'It's the details that matter.'

'It's a *Rose de Paris* boat tour, Papa. It has to come with roses. Right. I'm off. I'll see you at four. Hope it goes well!'

As his son climbs aboard his moped, Clément watches him, thinking. 'Lesbian roses,' he mutters under his breath. 'Where would I get lesbian roses?'

Nell and her mother are walking towards the little cubicle where *La Rose de Paris* is tethered. Nell is studying her phone, and then she looks up and smiles. 'There she is! Isn't she gorgeous?'

'Oh,' says Lilian. 'This is just darling.'

As they walk down to the quayside, Clément is coming towards them, his hand outstretched. 'Mesdames? Good afternoon. My name is Clément Thibauld. Allow me to welcome you aboard our boat. I hope you had a pleasant stay in Paris so far?' He helps Lilian aboard and then reaches his hand out to Nell, who is peering towards the kiosk.

'Today we will show you Paris's most beautiful sights. The sun is shining, and you will fall in love with our city and never want to go home. May I offer you a glass of champagne?' Nell winces for her mother, who was drinking with Louis the porter until 4 a.m., but Lilian accepts delightedly.

'Why, thank you. I'm loving this already!'

Nell gazes around her. She stays standing even as her mother accepts a glass, scanning the people walking along the top of the quayside for a familiar face.

'Can I help you, Mademoiselle?' says Clément, appearing beside her.

'Oh. No,' says Nell. 'I just . . . Your website – there were . . . two of you?'

'Ah. You mean my son. He is not working today. But I can assure you I have a lifetime of experience of sharing Paris's finest sights. You will not be disappointed. Here –'

Nell tries to smile as he hands her a glass. Then he stoops and, with exaggerated courtesy, presents Lilian with a rose. She holds it up, sniffs it, exclaims at how lovely it is.

'You like roses?' says Clément.

'But of course!' says Lilian. 'Who doesn't?'

'Oh . . . you never know. But this is good. If you are both comfortable, we'll push off.'

Nell and her mother listen as Clément talks them through the sights along the Seine, tells them about the menu he has prepared, remarks on the unusual stillness of the river. Lilian drinks two more glasses of champagne, quickly, and grows quite giggly. Nell appears to be listening, but her attention is repeatedly drawn to the shore, as if even then his face might appear among the crowds. Lilian leans over.

'You could go to that café. He'll probably be there.'

'Maybe,' says Nell, looking down at her hands.

'Maybe? You can't duck out now.'

Nell takes a sip of her drink. 'He never got in touch, Mum. He probably has another girlfriend by now. Or he'll be back with his ex.'

'Then you just say hello and that it's nice to see him again, and then you find another hot waiter to get jiggy with.' Lilian laughs at Nell's shocked face. 'Oh, come on. It's Paris, sweetheart. Nothing counts if you're more than a hundred miles from home. Ooh! This champagne has gone straight to my head.'

Half an hour later, Nell's mother is snoring gently against Nell's shoulder. Nell sits, wistfully gazing out at the river as Clément's boat moves through the water below Notre-Dame.

'And in nineteen thirty-one a woman shot herself at the altar of the cathedral with her lover's pistol –' He turns. 'Your friend is okay?'

'Oh, Mum's just burned herself out through over-excitement. She's still adjusting to life in the fast lane.'

'Your mother?'

'Yes. I promised to bring her on this boat. It's kind of a long story.'

Clément tilts his head. 'Mam'selle, I am all ears.'

Nell hesitates, wondering how much to tell him. It all seems faintly ridiculous now – the long weekend, her enduring crush, the way she has had to stop herself from emailing the website forty times a day, just to see if she can speak to him again. The whole three days have acquired a kind of dreamlike quality in her memory, as if she might have imagined them.

'Well,' she says when Clément is evidently still wait-ing, 'I came here six months ago. On this actual boat. And I kind of fell in love with . . . Oh, it sounds stupid to say it out loud. But it was one of those weekends that . . . that just changes you.'

Clément is staring at her. She wonders if she looks as stupid as she feels.

'What did you say your name is, Mademoiselle?'

'Nell.'

'Of course. Nell, will . . . will you excuse me for a moment, please?'

As she sits down, Clément makes his way to the front of the boat and pulls his phone from his pocket. Nell feels rather silly for having said anything to him. She turns to her mother, who is still snoring, openmouthed, on the bench cushion, and gives her shoulder a gentle shake. Nothing.

'Mum? Mum? You need to wake up now. We're coming to the end.'

'The end?' says Clément, appearing beside her. 'Who says we're near the end? We go one more time!'

'But your website says –'

'It says you are in Paris! And this is too nice a day to walk the streets. Have I shown you the Pont Neuf? I think you must see it close up . . .'

In the little café in rue des Bastides, Fabien is ending his shift, untying his apron and hanging it up on his peg when his phone dings. He stares at it, then shakes his head.

'You're really going to turn your phone off for a whole weekend?' says Émile, who is changing his T-shirt.

'It's the only way I'm going to finish this thing. The editor wants the new draft by Monday.'

Émile shrugs his way into the clean shirt, beaming at the woman who has paused outside the restaurant window, temporarily shocked into immobility by the sight of his bare torso. She grins back at him, shakes her head, and walks on.

'And after you hand it in on Monday, we head for Le Sud, yes?'

'Yes! I am so ready to stop staring at that computer screen.'

From Fabien's pocket his phone dings again.

'You're not going to check your messages?'

'It's just my dad. More obsessing over details. Homosexual flower choices or some such.'

Émile slaps him on the shoulder. 'Okay, man. *Bonne chance*. See you on the other side!' They clasp each other in a brotherly hug, and Émile stands back to look at him.

'Hey. You idiot. I'm proud of you! My best friend is going to publish a book!'

Fabien watches him go, and his phone dings again. He sighs and decides to ignore it, but then it dings three, four, five times. He picks it up, irritated, and stares at the little screen. Then he runs outside to his moped and climbs on.

Clément is talking so furiously that with his thick French accent Nell is barely able to understand what he says. She is confused and, frankly, a little concerned. They have done the circuit twice now, and he shows no sign of wanting to dock. Beside her, Lilian continues to doze gently.

'And now we come to the Pont des Arts. You will see that many of the padlocks have been removed. This is as a result of –'

'Mr Thibauld?' Nell leans over, her voice lifting to be heard against the engine. 'This is really kind of you, but you told us this story the first time around.'

'But did I tell you the names of the city officials involved? This is a very important part of the story.' He looks strange, almost manic. For the first time Nell feels properly uncomfortable.

'Look, I really need to get my mother back to the hotel. She needs a coffee.'

Clément clambers back towards them. 'I have coffee! Did you want some more gâteau? Let me serve you some. You know Paris has the best pâtissiers in the whole –'

She wonders briefly if there are any life rafts she could employ when the air is suddenly split by a whistle. Nell looks up, and there, unbelievably, standing on the bridge, is Fabien.

'Oh, thank God,' the old man says weakly, and sits down.

'Nell?' Fabien shouts. He waves one arm in a huge arc.

'Fabien?' She lifts a hand to her brow.

As Clément steers *La Rose de Paris* towards the path, Fabien runs along the bridge, his long legs eating the ground. He swings around the railing, his feet light, and as the boat comes to a near halt, he jumps aboard and stands there before her.

Clément looks over at his son, his enormous, uncomplicated smile. 'I will make madame some coffee,' he says quietly.

Nell stares at Fabien. Here is the man who has strolled through her dreams, sat opposite her, held her, laughed with her. And yet he is someone else entirely. They stutter a hello, grinning stupidly.

'It's really you!'

'It's really me.'

'It – I couldn't believe it when my father told me. Look, I . . . I brought something to show you.' He reaches into his jacket and pulls out a bound manuscript, its pages a little tattered at the edges. Nell takes it and reads the title.

'*Un Week-end á Paris. A Weekend in Paris.*'

'There's going to be an English-language edition. As well as a French one. I have a publisher and an agent and everything. And they want a second book, too.'

She flips through the pages, hearing the pride in his voice, marvelling at the dense prose. 'It's about . . . a girl who finds herself alone in Paris. But not for long.'

'And these are –' Nell stops at an open page.

'Pros and cons.'

Nell nods to herself. 'Nice.'

Finally she closes the manuscript. 'So . . . how are you? Have you . . . seen Sandrine?'

Fabien nods. Nell tries not to look disappointed. Of course he has. Who would leave a man like Fabien?

'She came to the apartment a couple of weeks ago, to pick up her bracelet. She couldn't believe how I had changed – you know, the book and the website . . .'

Fabien stares down at his feet.

'But I looked at her, and all I felt was this . . . this weight. Of all the things I was expected to be. Like those padlocks, you remember? And I realized that when you came, Nell, it was like . . .'

He looks up, and their eyes meet.

'*Bouf?*' says Nell.

His eyes stay on hers, and then he begins to pat his pockets. 'Look . . . look,' he says. 'I want to show you something else.'

Nell glances over at her mother, who is finally coming to on the bench, wiping at her eyes and blinking against the light. 'What's going on?' she says blearily.

'My son is finding his cojones,' says Clément fondly.

'Did we eat those, too?' murmurs Lilian. 'I kind of zoned out after the terrine.'

Fabien reaches into his inside pocket and presents Nell with a ticket. She studies it, realizing with a jolt what she is looking at.

'You were coming to England?'

'I wanted to surprise you. To show you that I am a person who does things now. I make things happen. And to tell you – I am done with stages. Nell, I realize we hardly know each other, and I understand that you said it would ruin everything, but . . . I have thought about you so much . . . You see, I don't think you were my mistake. I think you may be my best thing.'

He reaches out a hand, and she takes it. She stares at their entwined fingers for a moment, trying not to smile as ridiculously widely as she wants to. And then she gives in to it, and abruptly, awkwardly, they step forward and hug each other. And then they hug each other again, holding on for a longer time this time. And then – because all this staying apart has become frankly impossible – they kiss. For long enough for Nell to stop caring who is watching; long enough for her to forget to breathe, to lose herself in it, to feel that all her edges have become blurred and that somehow the sounds of Paris and the feel of Fabien and the sky and the scents in the air have all become part of her. For so long that her mother finally starts to cough pointedly.

'So,' Nell says as they reluctantly extricate themselves. 'This book of yours. You never did tell me. How does it end?'

Fabien takes the seat beside her. 'You know, I think in the best stories the characters themselves decide. Especially the impulsive ones.'

Nell looks up at the padlocks glinting on the bridge, at her mother, who is drinking coffee with Mr Thibauld. She turns so that she is looking ahead at the Seine, glittering gently in the falling dusk. 'Well,' she says, 'I always did like a story with a happy ending . . .'

# Between the Tweets

'I have a problem,' the man said.

'Everyone who comes here has a problem,' said Frank.

The man swallowed. 'It's a woman.'

'It usually is,' said Frank.

'She . . . she claims we've been having an affair,' he said.

Frank leaned back in his chair, pressing the tips of his fingers together. He'd liked to do that ever since his last secretary told him it made him look intelligent. 'Yeah. They usually do.'

I sat in the corner, my gaze flickering between my coffee and the man's skin, trying to work out which shade was darker. This was beyond Werther's Original. This was beyond Footballer's Wife. This was Daytime Television Grade. And that's when I realized who it was.

'I haven't had a bloody affair!' Declan Travis, former presenter of *Rise And Shine!*, looked at Frank and then at me. '*Really*. I haven't.'

Frank nodded. He usually did at this stage. It was a nod that managed to imply agreement while conveying that truth wasn't necessarily the issue. Nobody came to Frank Digger Associates unless he had something to hide.

'So what do you want from us, Mr Travis?'

'Look, I'm a family man. My reputation is built on my wholesome image. I'm at a very sensitive stage in my career. You're in the business of reputation management. Well, I need you to make this go away. I can't have it in the papers.'

Frank turned slowly towards me and cocked an eyebrow.

'The papers are the least of your worries,' I said.

'Bella's our resident geek. Sorry – digital manager,' Frank explained.

'Reputation is an online issue these days. Death by a thousand pixels. It's a whole new world.'

Declan Travis blinked at me. He had assumed I was the secretary. 'OK, Mr Travis,' I said, opening my laptop. 'I need you to tell me everything you know about this woman. Email, Twitter handle, Facebook profile, Snapchat, WhatsApp – the lot.' He looked at me as if I were speaking Polish. They usually did.

According to Travis it had begun several weeks previously. His teenage son, who liked to fiddle about on computers, as he put it, had idly Googled his father's name and found a young woman with a lot to say. Her Twitter name was @Blond_Becca. Her profile picture consisted of two blue eyes and a peroxide fringe. It was impossible to get any accurate picture of her. I scrolled back through her tweets.

*Declan Travis: Not the family man he likes to make out.*

*I was Declan Travis's lover for two years. Why won't anyone believe me?*

*He likes to make out he's a family man, but he's a dirty, lying sex
maniac. He's used me and ruined my life.*

'What do you think?' Frank came in behind me and
stared at my screen.

I frowned. 'Hard to say without her real name. I'll
engage with her, see if I can work out what's going on.
Then I'll work out how to discredit her.'

Frank squinted, brushed crisp crumbs from my
screen. 'Do we think she's telling the truth?'

I stared at @Blond_Becca's Twitter feed. She was one
determined woman. 'I'm not sure *he* is.'

I set up a new Twitter account, under the name Alexis
Carrington. It's a favourite: nobody young enough to
spend time on social media knows who she is. Then I
sent: *Why should anyone believe you?*

The answer came back within minutes. *Why would I lie?
He's not been on TV for two years, and he's at least twenty years older
than I am!*

She had a point.

*So what is this?* I typed. *Kiss and tell? Why not just sell your story
straight to the tabloids? You could make £20K minimum.*

*I don't want money,* she replied. *I just want the truth to come out.
He seduced me, he promised me we'd be together, and then he dumped*

*me. He's a fraud. He's a —* At this point she ran out of characters. But I got the gist.

She had thirteen thousand followers. I checked the analytics: up from six thousand five days previously.

'It's not good,' I told Frank. 'She doesn't want money.'

'They all want money,' he said.

'Not this one. I told her she could make twenty K, and she wasn't interested.'

He swore under his breath. 'Then we've got a live one. See if we can make her go away. If not, take it up a level.'

Travis rang that afternoon. Two tabloid newspapers had called to quiz him about the rumours. The newspapers loved Twitter; there was no such thing as a slow news day if you could report Kerry Katona and the blond one from *Made in Chelsea* battling it out in 140 characters. All they needed was a DECLAN TRAVIS IN AFFAIR RIDDLE headline and they had a five-hundred-word page lead and an excuse for a picture of a reality-television model with her face blacked out.

'They're camped outside my door!' he yelled down the phone. 'My wife is going nuts. My kids won't speak to me. My agent says this is killing negotiations with ITV2. You have to *do* something.'

'We're issuing a statement,' I said soothingly. 'We'll deny everything and threaten to sue anyone who says otherwise. Secondly, we've set up your own Twitter account. We'll use it to put out positive messages, pictures of you with your family. And we're closing in on

"Becca." But, Mr Travis –' I hesitated. It wasn't hard; I had just opened a packet of Bacon Frazzles, and the smell was frankly disarming.

'What?'

'Are you really telling us everything? If you don't give us the full picture, we can't fight this for you.'

His voice was a whinny. 'I'm telling you the truth. I have no idea who this woman is. Or why the hell she's trying to destroy my life.'

I don't know why I didn't believe him. It's not as if these kiss-and-tell girls didn't exist, all hair extensions and pole dancer's shoes, so desperate for attention that they would claim to have slept with the entire Sunday league for two weeks of fame, a couple of ladmag covers and a run on a reality show. But @Blond_Becca was different. I hadn't come up against anyone who cared about 'the truth' before. It made me nervous.

By that evening she had twenty-eight thousand followers.

I direct-messaged her. I typed, *I'm a friend of Declan's. I don't believe he slept with you. He's a good guy.*

*That's what he wants everyone to think. I have proof,* she replied. I waited.

*He has a scar on his left buttock the same shape as ET's head.* When I put that detail to Declan, the colour actually drained from his face. 'That could be anyone,' he spluttered. 'It could be my masseur. It could be the woman who does my spray tan.'

And then I told him about the other identifying feature she had mentioned, and Frank's eyebrows shot somewhere into his hairline, and he said that it was probably a little early in the day for talk like that, thank you, Bella, and took Mr Travis out for a restorative drink.

Declan Travis became a nightmare for Frank Digger Associates. Two newspapers ran the story the following day. TV'S MR CLEAN IN AFFAIR DRAMA, said one headline, WIFE GRIM-FACED AS SHE LEAVES FAMILY HOME. Another said simply, DIRTY DECLAN? accompanied by a selection of pictures from his finer moments on breakfast television.

Mostly involving girls in bikinis.

'We've got forty-eight hours before the broadsheets pick it up,' Frank said, scratching his head. They would run features titled 'Why do men find it so hard to stay faithful any more?' Travis, meanwhile, was apoplectic. He was chewing Valium like they were Smarties. His agent was on the phone fourteen times a day. @Blond_Becca had fifty-four thousand followers. I had spent two days creating fake Twitter accounts to contradict her. Frank glared at me. 'It's a code red,' he said.

'Will he pay?' I said.

'Oh, he'll pay,' said Frank.

I rang Buzz. 'I need you to trace an account,' I whispered. 'The usual terms.' Three hours later when he called me back, I scribbled the address on to my pad.

And then I sat back and stared at what I had just written.

She was online that afternoon. I sat in the car and tapped the Twitter app on my phone.

*Hello, Becca,* I messaged her.

*Do you believe me now?* she wrote.

*Yes. I believe you slept with Declan Travis. Perhaps we could talk about this further?*

*I told you. I'm not interested in going to the papers. I don't care what they're saying.*

*I wasn't talking about the papers. Come out to the car. I'm parked right outside your house.*

Sally Travis was the kind of blonde who would once have been called 'perky', had passed through 'foxy', and could now be described as 'well preserved and probably lusted after quietly by the chairman of the golf club'. She opened the door of my car, waited while I brushed the crumbs off the passenger seat, and sat down.

'I had to do something,' she said. She lit a cigarette with perfectly manicured fingers and blew out a large, perfectly constructed smoke ring. 'He's past it. He's been offered nothing in six months but *Pets in Crisis* and the holiday cover for *Anthea's Antiques*.'

'He doesn't know you're behind this?'

'Of course he doesn't know,' she said wearily. 'He's thick as two short planks, bless him. If he knew the truth, he would have blurted it out weeks ago. I just thought this way we could raise his profile, make him . . . exciting again. You know, relevant.'

I stared at her. 'He's going insane with worry.'

She narrowed her eyes. 'I know you think I'm awful. But look – I just got off the phone with his agent. This morning alone we've been offered a slot on *Loose Women* and two exclusives with the Sundays. Best of all, morning telly has come knocking again. It's what he loves.'

She raised a small smile. 'Oh, I know he's a bit shaken now, but I'll fill the kids in. And once he sees what's come out of it, he'll be absolutely delighted.'

She exhaled and blew another perfect smoke ring out the window.

'Besides, I can't have him under my feet all day, Bella. He drives me nuts.' She turned to look at me. 'What?' she said.

Her high heel crunched on a stray Frazzle.

'I don't suppose you want a job?' I said.

I was back in the office by four. The traffic on the M3 was awful, but I hadn't cared. I had sung along to a CD, eaten two packs of emergency Pickled Onion Monster Munch, and pondered the subtle complexities of enduring love. It wasn't a subject that came up much in my line of work.

Sally Travis and I had talked it out over a further half hour. We had agreed that @Blond_Becca would disappear as abruptly as she had arrived. Declan would remain blissfully ignorant. Nobody would be able to pin anything on him, but the faint hint of marital naughtiness would perversely do him no harm with the housewives. And we would place a four-page spread in the next edition of *OK!* – DECLAN AND SALLY TRAVIS: 'STRONGER THAN EVER AFTER TWENTY YEARS OF MARRIAGE'. The wives would read it out of sympathy for Sally. The husbands would leaf through with a flicker of envy that the old dog still had it. I had called a contact at the magazine, and they were totally up for it. That fee alone would cover Frank Digger Associates' expenses.

I walked straight into Frank's office without knocking and sat down on the leather sofa.

'You can tell Declan that Becca is no longer a problem. All he has to do is sit back and watch those career offers roll in.' I crossed my feet on his glass coffee table with an air of studied nonchalance.

It took me a few minutes to realize that he didn't look happy.

'What?'

'Have you not listened to your flipping radio?'

'No,' I said. 'It's busted. Why?'

Frank put his head in his hands. 'I couldn't stop him.'

'Stop him from what?' I said. 'Frank, I don't understand. What's going on?'

'I couldn't stop him from speaking out.' Frank shook his head in disgust.

'You were right all along, Bella. Declan Travis has just gone on telly and admitted to a three-year affair with his ruddy makeup girl.'

# Love in the Afternoon

They are allowed into the room on the dot of two. No earlier. Hotel policy, the receptionist explains. 'It has actually been free since eleven, but management say if we do it for one . . .' She taps her nose knowingly.

Sara nods. She hasn't minded waiting. It has given her some time to acclimatize. She had not expected to be here today, at a four-star Jacobean hotel in deepest Suffolk, with rolling manicured lawns and a dress code. She had expected to be home, sorting through school uniforms and unloading the detritus of lunch boxes and gym bags, perhaps doing a supermarket run. The usual weekend routine.

But Doug had swept into the kitchen shortly after breakfast, their children hovering behind him, and announced theatrically that she should put down her rubber gloves and put on some makeup.

'Why?' she'd said absently. She had been trying to listen to the radio.

'Because we are dropping the kids at my mother's, and then I am whisking you away for a night.'

She had stared at him.

'For your anniversary,' their daughter added.

'We knew all about it,' said Seth, their youngest. 'Dad did it as a surprise.'

She had peeled off her rubber gloves. 'But . . . our anniversary was weeks ago.'

'Well . . . happy belated anniversary.' He'd kissed her. Behind him, Seth had made retching noises.

'But . . . who's going to look after the dog?' she said.

Irritation flickered across his features. 'We'll leave some food out for him. It's only twenty-four hours.'

'But he'll be lonely. And he'll mess.'

'Then we'll take him to my mother's.'

His mother hated dogs. Sara made a mental note to order flowers for Janice as an apology. *I don't want to go away*, she thought suddenly. *I want to get the house straight. I want you to fix the bathroom light switch, like you've been promising you would for the past two months.* But she forced her mouth into an obliging smile as her daughter pointed to a weekend bag.

'I've put your blue dress in,' Tamsin said. 'And the satiny high heels.'

'Come on, come on!' Doug clapped his hands like the organizer of an errant tour group. In the car he placed a hand on her knee. 'OK?' he said.

'Who are you?' she said. 'And what have you done with my husband?' The children laughed. At their grandparents' they would watch satellite television and steal glasses of their grandmother's sherry before supper.

\*

The room overlooks a lake. It is dominated by the widest bed she has ever seen. She thinks absently that the children and the dog could have come, too, and there still would have been room for one more. There is tea and coffee and even home-baked biscuits in a small tin. He mentions this twice, as if reaffirming what a splendid hotel it is. He tips the man who brings up their cases, patting his pockets for change, and then, as the door closes, it is just the two of them, their eyes sliding together in the silence.

'So,' he says.

'So.'

'What shall we do now?'

They have been married for fourteen years. Once this question would have remained unasked. Once, maybe thirteen years ago, they sloped off to bed in the afternoon, dragging plates of toast that would end up untouched and congealing on the floor. There had been something deliciously decadent about stealing away in daylight hours when the rest of the world was working.

Now she is wondering whether her daughter packed her contact lenses and when she will find time to wash the school uniform.

She regards him, this man, pacing the room as he unpacks his clothes, smooths trousers carefully on to hangers. It is five weeks and two days since they last made love. That occasion had ended prematurely when Seth had been sick and yelled down the corridor that his duvet cover needed changing. She remembers feeling faintly relieved at the time, as if she had been excused games at school.

'You want to go for a walk?' he says. He is peering through the French windows. 'Grounds look nice.'

He has made all this effort, has shown that after all this time he can be generous, impulsive, unpredictable. Shouldn't she at least do the same?

She sits on the bed, leans back in a position that could possibly be construed as seductive, and tries not to feel self-conscious.

'We could . . . just stay here,' she says, stretching a leg. She realizes she is blushing.

He turns towards her. 'Great idea. Let's get a DVD,' he says. 'You can rent them from the front desk. They've got *Snakes on a Plane* – I've wanted to see that for ages.'

It is four fifteen, and she is lying on the oversized bed, watching a film about snakes on a plane. Her husband is beside her, his socked feet twitching as he laughs. She stares out of the window at the blue sky. When had they become like this? Not after their eldest son's birth. She remembered the health visitor telling them baldly to get intimate as soon as possible. 'Go to bed when he sleeps,' she had advised as they stared, whey-faced, felled by the first weeks of new parenthood. 'His afternoon nap. *Enjoy* each other.' They had looked at this woman and then at each other as if confirming that she was indeed mad. Go to bed? When the flat was drowning in nappies and soiled babygrows? When her body still leaked unpredictably from unmentionable places? But they had, and now, she realizes, it had been glorious. They had giggled at the naughtiness of it, exultant at the existence of their son and their part in creating him.

'What time are we going home tomorrow?'

'What?' He drags his attention from the screen.

'I just remembered – we need to pick up Seth's violin from the Thomases. He left it there on Friday. And his violin lesson is on Monday morning.'

'Do we have to think about that now?' he says irritably.

'It's better than thinking about pythons.' She has not shaved her legs or her armpits. She realizes that she actually hates surprises.

'You don't like this film?'

'It's fine.'

He studies her face. 'I knew it. You *did* want the one with Kate Winslet.'

'No . . . I just need to sort things before I can relax.'

He speaks with exaggerated patience. 'Just . . . forget . . . the . . . kids . . . for . . . five . . . minutes.'

'You can't simply parachute me out of our life and expect me to pretend that nothing needs doing.'

He pauses the DVD and hoists himself up on to one elbow.

'Why?' he demands. 'Why can't you switch off?'

'Because someone has to remember this stuff, Doug, and it isn't usually you.'

He pulls a face. 'Oh. That's nice . . .'

'I'm only stating a fact.'

'Well, what do I have to do?' he says. 'You moan that I take you for granted, and when I finally do the thing you say you want, give you a bit of romance, you witter on about music lessons and have a go at me.'

'Romance? You call watching a DVD about snakes *romance*? Jeez, Doug. I'd hate to see what you came up with when you *weren't* in a romantic mood.'

He stares at her, admits the first sign of awkwardness. 'OK. Well, what do you want to do?'

'I thought . . .' she begins. She sighs, picks at the silky bedcover. 'I thought . . .'

He is gazing at her intently. 'Oh. *You* thought we would be . . .'

She bridles. 'You make it sound like I was expecting something bizarre.'

'You want to make love, fine.' He shrugs. 'We can watch the end of the film later.'

'Oh, last of the great romantics.'

'Bloody hell, Sara. What am I supposed to say?'

'Nothing,' she says furiously. *'Nothing.'*

'No, that's right. Because I *can't* say anything bloody right. Or *do* anything right.'

He switches off the DVD as if under protest, and they sit in silence, absorbing the distant sounds of the hotel, the sporadic footfalls in the corridor, the muffled clatter of a room-service tray being removed. She observes, surreptitiously, the way his stomach strains against his waistband. He will not buy the next size up in trousers, even though he plainly needs them. The children call him 'Muffin Top' behind his back.

'We're booked for dinner at eight,' he says finally. 'The food is meant to be fantastic.'

'Good.'

'I asked Tess to pack that blue dress of yours. The one I like.'

'It doesn't actually fit me very well,' she says tentatively. 'Do you know if she packed anything else?' She suspects she will not be able to eat anything at all if she is not to split that dress at the seams.

'Don't know. We could go downstairs for a bit,' he says. 'I think they do a nice tea. You can have it on the lawn.'

She shakes her head, picturing calorie-laden cake, doilied éclairs.

Straining seams.

'Not if we've got a big supper.'

'Well . . .' He pats the bed, smiles tentatively. 'Do you want to . . . ?'

There is a long silence.

She hugs her knees. 'To be honest, not really. Not right now.'

He rolls his eyes. 'Well, what *do* you want to do?'

'Don't make that face,' she says.

'What face?'

'For years, Doug, you have forgotten my birthday. And our anniversary. And Valentine's Day. And now you make one grand gesture, and suddenly it's all OK? One DVD on a queen-size bed and I'm to forget it all?'

He is sitting up now, swinging his legs round so that his back is to her. 'Oh, there's always something wrong. I can never get it right. I come home every night, I earn a good salary, I help with our kids. I book us a romantic break. But no. It still isn't enough.'

'I am grateful,' she protests. 'But it's daytime. It feels . . . awkward. It's like going . . . from nought to sixty.'

'But we don't have a two-week holiday! What the hell do I do, Sara? I feel like nothing is enough for you.'

'Don't lay this all on me,' she snaps. 'Don't blame me if I've completely forgotten the art of seduction. It takes two *not* to tango, you know.'

'Fine!' he yells. 'Let's forget it. Let's just bloody well pack up and go home. I'm going to use the bathroom,' he says, and slams the door.

'You forgot your crossword!' she retorts, and hurls the newspaper after him.

There is silence.

She stares at her reflection, this cross, tired-looking woman in a pale blue shirt. She stares, and slowly she pictures a different kind of woman: tousle-haired, voracious, happy to pounce on her beloved in any tiny window of lascivious opportunity. Her neighbour Kath once confided that she and her husband often had a 'quickie' after getting the kids off to school. 'We've got it down to six minutes,' she said. 'So he doesn't miss the eight-forty.'

Sara stares, then pouts tentatively at her reflection, feeling immediately foolish. Then she flinches as she hears the knock on the door.

'Room service.'

Doug cannot hear over the extractor fan. She opens the door, and a man wheels in a trolley bearing a champagne bucket and glasses.

'Mr and Mrs Nicholls,' he says.

'Oh,' she says as the man begins to open the bottle, humming under his breath. 'Gosh. That's . . . very kind.' She is not sure what to do. She gazes out of the French windows, as Doug had done. She feels guilty and horrible. She wonders briefly if she should be trying to find a tip.

'Great, these corporate jollies, aren't they?' the man says cheerfully.

'Sorry?'

'The free trips. You're the fourth lot we've done for Trethick Johnson this week. Your husband is management, is he? All the management are getting the free champagne as well. Think some of them would have preferred cash bonuses, though.'

She stares at him for a moment, then accepts the glass he proffers.

'Yes,' she says, staring at it. 'Yes, I suppose they would.'

'Still, champagne is champagne, right?' He salutes as he leaves the room. 'Enjoy.'

She is sitting on the bed when Doug eventually emerges. He glances at the champagne bucket, then at her. He looks burdened, beaten. She thinks about how hard he has worked these last few months.

'What's this?'

She considers this for a moment. 'Special offer,' she says finally. 'I think it comes with the room.'

He nods, accepting this, then glances up at her again. 'Sorry,' he mutters.

She holds out a glass. 'And me,' she says.

'You're right. It's all a bit –'

There are new, deep grooves that cut from his nose halfway down his chin.

'Doug. Don't.' She raises a smile. 'Champagne is champagne, right?'

They sit beside each other on the bed. Slowly, they move their feet so that they are touching. He tilts his glass to hers. The bubbles are like little lead shots disappearing down her throat, like ammunition.

'I was thinking. I'll fix that bathroom light when we get back,' he says. 'Shouldn't take long.'

She has another long sip of her champagne and closes her eyes.

Outside, she can hear people taking tea on the lawn,

the hiss of tyres on a gravel drive. Laughter ripples its way up to their window. She opens her eyes and leans her head gently against his shoulder.

It is twenty to five in the afternoon.

'You know,' she says, 'it's still several hours until suppertime . . .'

# A Bird in the Hand

They always argued on the way to parties. She never could just relax, Simon would claim as he started the car. Not when they were already half an hour late, she couldn't, no, she retorted, still fixing her hair in the passenger mirror.

It might have been the fact that she always seemed to be seated next to the bore. (She occasionally timed how long it took for a man to ask her what she did; her current record was a little under two hours.) It might have been the fact that she always seemed to be the designated driver. (This was never up for discussion – she would ask him, *Who's driving?* And be met, inevitably, with a jokey look of horror and a confession that he'd already had several large ones.) But worse, this party was taking place in a marquee, a fact she had remembered fifteen minutes after she finally left home. In grey satin stilettos.

'You OK if I drink?' Simon said as they pulled up in the gravel car park. 'I drove last time, if you remember.'

Krista Nightingale (Beth always suspected she'd made up her name) was a life coach and former neighbour. No mundane dinner parties for her; her 'gatherings' took place in disused fire stations or candlelit churches. She was always investigating new methods of detoxification or disappearing on freebie trips with rich clients. Simon had urged Beth to ask her how she might do the same ('You're good at bossing people'), but Beth had never been any good at networking. It all seemed so calculating somehow, complimenting someone on her handbag while trying to plunder her address book.

'Wow,' said Simon, eyeing the crimson maharaja-style tent that spanned the length of Krista's garden. Around it flower beds sat in full-blooming glory, wafting scent into the warm evening air. Chinese lanterns dangled from the trees, sending a soft red glow into the sunset.

'Hessian flooring,' Beth said despairingly.

'Oh, come on, love. Look on the bright side. It's gorgeous!'

'Gorgeous if your heels aren't going to sink into that ground like meat skewers.'

'Well, wear different shoes.'

'That might have been useful advice half an hour ago.'

'You can borrow my shoes.'

'Funny.'

'Beth! Don't you look gorgeous!' Krista picked her way across the matting. She was one of those women who moved effortlessly among people, collecting pieces of information that she then redistributed in perfectly appropriate parcels, like some kind of social Robin Hood.

'Everyone else is here. No, don't worry! Don't worry!'

She waved a hand as Beth began to apologize. Beth stared at that perfectly untroubled brow and wondered about Botox. 'The food is running late anyway. Here, let me get you both a drink.'

'I'll sort us out. This looks absolutely amazing, Krista. Just point me towards the bar.' Simon kissed Krista's cheek and disappeared. He would be there for a good half an hour, Beth thought. Picking at snacks.

And waiting for her bad mood to evaporate.

Krista was steering her into the tent. 'You know the Chisholms, don't you? And the McCarthys? Hmm. Oh, look,' she said. 'Let me introduce you to Ben. He's in the same line of work as you.'

And there he was, standing in front of her, slowly lifting a hand.

'Actually,' he said, as Beth's mouth dried to powder, 'we've already met.'

Her gaze slid sideways to where her husband was standing, picking his way through the Bombay mix. 'Yes.' She looked at Krista and swallowed, recovering her smile. 'We . . . we used to work together.'

Krista looked delighted. 'Oh, really? What a coincidence! What did you do?'

'We used to put brochures together. I wrote the words, Ben did the images.'

'Until Beth left.'

'Yes. Until I left.'

They stared at each other for a moment. He looked exactly the same, she thought, no – *better,* damn it – and then she was suddenly aware of the redheaded woman beaming at her.

Ben's gaze dropped briefly to his feet. 'And this is my wife, Lisa.'

'Congratulations.' Her smile was swift and seamless. 'When did you get married?'

'Eighteen months ago.'

'That was quick. I mean . . . you weren't married when we worked together.'

'It was a whirlwind romance, wasn't it, sweetie?' The woman slid her arm across his shoulder, just a hint of possession in the way her hand lingered on his collar.

Ben nodded. 'And your husband? Are you . . .'

'Am I what? Still with him?' It was snappier than she'd intended. She half laughed, trying to make it seem like a joke.

' . . . here with him?'

She recovered. 'Yes. Of course! He's just over there. By the bar.'

His gaze paused just a little too long, assessing. 'I don't believe I ever met him.'

'No, I don't believe you did.'

She felt Krista's hand on her back. 'We'll be sitting down in two minutes. Will you excuse me while I see how the pakoras are doing? Beth, you're not vegan, are you? I'm sure somebody said they were vegan. Because we have some curried tofu.'

'Nice to see you, Beth.' Ben was already turning away.

'You, too.' She kept her smile on her face the whole way across the room to Simon.

'I've got a headache.'

Simon threw a peanut into his mouth. 'But I haven't even got my pants off.'

'Funny. Do we really have to stay? I'd much rather go home.' She glanced around the crowded tent. As night fell, the smell of roses and freshly cut grass mingled with those of Indian spices. From his cross-legged position on a cushion in the corner, a sitar player picked lush tunes. English people were no good at sitting on the floor, she thought absently. Not bendy enough. Across the room a man was wrapping a napkin around his head in a feeble facsimile of a turban, and she winced for him.

'I really have got a headache.'

Simon allowed the barman to refill his glass. 'You're just tired. We can't walk out even before the food.' He gave her a squeeze and a quizzical look. 'Just hang on another couple of hours. You'll feel better once we eat.'

There was an empty seat on her left. She knew as soon as she saw the name carefully inscribed beside it that it had been inevitable.

'Oh,' he said when he saw it.

'Yes,' she said. 'Lucky you.'

'Lucky both of us.'

Why had she agreed to come tonight? There'd been eighty-nine excuses she could have made, including the fact that she had rare medical conditions to investigate on Google, perhaps an afghan to crochet out of the cat's sheddings. But how had she ended up within inches of this man – a man who not even two years earlier had turned her life inside out?

The man who had transformed her from invisible, un-appreciated wife to sex goddess, flirtatious fox. Adulterer.

She swivelled determinedly towards the florid man on her right. 'So,' she began, 'what is it that you do? Tell me everything about yourself. Everything!'

Even before she finished her starter, Beth knew every-thing she was ever going to need to know about damp-proofing, about Vandex plastering and water ingress. Not that she had really registered much that the large man said anyway; her every sense was trained on Ben on her left, on Ben laughing, talking to the woman beside him.

But then after a series of involved observations about ultra-membranes and cavity walls, Henry the Damp-Proof Consultant decamped to have a cigarette in the garden, and it was just the two of them, marooned on their part of the table.

They sat in silence for a few minutes, gazing at the flower arrangements.

'Lovely party.'

'Yes.'

'You look well,' he said.

'Thank you.' She wished she had worn the red dress. Why hadn't she worn the red dress?

'Are you working?' he asked.

'Yes. A small marketing company in town. You?'

'I'm still at Farnsworth's.'

'I see.'

They lapsed back into silence while a teenage waitress self-consciously handed them fresh plates.

Beth refilled her glass. 'Congratulations. On getting married.'

'Thank you. It was unexpected.'

'You make it sound like an accident.' She took a large slug of wine.

'No. Just unexpected, as I said. I didn't think I was going to get involved with anyone. Not for a long time.'

'No. You never were a big one for commitment, were you?'

She felt his eyes on her and flushed. Shut up, she told herself. Simon is only a matter of feet away.

His voice dropped to a murmur. 'Are we really going to do this?'

Beth felt a kind of recklessness building within her. How many times had she wanted to have this conversation? How many times had she rehearsed all the things she wanted to say to him? When they had sat down at the table, she'd half expected him to simply get up and leave. How could he sit there eating and drinking and behave as if nothing had happened after all?

'You really want to get into this now, Beth?'

She lifted her glass. Her husband was laughing at

something Krista was saying. He looked over and winked at her.

'Why not?' she said, waving back. 'It's only been two years. I figure that's a pretty decent period of time to put off an argument.'

'It's funny.' He spoke through a rictus grin. 'I don't remember you being this angry.'

'Angry?' she said sarcastically. 'Why would I be angry?'

'I don't know. Especially as, if I remember correctly, you were the one who made all the decisions.'

'Decisions?'

Ben leaned a little closer to her. 'Not to meet me? Not even to discuss what we had promised to discuss?'

'*Not to meet you?*' She turned and stared at him. 'Are we talking about the same relationship?'

'Beth darling, would you mind passing the wine?' Krista's voice broke across the conversation.

She held it up abruptly as if she had won a prize. 'Certainly,' she said, her voice unnaturally loud.

'The day you left,' he hissed beside her, 'you were going to meet me in the Old Hen, so that we could discuss our future. And you never even turned up. I knew you were having trouble working things out, but not a call, not an explanation? Nothing?'

'The Old Hen?'

Krista's voice again. 'And the white? Sorry, darling. Just can't reach from here.'

'Sure!' She leaned forward with the chilled bottle.

'And you knew I couldn't reach you once you had

handed in your work phone. What was I supposed to think? Don't you believe that after everything we'd been through, everything we'd promised each other, that I deserved a little more than just a no-show?'

Her voice dropped to a whisper. 'It was the Coach and Horses. We were due to meet at the Coach and Horses. And *you* were the one who didn't turn up.'

Their eyes locked.

Lisa appeared between them. Beth noticed, with vague satisfaction, that Ben flinched slightly at her hand on his shoulder. 'What did you think of the lentil pâté, darling?'

'Delicious!' His smile landed on his face like it had been dropped there.

'I thought you'd enjoy that. Krista's going to give me the recipe.'

'Great!'

There was a brief, awkward silence.

Lisa nodded wryly. 'Business, eh? It's OK . . . you two can get back to your marketing discussions now. I'm trying to locate the Ladies.'

'Over there.' Beth pointed through the crowd of people. 'In the main house.'

'The Coach and Horses?' Ben repeated as his wife disappeared.

The rice had arrived in front of Beth. She passed it to Ben, feeling an electric jolt as their hands made contact. 'Two hours I waited.'

They stared at each other. For a moment the tent

disappeared. She was there on a wet Thursday, weeping into her sleeve in an empty pub.

'Did I hear you two talking about pubs?' Henry had arrived back on her right.

'Yes.' She swallowed. 'The Coach and Horses.'

'Oh, I know that one. Up by the ring road, isn't it? Isn't it quite busy?'

Her eyes met Ben's. 'Not as busy as some of us would like, apparently.'

'Shame. A lot of pubs seem to be headed that way around here. It's the landlords, you know. Charge them extortionate amounts. They'll put them all out of business.'

They sat and ate the main course, something containing chicken breast. She didn't know.

She could no longer taste anything.

'Do you want some more wine?'

She watched his hand as he poured, remembering how much she had loved the shape of his fingers. Perfect men's hands, long, strong fingers with squared-off ends, lightly tanned as if they'd been working outside. She had always compared her own husband's unfavourably to them and hated herself for doing so.

'I don't know what to say,' he told her.

'There's nothing *to* say. You're married, I'm married. We've moved on.'

She felt the faintest pressure and realized with shock that it was his thigh against hers.

'Have you?' he said quietly, and the words went through her like a seismic tremor. 'Really?'

She had eaten half a chocolate mousse, and the coffee cups were empty in front of them. She fingered her wineglass, watching as Ben's redheaded wife talked animatedly to a group of people at the other end of the long table. That could have been me, Beth thought.

'All this time,' Ben said, quietly, 'both of us believing the other had bailed out.' His leg was still resting against hers. She didn't like to think how she would feel when it was taken away.

'I just figured you'd tired of my indecision.'

'I'd waited the best part of a year. I would have waited another.'

'You never said that.'

'I hoped I wouldn't have to.'

She had grieved for him. Privately, hiding it from her unsuspecting husband. Tears in the bath or in the car, tears of loss for what might have been and of guilt for what *had* been. But even then with a vague relief that a decision had been reached. She was not naturally a duplicitous person; this *thing* had left her incapable of concentrating on anything – work, house, family. And the prospect of breaking Simon's heart had been almost too much to bear.

Ben leaned in towards her, his eyes trained on the dance floor. 'What do you think would have happened to us?'

She kept her own eyes straight ahead. Her husband was talking to Krista. They broke off briefly to laugh at someone who had fallen from his chair.

'I think . . . speculating on that would drive one mad.'

His voice was a low murmur. 'I think we would be together now.'

She closed her eyes.

'In fact, I know it.'

She turned to look at him. His eyes were soft, searching, terrifying.

'Nobody ever made me feel like you do,' he said.

The world stalled around her. She felt her blood rising, her heart race. Two years fell away.

Then she looked up, and as she did, she saw Lisa at the other end of the table. Lisa had turned from the group of people and was watching them both, her expression briefly unguarded, bearing the tense weariness of the constantly vigilant. She smiled awkwardly at Beth, then looked down at the table. Beth felt the colour rise to her cheeks.

*Yes. That could have been me.*

She looked over at her husband, laughing. Unaware. Blameless. *We're doing OK, aren't we?* he'd said the previous Sunday evening. Uncharacteristically, he had studied her face as he said it. She took a last sip of her drink and sat very still for a moment. Then she stood, feeling for her handbag at her feet.

'Beth?'

'It was good to see you, Ben,' she said.

Incomprehension flickered across his face. 'You never told me where you worked,' he said hurriedly. Henry the Damp-Proof Consultant sat a short distance away, nodding in time to the music.

'Maybe . . . we could have lunch sometime? We've hardly begun to catch up.'

She looked over again at Lisa. She put her hand gently on his arm, just for a moment. 'I don't think so,' she said. 'We've both moved on, haven't we?'

'I'm sorry – what did you say you did?' Henry called out as she left the table.

Simon was standing near the bar, picking his way through what remained of the canapés. He would be searching for cashew nuts, his favourites. He found one and held it aloft like a prize before tossing it into his mouth. She realized she'd never seen him miss.

'Let's go home,' she said, placing her hand on his shoulder.

'Still tired?'

'Actually, I thought we could have an early night.'

'Early night?' He glanced at his watch. 'At a quarter past twelve?'

'Gift horse, mister,' she said.

'Ah. I'm not looking. Promise.' He smiled, helping her on with her jacket.

Perhaps she imagined, rather than really saw, the way he glanced behind him at where she'd been sitting, a flicker of something unreadable on his face. But with her husband's arm around her, just enough to stop her heels from sinking too far into the matting, Beth made her way carefully through the tables to the entrance of the tent and home.

# Crocodile Shoes

She is peeling her way out of her swimsuit when the Yummy Mummies arrive. Glossy and stick thin, they surround her, talking loudly, rubbing expensive moisturizer into shiny legs, completely oblivious to her.

These are women with designer gymwear, perfect hair, and time for coffee. She imagines husbands called Rupe or Tris who carelessly toss envelopes containing awesome bonuses on to their Conran kitchen tables and sweep their wives into bear hugs before booking impromptu dinners out. These women do not have husbands who stay in their pyjama bottoms till midday and look hunted whenever their wives mention having another go at that job application.

Gym membership is a luxury they really cannot afford these days, but Sam is tied into paying for it for another four months, and Phil tells her she might as well make the most of it. It does her good, he says. He means it does them both good for her to get out of the house and away from him.

'Use it or lose it, Mum,' says their daughter, who eyes Sam's increasingly indistinct hip-to-waist ratio with barely concealed horror. Sam cannot tell either of them how much she hates the gym: its apartheid of hard bodies, the carefully disguised disapproval of the twenty-something personal trainers, the shadowed corners where she and the other Lumpy People try to hide.

She is at that age, the age where all the wrong things seem somehow to stick – fat, the groove between her eyebrows – while everything else – job security, marital happiness, dreams – seem to slip effortlessly away.

'You have no idea how much they've put up the prices at Club Med this year,' one of the women is saying. She is bent over, towelling her expensively tinted hair, her perfectly tanned bottom barely covered by expensive lace knickers. Sam has to wiggle sideways to avoid touching her.

'I know! I tried to book Mauritius for Christmas – our usual villa has gone up by forty per cent.'

'It's a scandal.'

*Yes, it's a scandal,* Sam thinks. *How awful for you all.* She thinks of the camper that Phil bought the previous year to do up. We can spend weekends by the coast, he'd said cheerfully. He never got beyond repairing the back bumper. Since he lost his job, it has sat there on the drive, a nagging reminder of what else they've lost.

Sam wriggles into her knickers, trying to hide her pale, mottled flesh under the towel. Today she has four meetings with potential clients. In half an hour, she will meet Ted and Joel from Print, and they will try to win their company the deals they've been working on. 'We need this,' Ted had said. 'As in, if we don't get it . . .' He pulled a face. No pressure there, then.

'Do you remember that awful place in Cannes that Susanna booked?'

They are braying with laughter. Sam pulls her towel more tightly around her and heads to the corner to dry her hair.

When she returns, they are gone, an echo of costly scent lingering in the air. She breathes a sigh of relief and slumps down on the damp wooden bench.

It is only when she is dressed that she reaches under the bench and realizes that although the kitbag there looks exactly like hers, it is not hers. This bag does not contain her comfortable black pumps, suitable for pounding pavements and negotiating deals. It contains a pair of vertiginous, red, crocodile-skin Christian Louboutin sling-backs.

The girl at the desk doesn't blink.

'The woman who was in the changing rooms. She's taken my bag.'

'What's her name?'

'I don't know. There were three of them. One of them took my bag.'

'Sorry, but I usually work at the Hills Road branch. You're probably best off speaking to someone who works here full-time.'

'But I have meetings to go to now. I can hardly go in my trainers.'

The girl looks her slowly up and down, and her expression suggests that wearing trainers may be the least of

Sam's sartorial worries. Sam glances at her phone. She is due at the first meeting in thirty minutes. She sighs, picks up the kitbag and stomps off towards the train.

She cannot go into this meeting in gym shoes. This becomes obvious as soon as she reaches the publishers, whose marble-and-gilt offices make Trump Tower look positively Amish. It is also apparent in Ted and Joel's sideways glances at her feet.

'Getting down with the yoof, are we?' Joel says.

'Going to wear your leotard, too?' says Ted. 'Perhaps she's going to conduct negotiations via the medium of freeform dance,' and waves his arms a la Isadora Duncan. He waves his arms to the sides.

'Funny.'

She hesitates, then curses, rummages around in the bag, and pulls out the shoes. They are only half a size out. Without saying anything, she whips off her trainers in the foyer and puts on the red Louboutins instead. When she stands, she has to grab Joel's arm to stay upright.

'Wow. They're . . . um . . . not very you.'

She straightens, glares at Joel. 'Why? What's "me"?'

'Plain. You like plain stuff. Sensible stuff.'

Ted smirks. 'You know what they say about shoes like that, Sam.'

'What?'

'Well, they're not for standing up in.'

They nudge each other, chuckling. *Great*, she thinks. *So now I get to go to a meeting looking like a call girl.*

When she emerges from the lift, it is all she can do to walk across the room. She feels stupid, as if everyone is looking at her, as if it is obvious that she is a middle-aged woman in somebody else's shoes. She stammers her way through the meeting and stumbles as she leaves. The two men say nothing, but they all know that they will not get this contract. Nevertheless, she has no choice. She will have to wear the ridiculous shoes all day.

'Never mind. Still three to go,' says Ted kindly.

She is outlining their print strategy in the second meeting when she observes that the managing director is not listening to her. He is staring at her foot. Embarrassed, she almost loses the thread of what she is saying. But then, as she continues, she realizes it is he who is distracted.

'So how do those figures sound?' she says.

'Good!' he exclaims, as if hauled from a daydream. 'Yes. Good.'

She senses a brief opportunity, pulls a contract from her briefcase. 'So shall we agree on terms?'

He is staring at her shoes again. She tilts one foot and lets the strap slide from her heel.

'Sure,' he says. He takes the pen without looking at it.

'Don't say anything,' she says to Ted as they leave, jubilant.

'I'm saying nothing. You get us another deal like that, you can wear carpet slippers for all I care.'

At the next meeting, she makes sure her feet are on display the whole time. Although John Edgmont doesn't stare, she sees that the mere fact of these shoes makes him reassess his version of who she is. Weirdly, it makes *her* reassess *her* version of herself. She charms. She stands firm on terms. She wins another contract.

They take a taxi to meeting four.

'I don't care,' she says. 'I can't walk in these things, and I've earned it.'

The result is that instead of making their usual harried, sweaty arrival, she pulls up outside the final meeting unruffled. She steps out and realizes that she is standing taller.

She is a little disappointed, therefore, to discover that M. Price is a woman. And it doesn't take long to discover that Miriam Price plays hardball. The negotiations take an hour. If they go ahead, their margins will be down to almost nothing. It feels impossible.

'I just need to visit the Ladies room,' Sam says. Once inside, she leans forward over the basin and splashes her face with water. Then she checks her eye makeup and stares at herself in the mirror, wondering what to do.

The door opens, and Miriam Price steps in behind her. They nod politely while washing their hands. And then Miriam Price looks down.

'Oh, my God, I love your shoes!' she exclaims.

'Actually they're –' Sam begins. Then she stops and smiles. 'They're great, aren't they?'

Miriam points down at them. 'Can I see?'

She holds the shoe that Sam removes, examines it from all angles. 'Is this a Louboutin?'

'Yes.'

'I once queued for four hours just to buy a pair of his shoes. How crazy is that?'

'Oh, not crazy at all,' says Sam.

Miriam Price hands it back almost reluctantly. 'You know, you can always tell a proper shoe. My daughter doesn't believe me, but you can tell so much about someone from what they wear.'

'I tell my daughter the exact same thing!' The words are out of her mouth before she even knows what she's saying.

'I tell you what. I hate negotiating like this. Do you have a window for lunch next week? Let's the two of us get together and thrash something out. I'm sure we can find a way through.'

'That would be great,' Sam says. She manages to walk out of the Ladies without the slightest wobble.

She arrives home after seven. She is in her trainers again, and her daughter, who is just heading out, raises her eyebrows at Sam as if she is some kind of bag lady.

'This is not New York, Mum. You just look weird, like you lost your shoes.'

'I *did* lose my shoes.' She puts her head around the living room door. 'Hey.'

'Hey!'

Phil raises a hand. He is where she knew he'd be: on the sofa. 'Have you . . . done anything about supper?'

'Oh. No. Sorry.'

It's not that he is selfish. It's as if he cannot rouse himself to anything any more, even the cooking of beans on toast. The successes of the day evaporate. She makes supper, trying not to feel weighed down by it all, and then, as an afterthought, pours two glasses of wine.

'You'll never guess what happened to me today,' she says, handing one to him. And she tells him the story of the swapped shoes.

'Show me.'

She heads out into the hallway and puts them on. She straightens a little as she heads back into the living room, injects a little swagger into her walk.

'Wow.' His eyebrows shoot up to somewhere near his hairline.

'I know! I wouldn't have bought them in a million years. And they're a nightmare to walk in. But I pulled in three deals today, three deals we weren't expected to get. And I think it was all because of the shoes.'

'Not all of it, surely. But your legs look fantastic.' He pushes his way up so he is sitting straight.

She smiles. 'Thank you.'

'You never wear shoes like this.'

'I know. But I don't have a Louboutin-shoe sort of life.'

'You should. You look . . . you look amazing.'

He looks so lovely then, so pleased for her and yet so vulnerable. She walks over to her husband, sits on his lap, links her arms around his neck. Perhaps the wine has made her giddy. She cannot remember the last time she approached him like this. They gaze at each other.

'You know what they say about shoes like this?' she murmurs.

He blinks.

'Well, they're not made for standing up in.'

She is at the gym shortly after nine on Saturday morning. She is not here to thrash up and down the pool or strap herself to one of their merciless machines. She has a different ache, one that makes her blush faintly with remembered pleasure. She has come to return the shoes.

She pauses in front of the glass doors, remembering Phil's face as he woke her with a mug of coffee.

'I thought I'd start on that camper today,' he said cheerfully. 'Might as well make myself useful.'

It is then that she sees the woman at the reception desk. It is one of the Yummy Mummies, her hair in a glossy ponytail, railing at one of the staff. On the desk is a familiar gym bag. She hesitates, feeling a reflexive clench of inadequacy.

Sam looks down at the bag by her feet. She will not come to this gym again. She suddenly knows this as surely as she knows anything. She will not be swimming, or sweating or hiding in corners. She takes a breath, strides in and puts the bag down in front of the woman.

'You know, you really should check that you pick up the right bag,' she says as she grabs her own. 'It's a bit rich, taking someone else's shoes. Honestly, I wonder what kind of people this establishment lets in these days.'

Sam turns on her heel. She is still laughing when she reaches the train station. She has a bonus payment that is burning a hole in her pocket. And a pair of very unsuitable shoes to purchase.

# Holdups

Detective Inspector Miller wished he hadn't eaten the extra pickled onion. He could feel it there, sizzling through his stomach lining. He popped an antacid and observed the girl in the blue blouse and skirt seated opposite. A straightforward witness: no form, same job for years, still lived with her parents. Probably always would. She would do well in court.

'You understand what we're doing today?'

'Oh, yes.'

Her hands were pressed together in her lap, her expression open and straightforward. She seemed curiously composed, considering what she'd been through.

'You're not worried?'

'Not if it means they will stay behind bars, no.'

He looked at her steadily. 'OK. Before we go in, I'd just like to run through your statement again. So you were just opening up . . .'

Alice Herring sat on the floor, her skirt twisted, her shoulder throbbing.

The door slammed behind her, muffling the shouting in the shop. When she looked up, a man stood facing her, his gun raised.

She stared at him. 'Are you going to shoot me?'

'Shut up.' He was tall and thin, his face obscured by a tan stocking. She detected a slight Eastern European accent.

'You don't have to be rude. I'm only asking.'

'Please. Don't do anything stupid.'

'You're pointing a gun at an unarmed woman, with a pair of tights over your head. And you think *I'm* doing something stupid?'

He touched his head. 'It's not tights. It's a stocking.'

They flinched at the sound of furniture crashing next door. A muffled curse.

'Oh. Well,' she said. 'That makes all the difference.'

It had started like any other morning. Any morning, that is, where Mr Warburton's unlocking of the shutters had been interrupted by three masked men bursting into the jewellery shop, forcing them to the floor. *'Where's the safe? Open the bloody safe!'* The atmosphere became a vortex of noise and action, the men around her a blur.

She had leaped for the emergency button, but the big man had caught her wrist, wrenching it painfully behind her back. He had forced her down, pushing her through the doorway of Mr Warburton's office. She'd been vaguely annoyed, even as she fell, because it had been cake day.

On Friday mornings Mr Warburton often suggested a trip to the bakery, in the tone of voice of someone who had never considered this before. They knew he didn't like to admit it, but he was quite partial to a cream horn.

Alice straightened up, eyeing her captor. 'You know, you could lower the gun. I'm hardly going to overpower you.'

'You won't move?'

'I won't move. Look. Here I am. Sitting on the floor.'

He glanced towards the door. His tone was almost apologetic. 'This won't take long. They just want safe keys.'

'They need the PIN number. They won't get it from Mr Warburton.'

'They need keys. Is the plan.'

'Well, it's not a very good one.'

Alice sat gingerly and rubbed at her shoulder while the man watched. He seemed vaguely surprised by her lack of alarm – as far as it was possible to tell someone's true emotion through a film of 40 denier.

'I've never been in a robbery before ... You're not what I expected.'

He shot her a look, his foot tapping nervously. 'Why? What did you expect?'

'I don't know. Although it's hard to tell what you *are*, with ... you know, that thing over your head. Aren't you hot?'

He hesitated. 'A bit.'

'You've got sweat marks. On your top.' She pointed, and he looked down. 'That'll be the adrenalin, I expect. I'm sure there's heaps of adrenalin involved when you decide to burst in on a jewellery shop. I bet you didn't sleep last night either. I know I wouldn't.'

As she watched, he began to pace the room.

'I'm Alice,' she said eventually.

'I'm – I can't tell you my name.'

She shrugged. 'I don't get to meet many men in here. Unless they're buying presents for their wives. Or engagement rings. Which is not the best time to chat someone up.' She paused. 'Believe me.'

He stopped and turned towards her. 'Are you . . . chatting me up?'

'Just making conversation. There's not much else to do, is there? Short of fighting, or screaming, or smashing up the office.' They winced as they heard another crash next door. 'And your friends seem to be taking care of that department quite well.'

He glanced around, uncertain. 'You think I should smash up this office?'

'You should probably turn off the CCTV. I would imagine that's pretty elementary for robbers.'

He looked up.

'It's up there.' She pointed at the security camera.

He stood, raised his bat, and with a vigorous swing smashed the little box from the wall. Alice ducked out of the way to avoid the flying debris. She picked a tiny bit of glass from her sleeve.

'I hate CCTV. I always worry that Mr Warburton is watching me accidentally tuck my skirt into my knickers.' Alice stared up at the wall, at the oil painting of the sultry Spanish dancer. 'I tell you what, you could smash up that picture. I mean, I would. If I were a robber.'

'It's a terrible painting.'

'The worst.'

His grin was just visible under the fine mesh. 'You want to do it?'

'Can I?'

He handed her the baseball bat.

She looked down at it, then up at him.

'Are you sure you want to give me that?'

'Oh. No.' He took it back, then wrenched the picture off the wall. 'You could put foot through it if you want. Here.' He hurled it on to the floor in front of her.

She stood, waited a moment, then stomped on it enthusiastically, several times. She stepped back and grinned at him. 'That was strangely satisfying. I can sort of see why you do this.'

'It was very ugly picture,' he conceded.

Alice sat on her chair, and they were silent for a few moments, listening to the sound of drawers being ransacked outside.

She kicked distractedly at the ruined canvas. 'So do you do it often?'

'What?'

'Rob jewellers' shops?'

He hesitated, then sighed. 'This is my first time.'

'Oh . . . I'm not sure I've ever been anyone's first. So how did you end up . . . here?'

He sat down opposite her, dropping the baseball bat between his knees. 'I owe Big Kev – the tall one – money. A lot of money. I had business, and it fail. Stupidly I borrow from him, and now he says this is only way I can pay him off.'

'What's his interest rate?'

'I borrow two thousand, now eight months later he say I owe him ten.'

'Oh. That's not good. You'd have done better with a credit card. Mine's sixteen per cent APR. As long as you don't just pay off the interest every month. You wouldn't believe the number of people who get into trouble doing that. Here – you get points with mine, too. Look.'

As she pulled it from her pocket, they were interrupted by renewed crashing and swearing. He glanced anxiously towards the door.

'If that's the display cases, they're toughened glass.' Alice observed. 'And they shouldn't bother with the trays in the smaller window. They're mostly cubic zirconia. We call it the Value Range.'

'Value Range?'

'Not in front of the customers, obviously. My fiancé bought me one. I was so proud, until Mr Warburton announced it was fake, in front of everyone. I've been terrified of being deemed cubic-zirconia quality ever since.'

He shook his head. 'That is terrible. Are you still with this man?'

'Oh, no.' She sniffed. 'I realized pretty quickly I couldn't marry a man without a bookshelf.'

'No bookshelf?'

'Not even in his loo for the *Reader's Digest*.'

'Many people in this country don't read books.'

'He didn't have *one book*. Not even a true crime. Or a Jeffrey Archer. I mean, what does that tell you about someone's character? I should have known anyway. He went off with a girl from the pound store who put a hundred and thirty-four pouty pictures of herself on Instagram. I counted. I mean – who puts a hundred and thirty-four pictures of themselves on the Internet? All doing the duck face.'

'Duck face?'

'You know. That pout they do. Because they think it makes them look sexy.' She pouted exaggeratedly, and he stifled a laugh. 'I don't miss him at all, funnily enough. But I do feel a bit sad sometimes at the thought that –'

'Ssh!' The shouting had suddenly grown louder. The man with the stocking motioned at her to stay still, twisting his head round the doorframe. She heard murmured, urgent voices.

He turned back to her. 'They want PIN number to key cabinet. Is plan.'

'I told you. Mr Warburton's the only one who knows it.'

He leaned out again, and she heard muffled voices. He turned back to her.

'Big Kev says I must . . . abuse you. To make your boss give them this number.'

'Oh, he won't care. He doesn't like me much. He says I remind him of his ex-wife. You should have taken Clare. She works on Tuesdays. He's definitely soft on her. He gives her custard creams when he thinks nobody's looking.' She paused. 'She'll be gutted she's missed this. She loves a bit of drama.'

He closed the door and lowered his voice. 'You cry? Make it sound like I'm hurting you? Then maybe things happen.'

She shrugged. 'If it will help. But I honestly don't think Mr Warburton will be troubled by the idea of me in any kind of peril.'

'Really? Try.'

Alice took a deep breath, her eyes on his. *'Help! Ow! You're hurting me!'*

He shook his head dismissively. 'No. Is no good.'

'Well, it's not as if I've had much practice. I've never been good at acting. I was always Third Tree in the school play. Or Scenery Painted By.'

'You need to sound . . . breathless. Frightened.' He picked up a chair and hurled it across the room, raising his eyebrows as it crashed against the wall.

'But I'm *not* very frightened,' she hissed. 'I mean, you're plainly formidable. But . . .'

'But?'

'I've just got this feeling that you're not going to hurt me.'

This seemed to trouble him. 'You don't know anything about me.' He took a step closer, so that he towered above her. 'I could hurt you. Really.' And with that he picked up his baseball bat and demolished the coffee machine, sending cold brown liquid and shards of glass skittering on to the carpet.

She looked down at it. 'You're actually getting into this now, aren't you?'

'You are frightened . . . Alice?'

'I'm . . . certainly . . .'

He took a step closer to her, his baseball bat frozen in his hand. They stared at each other. Then he dropped it, and swiftly, they kissed.

'You,' he said softly as he pulled back, 'are definitely not cubic zirconia.'

'I've never kissed anyone through a stocking before,' she said.

'Is a little strange.'

'It really is. How about if I just . . . tear a hole . . . here, so our lips can meet . . .' With her fingernails she created a small gap.

When they stopped this time, his hands travelled to his nose. The hole had laddered and grown, spreading across his face so that all but his eyes were exposed.

'Jesus. What am I going to do?'

'Here,' she said, hitching up her skirt. 'You can have one of mine.'

He stood transfixed as she peeled one from her leg. 'It's nice to see your face,' she said, glancing up at him. 'You look . . . lovely, Mr . . . um . . .'

'Tomasz. My name is Tomasz. You, too.'

Her voice was soft, pliant. 'I'll put it on for you. If you like.'

They kissed again, breaking off as she slid her stocking tenderly over his head.

'I can't see,' he said when she pulled back.

'Oh, I know . . . they're a hundred denier. Tell you

what, I'll pull it a bit tighter just here . . . Then maybe you can –' She moved around behind him.

'What are you doing?'

'I'm so sorry.'

'For what?'

'This.' With a muffled clunk, she brought the baseball bat down upon his head.

So, said Detective Inspector Miller as they walked along the corridor. 'Are you ready to view the lineup?'

'Oh, yes, quite ready.'

'Miss Herring. Do you see the men who robbed Warburton's Jewellers?'

She stared at the row of men behind the glass, her fingers tapping on her lower lip. She turned to the detective. 'I'm sorry – it's hard to tell without their stockings.'

'Stockings?'

'On their faces. I'm ninety-nine per cent sure without, but if I saw them wearing them, I could be definite.'

Stockings were organized. This seemed to amuse her.

'Number one – for sure,' she said. 'He had the gun. And number three, him with the ears. He was the one that hit Mr Warburton.'

Inspector Miller took a step closer. 'Anyone else?'

She gazed through the glass. 'Mmm. No.'

Two of the officers exchanged looks. Inspector Miller peered at her face. 'You're absolutely sure? Your boss seems to think there were three men.'

'Oh, no, there were definitely two. The only other man in the shop was a customer, as I said before. He came in to look at engagement rings, I believe. Nice chap. Foreign accent.'

Miller's ulcer was burning again. 'Mr Warburton is very insistent. Three men, he said.'

She lowered her voice. 'But he did take quite a blow to the head, didn't he? And between you and me, his eyesight is absolutely terrible. All that peering at gemstones.' She smiled. 'Can I go now?'

Miller stared at her. He sighed. 'Fine. We'll be in touch.'

'Are you ready?'

He unfolded his long legs and got up from the park bench, smiling. 'You look nice, Alice.'

She lifted a hand to her hair. 'I just had my photograph taken for the local paper. I'm a have-a-go hero, apparently. "Local Girl Stops Robbery. Saves Customer."'

'You certainly saved me.'

She lifted a hand and ran a finger over the bump on his crown. 'How's the head?'

'Not so sore.' Tomasz took her fingers and kissed them. 'Where are we going?'

'I don't know. The library?'

'Oh, yes. I want you to show me this true crime. And then I buy you a . . . cream horn?'

'Now, that,' said Alice Herring, taking his arm, 'sounds like a plan.'

Honeymoon in Paris

# I

*Paris, 2002*

Liv Halston holds tight to the guard rail of the Eiffel Tower, looks down through the diamond-strung wire at the whole of Paris laid out below, and wonders if anyone, ever, has had a honeymoon as disastrous as this one.

Around her, families of tourists squeal and duck back from the view, or lean against the mesh theatrically for their friends to take pictures, while an impassive security guard looks on. From the west a glowering clump of storm clouds is moving towards them across the sky. A brisk wind has turned her ears pink.

Someone throws a paper aeroplane, and she watches it travel its corkscrew course down, buoyed by passing winds, until it grows too small and is lost from view. Somewhere down there, among the elegant Haussmann boulevards, and the tiny courtyards, the classically laid-out parks and the gently undulating banks of the Seine, is her new husband. The husband who had informed her, two days into their honeymoon, that he was really sorry but he was going to have to meet someone that morning for a work thing. The building he had been telling her about on the edge of the city. Just for an hour. He shouldn't be long. She'd be OK, wouldn't she?

The same husband she had told that if he walked out of the hotel room he could bugger right off and not come back.

David had thought she was joking. She had thought he was. He'd half laughed. 'Liv – this is important.'

'As is our honeymoon,' she had replied. The way they had stared at each other then, as if they were each facing someone they had never seen before.

'Oh, my. I think I'm gonna have to go back down.' An American woman, with a huge money-belt around her waist and hair the colour of gingerbread, pulls a face as she inches past. 'I can't do heights. You feel it creaking?'

'I hadn't noticed,' Liv says.

'My husband's like you. Cool as a cucumber. He could stand there all day. My nerves were shot coming up in that darned lift.' She looks at a bearded man, who is taking pictures intently with an expensive camera, shivers and makes her way towards the lift, holding on to the rail.

It is painted brown, the Eiffel Tower, the same shade as chocolate, an odd colour for such a delicate-looking structure. She half turns to say as much to David before realizing that, of course, he isn't there. She had pictured herself and David up here from the moment he suggested a week in Paris. The two of them, their arms wrapped around each other, perhaps at night, looking down at the City of Lights. She would be giddy with happiness. He would look at her the way he had when he proposed. She would feel like the luckiest woman in the world.

Then a week had become five days, because of an unmissable meeting in London on the Friday. And of those five days, only two had passed before another apparently unmissable meeting had popped up.

And now Liv stands, shivering – in the summer dress she had bought because it was the exact shade of her eyes and she'd thought he would notice – as the skies grow grey and a fine spit starts. And she wonders whether her schoolgirl French is up to hailing a taxi back to the hotel, or whether, in her current mood, she may as well trudge home in the rain. She joins the queue for the lift.

'Are you leaving yours up here too?'

'My what?'

The American woman is beside her. She smiles, nods towards Liv's shiny wedding band. 'Your husband.'

'He – he's not here. He's . . . busy today.'

'Oh, are you here on business? How gorgeous for you. He gets to do the work, and you get to have a lovely time seeing the sights.' She laughs. 'You worked that out right, honey.'

Liv takes a last look out at the Champs-Élysées and something settles in the pit of her stomach. 'Yes,' she says. 'Aren't I the lucky one?'

'Marry in haste . . .' her friends had warned her. They had said it jokingly but, given that she and David had known each other for all of three months and eleven days when he'd proposed, she could detect the faint edge of truth in it.

She hadn't wanted a big wedding: her mother's absence would have hung over it, colouring it a darker shade. So she and David had fled to Italy, to Rome, where she'd bought a white dress off the peg from an understated and terrifyingly expensive designer in the via Condotti and had understood almost none of the church ceremony until David slid a ring on to her finger.

David's friend Carlo, who had helped organize it and acted as one of their witnesses, had kidded her afterwards that she had just agreed to honour, obey and accept any further wives that David might wish to add to the collection. She had laughed for a solid twenty-four hours.

She had known it was right. She had known it from the moment she'd met him. She'd known it even when her father had looked downcast at the news, and masked it immediately with hearty congratulations, and she had realized guiltily that, while she had never particularly dreamed about her wedding, her surviving parent might have done. She'd known it when she'd moved her few belongings to David's house – the glass structure on top of a sugar factory by the Thames had been one of the first things he'd designed and built. Every morning in the six weeks between her wedding and her honeymoon she had woken up in the Glass House, surrounded by sky, gazed at her sleeping husband and known that they were right together. Some passions were too great not to act upon.

'Don't you feel . . . I don't know . . . a bit young?' Jasmine had been waxing her legs over her kitchen sink. Liv had sat at the table and watched her, smoking a contraband cigarette. David didn't like smoking. She had told him she'd stopped a year ago. 'I mean, I'm not being funny, Liv, but you do tend to do things on impulse. Like the whole cutting-your-hair-off-for-a-bet thing. And the jacking-in-your-job-and-going-round-the-world thing.'

'Like I'm the only person ever to do that.'

'You're the only person I know who did the two things on the same day. I don't know, Liv. It just . . . it all seems so fast.'

'But it feels right. We're so happy together. And I can't imagine him doing anything that makes me angry or sad. He's . . .' Liv blew a smoke ring towards the strip light ' . . . perfect.'

'Well, he's definitely lovely. I just can't believe you of all people are getting married. You were the one of us who always swore you wouldn't.'

'I know.'

Jasmine pulled up a sheet of wax and grimaced at its grim residue. 'Ouch. Fuck, that hurt . . . He's bloody fit, though. And that house sounds amazing. Better than this hole.'

'When I wake up with him I feel like I'm in the pages

of some glossy magazine. Everything is just so grown-up. I didn't bother bringing hardly any of my stuff. He has linen bed sheets, for God's sake. Actual linen sheets.' She blew another smoke ring. 'Made of linen.'

'Yeah. And who's going to end up ironing those linen sheets?'

'Not me. He has a cleaner. He says he doesn't need me to do that stuff. He's worked out I'm a rubbish house-keeper. In fact, he wants me to think about doing a postgrad.'

'A postgrad?'

'He says I'm too smart not to do something with my life.'

'Shows how long he's known you.' Jasmine rotated her ankle, looking for stray hairs. 'So. Are you going to?'

'I don't know. There's so much going on, what with moving into his house and getting married and every-thing. I feel like I should get my head round being married first.'

'A wife.' Jasmine grinned at her slyly. 'Oh, my God. Wifey.'

'Don't. It still freaks me out a bit.'

'Wifey.'

'Stop it!'

So, obviously, Jasmine had kept saying it until Liv flicked her hard with a tea-towel.

He's at the hotel when she returns. She had decided to walk, and the heavens had opened, so she's soaked through, her dress clinging to her wet legs. As she walks through Reception she swears the concierge gives her the look reserved for the kind of woman whose husband takes business meetings on their honeymoon.

David is on the telephone when she walks into their room. He turns, spies her, and breaks the call. 'Where have you been? I was getting worried.'

She pulls her wet cardigan from her shoulders, reaches into the wardrobe for a hanger. 'I went up the Eiffel Tower. And walked back.'

'You're soaked. I'll run you a bath.'

'I don't want a bath.' She does. She's thought of nothing else the whole, long, miserable walk back.

'I'll order up some tea, then.'

As he picks up the phone for room service she turns away, walks into the bathroom and shuts the door. She can feel David looking after her long after it has closed. She doesn't know why she's being mulish. She'd planned to be nice when she got back, to recover the day. It was only one meeting after all. And she *had* known what he was like, from their very first date, when he had driven her around London and told her about the background and design of modern glass and steel structures they passed.

But something had happened as she'd crossed the threshold of the hotel room. She'd seen him on the telephone and just the simple fact that she'd known, immediately, it was a work call had skewed her fragile sense of goodwill. *You weren't worried about me*, she thinks crossly. *You were discussing what thickness of glass to use on the new building entrance, or whether the roof brace could support the weight of the extra ventilation shaft.*

She runs a bath, filling it with expensive hotel bubbles, then slides in, letting out a sigh of relief as she immerses herself in the hot water.

Some minutes later, David knocks on the door and enters.

'Tea,' he says, and puts the cup on the side of the marble bath.

'Thank you.'

She waits for him to leave, but he sits down on the closed lid of the lavatory, leaning forwards, and watches her.

'I booked us a table at La Coupole.'

'For tonight?'

'Yes. I told you about it. It's the brasserie with the amazing murals painted by artists who –'

'David, I'm really tired. I walked a long way. I don't think I want to go out tonight.' She doesn't look at him as she speaks.

'I'm not sure I'll be able to get us reservations for another night.'

'Sorry. I just want to have some room service and go to bed.'

*Why are you doing this?* she yells at herself silently. *Why are you sabotaging your own honeymoon?*

'Look. I'm sorry about today, OK? It's just that I've been trying to get a meeting with the Goldsteins for months. And it just turns out they're in Paris, and they finally agreed to see my designs. This is the building I was telling you about, Liv. The big one. And I think they liked it.'

Liv stares at her toes, which emerge pink and shining from the water. 'Well, I'm glad it went well.'

They sit in silence.

'I hate this. I hate that you're so unhappy.'

She looks up at him, his blue eyes, the way his hair is always a bit messy, the way he is resting his face in his hands. After a moment's hesitation she reaches out a hand, and he takes it. 'Ignore me. I'm being silly. You're right. I know this building's a big deal for you.'

'It really is, Liv. I wouldn't have left you for anything else. This is the thing I've been working towards for months. Years. If I can pull it off, the partnership is made. My reputation is made.'

'I know. Look, don't cancel dinner. We'll go. I'll feel better after my bath. And we can plan our day tomorrow.'

His fingers close around hers. Because of the soap-suds it's hard for hers not to slip away.

'Well . . . here's the thing. They want me to meet their project manager tomorrow.'

Liv goes very still. 'What?'

'They're flying him over specially. They want me to meet them at their suite in the Royal Monceau. I thought maybe you could go to the spa there while I was with them. It's meant to be amazing.'

She looks up at him. 'Are you serious?'

'I am. I heard it was voted French *Vogue*'s best –'

'I'm not talking about the bloody spa.'

'Liv – this means they're actually keen. I have to capitalize on it.'

Her voice, when it emerges, is strangely strangulated. 'Five days. Our honeymoon is all of five days, David. Not even a week. You're telling me they couldn't wait to have a meeting for another seventy-two hours?'

'This is the Goldsteins, Liv. This is how billionaires do things. You have to fit around their timetable.'

She stares at her feet, at the pedicure she had booked at great expense, and remembers how she and the beautician had laughed when she'd said that her feet looked good enough to eat.

'Please go away, David.'

'Liv. I –'

'Just leave me alone.'

She doesn't look at him as he rises from the lavatory. When he closes the bathroom door behind him, Liv shuts her eyes and slides under the hot water until she can hear nothing at all.

# 2

*Paris, 1912*

'Not the Bar Tripoli.'

'Yes, the Bar Tripoli.'

For a big man, Édouard Lefèvre could bear an uncanny resemblance to a small boy informed of some imminent punishment. He looked down at me, his expression pained, and blew out his cheeks. 'Ah – let's not do this tonight, Sophie. Let's go and eat somewhere. Let's have an evening free of financial concerns. We're only just married! It's still our *lune de miel*!' He waved dismissively at the bar.

I reached into my coat pocket for the handful of IOUs I had folded in there. 'My beloved husband, we cannot have an evening free of financial concerns for we have no money to eat. Not a *centime*.'

'But the money from the Galerie Duchamp –'

'Gone on rent. You were behind from the summer, remember.'

'The savings in the pot?'

'Spent two days ago when you were minded to treat everyone in Ma Bourgogne to breakfast.'

'It was a wedding breakfast! I felt the need to mark

215

the occasion of our return to Paris somehow.' He thought for a moment. 'The money in my blue *pantalons*?'

'Last night.'

He patted his pockets, coming up only with his tobacco pouch. He looked so downcast I almost laughed.

'*Courage*, Édouard. It won't be so bad. If you prefer I'll go in and ask your friends nicely to settle their debts. You need have nothing to do with it. They will find it harder to refuse a woman.'

'And then we will leave?'

'And then we will leave.' I reached up and kissed his cheek. 'And we will go and get some food.'

'I'm not sure I'll wish to eat,' he grumbled. 'Discussing money gives me indigestion.'

'You will wish to eat, Édouard.'

'I don't see why we have to do this now. Our *lune de miel* is meant to last a month. A month of nothing but love! I asked one of my society patrons and she knows all about such things. I'm sure there is money somewhere in my . . . Oh, hang on, here's Laure. Laure! Come and meet my wife!'

In the three weeks that I had been Madame Édouard Lefèvre, and, in truth, for some months beforehand, I had discovered that the number of my new husband's creditors was even greater than his skills as a painter. Édouard was the most generous of men – but with little, financially, to support such generosity. He sold his paintings with an ease that must have been the envy of his friends at the Académie Matisse, but rarely bothered to

demand anything as unpleasant as cash for them, set-
tling instead for a steadily growing pile of tattered IOUs.
Hence Messieurs Duchamp, Bercy and Stiegler could
afford both his exquisite artistry on their walls and food
in their bellies, while Édouard lived for weeks on bread,
cheese and *rillettes*.

I had been horrified when I uncovered the state of his
finances. Not because of his lack of funds – I had known
when Édouard and I met that he could not be wealthy –
but because of the casual disregard with which these
so-called friends seemed to treat him. They promised him money, which never came. They accepted his
drinks, his hospitality, and gave little back. Édouard
would be the man suggesting drinks for all, food for the
ladies, good times for everyone, and when the bills
came, he would somehow find himself the last soul in
the bar.

'Friendship matters more to me than money,' he had
said, when I went through his accounts.

'That is a perfectly admirable sentiment, my love.
Unfortunately friendship will not put bread on our
table.'

'I have married a businesswoman!' he exclaimed
proudly. In those days after our wedding, I could have
announced I was a lancer of boils, and he would have
still been proud of me.

I had been peering through the window of the Bar
Tripoli, trying to make out who was inside. When I
turned back, Édouard was talking to this Madame

Laure. This was not unusual: my husband knew everyone in the fifth and sixth arrondissements. It was impossible to walk a hundred yards without him exchanging greetings, cigarettes, good wishes. 'Sophie!' he said. 'Come here! I want you to meet Laure Le Comte.'

I hesitated for only a second: it was clear from her rouged cheeks, her evening slippers, that Laure Le Comte was a *fille de rue*. He had told me when we'd first met that he often used them as models; they were ideal, he said, being so unselfconscious about their bodies. Perhaps I should have been shocked that he wished to introduce me, his wife, to one, but I had quickly learned that Édouard cared little for conventional etiquette. I knew he liked them, respected them, even, and I did not want him to think less of me.

'A pleasure to meet you, Mademoiselle,' I said. I held out my hand, and used the formal *vous* to convey my respects. Her fingers were so ridiculously soft that I had to check I was actually holding them.

'Laure has modelled for me on many occasions. You remember the painting with the woman on the blue chair? The one you're particularly fond of? That was Laure. She's an excellent model.'

'You're too kind, Monsieur,' she said.

I smiled warmly. 'I do know the painting. It's a beautiful image.' The woman's eyebrow lifted just a fraction. I realized afterwards that it was unlikely she was often complimented by another woman. 'I always think it an oddly regal work.'

'Regal. Sophie is quite right. That is exactly how you appear in it,' Édouard said.

Laure's gaze flickered between us, as if she was trying to work out whether I was mocking her.

'The first time my husband painted me I looked like the most awful old maid,' I said quickly, wanting to put her at ease. 'So severe and forbidding. I think Édouard said I looked like a stick.'

'I'd never say such a thing.'

'But you thought it.'

'It was a terrible painting,' Édouard agreed. 'But the fault was entirely mine.' He looked at me. 'And now I find it impossible to paint a bad picture of you.'

It was still hard not to meet his gaze without blushing a little. There was a brief silence. And I looked away.

'My congratulations on your wedding, Madame Lefèvre. You are a very lucky woman. But, perhaps, not as lucky as your husband.'

She nodded to me, and then to Édouard, as she lifted her skirts slightly from the wet pavement and walked away.

'Don't look at me like that in public,' I scolded him, as we watched her go.

'I like it,' he said, lighting a cigarette and looking ridiculously pleased with himself. 'You go such an endearing colour.'

Édouard saw a man he wanted to speak to over in the *tabac*, so I let him go, walked into the Bar Tripoli and stood at the counter for a few minutes, watching

Monsieur Dinan at his usual spot in the corner. I asked for a glass of water, and drank it, exchanging a few words with the barman. Then I walked over and greeted Monsieur Dinan, removing my hat.

It took him a few seconds to register who I was. I suspected it was only my hair that gave me away. 'Ah. Mademoiselle. And how are you? It's a chill evening, is it not? Is Édouard well?'

'He is perfectly fine, Monsieur, thank you. But I wonder if I might have two minutes to discuss a private matter.'

He glanced around the table. The woman to his right gave him a hard look. The man opposite was too busy talking to his companion to notice. 'I do not believe I have any private matters to discuss with you, Mademoiselle.' He looked at his female companion as he spoke.

'As you wish, Monsieur. Then we shall discuss it here. It is a simple matter of payment for a painting. Édouard sold you a particularly fine work in oil pastels – *The Market at Grenouille* – for which you promised him . . .' I checked my paper '. . . five francs? He would be much obliged if you could settle the sum now.'

The convivial expression disappeared. 'You are his debt collector?'

'I believe that description is a little strong, Monsieur. I am merely tidying Édouard's finances. And this particular bill is, I believe, some seven months old now.'

'I am not going to discuss financial matters in front of my friends.' He turned away from me in high dudgeon.

But I had half expected this. 'Then I'm afraid, Monsieur, that I will be forced to stand here until you are ready to discuss it.'

All pairs of eyes around the little table had now landed on me, but I did not so much as colour. It was hard to embarrass me. I had grown up in a bar in St Péronne; I had helped my father throw out drunks from the age of twelve, had cleaned the gentlemen's WC, had heard talk so bawdy it would have made a street girl blush. Monsieur Dinan's theatrical disapproval held no terrors for me.

'Well, you will be there all evening, then. For I do not have such a sum on me.'

'Forgive me, Monsieur, but I was standing at the bar for some time before I came over. And I could not help but notice that your wallet was most generously stocked.'

At this his male companion began to laugh. 'I think she has the measure of you, Dinan.'

This seemed only to enrage him.

'Who are you? Who are you to embarrass me so? This is not Édouard's doing. He understands the nature of a gentleman's friendship. He would not come here so gauchely, demanding money and embarrassing a man in front of his friends.' He squinted at me. 'Hah! I remember now . . . You are the shop girl. Édouard's little shop girl from La Femme Marché. How could you possibly understand the ways of Édouard's circle? You are . . .' he sneered '. . . *provincial*.'

He had known that would hurt. I felt the colour rising

slowly from my chest. 'I am indeed, Monsieur, if it is now a provincial concern to eat. And even a shop girl can see when Édouard's friends have taken advantage of his generous nature.'

'I've told him I will pay him.'

'Seven months ago. You told him you would pay him seven months ago.'

'Why should I answer to you? Since when did you become Édouard's *chienne méchante*?' He actually spat the words at me.

Briefly, I froze. And then I heard Édouard's voice, behind me, reverberating from somewhere deep within his chest. 'What did you call my wife?'

'Your *wife*?'

I turned. I had never seen my husband's expression so dark. 'Are you deaf as well as charmless now, Dinan?'

'You married her? That sour-faced shop girl?'

Édouard's fist shot out so fast that I barely saw it. It came from somewhere behind my right ear and caught Dinan so hard on the chin that he actually lifted a little into the air as he flew backwards. He crashed down in a pile of chairs, the table overturning as his legs swung over his head. His female companions shrieked as the wine bottle broke, spraying Medoc over their clothes.

The bar fell quiet, the fiddler stopping mid-note. The air felt electrified. Dinan blinked, struggling to right himself.

'Apologize to my wife. She is worth a dozen of you.' Édouard's voice was a growl.

Dinan spat something, possibly a tooth. He lifted his chin, a thin scarlet trickle bisecting it, and muttered, so quietly that I thought only I could have heard him: *'Putain.'*

With a roar, Édouard went for him. Dinan's friend launched himself on Édouard, throwing punches at his shoulders, his head, his broad back. They bounced off my husband as if they were gnats. I could just make out Édouard's voice: 'How *dare* you insult my wife?'

*'Fréjus*, you blackguard!' I turned to see Michel Le Duc landing a punch on someone else.

*'Arrêtez, Messieurs! Arrêtez-vous!'*

The bar erupted. Édouard pushed himself upright. He shook Dinan's friend from his shoulders, as if he were shrugging off a coat, and swung a chair behind him. I felt, as much as heard, the wood crack on the man's back. Bottles skimmed the air over our heads. Women shrieked, men swore, customers scrambled for the doors, while street boys ran in through them to join the mêlée. In the chaos, I saw my moment. I stooped, and pulled the groaning Dinan's wallet from his jacket. I took a five-franc note from it and tucked a piece of handwritten paper in its place.

'I have written you a receipt,' I shouted at him, my mouth close to his ear. 'You may need it if you ever choose to sell Édouard's painting. Although, frankly, you would be a fool to do so.' And then I straightened. 'Édouard!' I called, looking around for him. 'Édouard!' I was unsure whether he had heard me above the commotion.

I ducked to avoid a bottle and made my way through the scrum towards him. The street girls were laughing and catcalling in a corner. The *patron* was shouting and wringing his hands, the fight spilling out on to the street now, tables crashing. There was not a man in there who wasn't throwing punches – indeed, they had all embraced the prospect of pitched battle with such relish that I wondered if it was a fight at all.

'Édouard!'

And then I spied Monsieur Arnault in the corner by the piano. 'Oh, Monsieur Arnault!' I yelled, as I fought my way over to him, holding up my skirts as I trod over the bodies and the upturned chairs. He was sliding along a banquette, evidently hoping to make his way to the door. 'Two charcoal sketches! The women in the park? You remember?' He glanced at me and I mouthed the words: 'You owe Édouard for two charcoal sketches.' I crouched, one hand raised to protect my head and used the other to pull the IOUs from my pocket, flicking through them and ducking to avoid a shoe. 'Five francs for the two, it says here. Yes?'

Behind us, someone screamed as a tankard hit a window, smashing it.

Monsieur Arnault's eyes were wide with fear. He peered swiftly behind me, then scrabbled in his pocket for his wallet. He peeled off the notes with such haste that I discovered later he had given me two francs too many. 'Take it!' he hissed, then bolted for the door, his hat pressed to his head.

And there we had it. Eleven – no, twelve francs. Enough to keep us going.

'Édouard,' I called again, scanning the room. I could just make him out in the corner, where a man with a ginger moustache, like a fox's brush, was swinging vainly at him, as Édouard held him by the shoulders. I put my hand on his arm. My husband looked at me blankly, as if he had forgotten I was there. 'I have the money. We should go.'

He didn't seem to hear me.

'Really,' I said. 'We should go now.'

He dropped the man, who slid down the wall and felt in his mouth with a finger, muttering something about a chipped tooth. I had hold of Édouard's sleeve now, pulling him towards the doors, my ears ringing with the din, fighting my way through the men who had come in from outside. I cannot believe they had any idea what the fight was about.

'Sophie!' Édouard pulled me backwards sharply as a chair swung in a great arc before my face, close enough for me to feel the disturbance it created in the air. I cursed with fright, and blushed that my husband had heard me.

And then we were outside in the evening air, onlookers gazing in at the windows, through cupped hands, the distant sound of shouting and breaking glass in our ears. I stopped by the empty tables and brushed my skirts down, dislodging splinters of glass. Beside us a bloodied man sat on a chair, holding his ear with one hand, and smoking contemplatively with the other.

'Shall we go and eat, then?' I said, smoothing my coat and glancing up at the sky. 'I think it may rain again.'

My husband pulled at his collar, then ran his hands through his hair, letting out a short breath. 'Yes,' he said. 'Yes. I'm ready for some food now.'

'I must apologize for cursing. It was not very ladylike.'

He patted my hand. 'I did not hear a thing.'

I reached up to pull a wooden splinter from the shoulder of his coat, and flicked it away. I kissed him. And arm in arm we walked briskly towards the Panthéon, the sound of the gendarmes' clanging bell echoing over the Paris rooftops.

I had moved to Paris two years previously, and had lived in lodgings behind the rue Beaumarchais, as did all shop girls who worked at La Femme Marché. The day I had left to be married, all the girls lined up on my corridor and cheered and banged saucepans with wooden spoons.

We were married in St Péronne, and in the absence of my father I was given away by Jean-Michel, my sister's husband. Édouard was charming and generous, and behaved like the perfect groom for the three-day celebrations, but I knew how relieved he was to escape the provincial confines of northern France and make his way swiftly back to Paris.

I cannot tell you how happy I was. I had never expected to love, let alone marry. And I would never have admitted as much in public but I loved him with such a passion that I would have stayed with Édouard Lefèvre even if he had not wanted to marry me. In fact, he had so little time for convention that I had assumed it would be the last thing he wanted.

But it was he who had suggested marriage.

We had been together a little under three months when Hans Lippmann visited his studio one afternoon (I was washing our clothes, as Édouard had forgotten to put by any money to pay his laundress). Monsieur Lippmann was something of a dandy and I had been a little embarrassed that he saw me in my house garments. He walked around the studio, admiring Édouard's latest works, then paused in front of the painting he had done of me on the evening of Bastille Day, when he and I had first revealed our feelings for each other. I remained in the bathroom, scrubbing away at Édouard's collars, trying not to be embarrassed that I knew Lippmann was looking at a picture of me in my underclothes. Their voices dropped for a few minutes and I couldn't hear what they were saying. Eventually curiosity overcame me. I dried my hands and walked out into the studio to find them gazing at a series of sketches Édouard had done of me sitting by the large window. Monsieur Lippmann turned and, after the briefest of greetings, asked if I would model for him too. Fully dressed, of course. There was something fascinating about the angles of my face, something about my pale skin, he said. Didn't Édouard agree? Why, he must do – he had seen it himself. He laughed.

Édouard didn't.

I was about to say yes (I liked Lippmann: he was one of the few artists who treated me as an equal), but I saw Édouard's smile tighten.

'No. I'm afraid Mademoiselle Bessette is far too busy.'

There was a brief, awkward silence. Lippmann gave us an amused glance.

'Why, Édouard, we have shared models before. I merely thought that –'

'No.'

Lippmann looked at his feet. 'If you say so, Édouard. A pleasure to meet you again, Mademoiselle.' He tipped his hat to me and left. Édouard did not wish him goodbye.

'You funny thing,' I said to him later. He was in the tub, and I was kneeling on a cushion behind him, washing his hair. He had been quiet all afternoon. 'You know I have eyes only for you. I would have worn a nun's habit for Monsieur Lippmann if it meant keeping you happy.' I poured a jug of water slowly over the back of his head, watching the suds slide away. 'Besides, he's married. Contentedly so. *And* he's a gentleman.'

Édouard was still silent. Then he turned his whole body abruptly, so that a slew of water went over the side of the tub. 'I need to know you are mine,' he said, and his face was so anxious, so miserable, that it took me a moment to speak.

'I am yours, you fool.' I took his face between my hands and kissed him. His skin was wet. 'I have been yours since the first time you came to La Femme Marché and bought fifteen ridiculous scarves in your determination to see me.' I kissed him again. 'I was yours from the moment you told Mistinguett I had the best ankles in Paris, after she tried to humiliate me because I wore clogs.' I kissed him again. He closed his eyes. 'I was yours from the moment you drew me and I realized nobody else would ever look at me like you do. As if you saw only the best of me. As if I was someone more magnificent than I knew.'

I took a towel and tenderly rubbed the moisture from his nose and eyes. 'So, you see? There is nothing to fear. I am yours, Édouard, utterly and completely. I cannot believe you would doubt it.'

He looked at me, and his big brown eyes were steady and oddly determined. 'Marry me,' he said.

'But you always said –'

'Tomorrow. Next week. As soon as we can.'

'But you –'

'Marry me, Sophie.'

So I married him. I never could deny Édouard anything.

The morning after the fight at Bar Tripoli, I slept late. We had become giddy with our riches, eaten and drunk too much, and stayed awake until the small hours, lost in each other's bodies, or in fits of giggles as we remembered Dinan's outraged expression. I raised my head blearily from the pillow, and pushed my hair from my face. The small change that had been on the table was missing: Édouard must have gone for bread. I became dimly aware of the sound of his voice in the street below, and let my memories of the previous evening flow and recede in a happy blur. Then, when he did not sound as if he were coming upstairs, I pulled a robe around me and went to the window.

He had two baguettes tucked under his arm and was talking to a striking blonde woman in a fitted dark green coat-dress with a broad-brimmed fur hat. As I looked down, her gaze slid up to me. Édouard, following it, turned and lifted a hand in greeting.

'Come downstairs, *chérie*. I want you to meet someone.'

I did not want to meet anyone. I wanted him to come upstairs and for me to wrap my legs around him and smother him in kisses as we ate. But I sighed, pulled the robe around me, and walked downstairs to the front door.

'Sophie, this is Mimi Einsbacher. An old friend of mine. She has bought several paintings, and posed for some of my life drawings too.'

Another? I thought absently.

'Congratulations on your marriage. Édouard gave me . . . no clue.'

There was something about the way the woman looked at me when she said this, her flicker of a glance towards Édouard, that made me uneasy.

'*Enchantée*, Mademoiselle,' I said, and held out my hand. She took it as if she were handling a dead fish.

We stood there, studying our feet. Two road sweepers

were working on opposite sides of the street, whistling in tandem. The drains were overflowing again, and the smell, teamed with the amount of wine we had consumed the previous evening, made me feel suddenly queasy.

'You will excuse me,' I said, backing into the doorway. 'I am hardly dressed for company. Édouard, I will light the fire and put the coffee on.'

'Coffee!' he exclaimed, rubbing his hands. 'So very good to see you, Mimi. I will come – sorry, *we* will come and see your new apartment soon. It sounds marvellous.'

He was whistling as he came up the stairs.

While Édouard shed his outer clothes, I poured him a cup of coffee and climbed back into bed. He put a plate between us, broke me off a piece of bread and handed it to me.

'Did you lie with her?' I didn't look at him as I spoke.

'Who?'

'Mimi Einsbacher.'

I have no idea why I asked him this; I had never done such a thing before.

He gave a slight shake of his head, as if it were of no consequence. 'I may have done.' When I said nothing he opened an eye and looked at me gravely. 'Sophie, you know I was not a priest before I met you.'

'I do.'

'I am just a man. And I was alone for a long time before we met.'

'I know this too. I would not wish you to be any

different from the way you are.' I turned and kissed his shoulder lightly.

He reached out and pulled me to him, letting out another great sigh of contentment. His breath was warm on my eyelids. He slid his fingers into my hair and tilted my head back so that I was looking at him. 'My darling wife. You need only remember this: I never knew happiness until I knew you.'

*What should I care for Mimi and her ilk?* I thought, as I dropped my bread and slid my leg across him, breathing in his scent, taking possession of him yet again. They were no threat to me.

I almost convinced myself.

Mimi Einsbacher just happened to be passing as we came out of the studio the following Wednesday (I was rushing to *la poste* to send a letter to my sister); it made sense for Édouard to have breakfast with her. What was the point in him eating alone? And then again, two days later. It was a cold November day, and Édouard was placing my good felt hat on my head as I pulled open the huge oak door that led on to rue Soufflot. I was laughing and batting away his hands. 'You have it back to front! Édouard! Stop! I will look like a madwoman!' His great hand rested on my shoulder where it met my neck. I loved the weight of it.

'Why, good morning!' Mimi was dressed in a mint green cape and fur stole. Her waist was pulled in so tightly that I suspected her lips were blue under the red stain. 'What a happy surprise!'

'Mademoiselle Einsbacher. How fortunate we are to see you again so soon.' My hat felt suddenly skewed and ridiculous on my head.

'Mimi! How delightful.' Édouard released my shoulder, bent his head and kissed her gloved hand. I protested inwardly at the sight, and then chided myself: Don't be childish. Édouard chose you, after all.

'And where are you off to this brisk morning? Back to the post office?' She held her bag neatly in front of her. It was crocodile skin.

'I have an appointment in Montmartre with my dealer. My wife is off to buy us some food.'

I turned the hat around on my head, wishing suddenly I had worn my black one. 'Well, I might,' I said. 'If you behave yourself.'

'See what I endure?' Édouard leaned forwards to kiss my cheek.

'Goodness. She's very hard on you, I am sure.' Mimi's smile was unreadable.

Édouard wrapped his muffler around his neck, surveying the two of us for a moment. 'You know, you two should get to know each other. It would be good for Sophie to have a friend here.'

'I am not without friends, Édouard,' I protested.

'But all your shop friends are busy during the day. And they live over in the ninth. Mimi is someone you could meet for coffee when I'm busy. I hate to think of you alone.'

'Really.' I smiled at him. 'I'm quite content in my own company.'

'Oh, Édouard is quite right. You don't want to be a drain on him, after all. And you are hardly familiar with his circle. Why don't I accompany you? As a favour to Édouard. I'd be delighted.'

Édouard beamed. 'Marvellous!' he said. 'My two favourite ladies, taking a jaunt. I'll wish you both good day then. Sophie, *chérie*, I'll be home for dinner.'

He turned and walked off in the direction of rue St Jacques.

Mimi and I gazed at each other and, just for a moment, I thought I detected something glacial in her eyes.

'How lovely,' she said. 'Shall we walk?'

# 3

They'd had the morning planned: a lazy start, breakfast at Café Hugo on place des Vosges, a wander around the little shops and boutiques of the second, perhaps a walk along the Seine, stopping off to look at the second-hand book stalls. David would disappear after lunch to his meeting for perhaps two hours; Liv would use the magnificent spa at the Royal Monceau while he discussed business. They would meet in the bar for an afternoon cocktail, have a relaxed dinner at a local brasserie. The day had been salvaged. She would be nice. She would be understanding. This was what marriage was about, after all: the great art of compromise. She had told herself this several times since waking up.

And then, during breakfast, David's phone rings.

'The Goldsteins,' she says, when he finally stops talking. Her *tartine* sits untouched in front of her.

'Change of plan. They want to meet me this morning, at their offices near the Champs-Élysées.'

When she doesn't say anything, he puts his hand over hers and says, 'I'm really sorry. I'll be gone for a couple of hours at most.'

She cannot speak. Great fat salty tears of disappointment are building behind her eyes.

'I know. I'll make it up to you. It's just –'

'– that this is more important.'

'This is our future, Liv.'

Liv looks at him, and she knows her frustration must be clear in her expression. She feels perversely angry with him for making her behave like this.

He squeezes her hand. 'Come on, sweetheart. You can do something I didn't particularly want to do, and I'll come and meet you. It's not like it's hard to kill a couple of hours here. It's Paris.'

'Sure. I just hadn't realized my honeymoon was going to be five days in Paris thinking up ways to kill time.'

There is a slight edge to his voice: 'I'm sorry. I don't have a job that I can just switch off.'

'No. You've made that very clear.'

It had been like this all the previous evening at La Coupole. They had struggled to find safe subjects to talk about, smiled stiltedly, an unacknowledged conversation running underneath their too-polite spoken one. When he did speak she had winced at his obvious discomfort. When he didn't, she had wondered if he was thinking about work.

When they returned to their suite, Liv had turned away from him on the bed, somehow too angry to want him to touch her – then lain there panicking when he didn't even try.

In the six months they had been together she wasn't

sure they had ever argued with each other until they'd come to Paris. The honeymoon was slipping away, she could feel it.

David breaks the silence first. He refuses to let go of her hand. He leans over the table and pushes a strand of hair back from her face tenderly. 'I'm sorry. This really will be it. Just give me a couple of hours and I promise I'll be all yours. Maybe we'll extend the trip, and I'll . . . make up the hours.' He tries to smile.

She turns to him then, disarmed, wanting them to feel normal again, wanting them to feel like *themselves*. She stares down at her hand in his, the brassy shine of her new wedding ring, still unfamiliar on her finger.

The last forty-eight hours have left her completely unbalanced. The happiness she has felt for the last few months seems suddenly fragile, as if it is built on shakier foundations than they had realized.

She searches his eyes. 'I do love you, you know.'

'And I love you.'

'I'm a horrible, needy, grumpy girlfriend.'

'Wife.'

A reluctant smile spreads across her face. 'I'm a horrible, needy, grumpy wife.'

He grins and kisses her, and they sit on the edge of the place des Vosges, listening to the roar of the mopeds outside, the traffic crawling up towards rue Beaumarchais. 'Luckily, I happen to find horrible and grumpy desperately attractive traits in a woman.'

'You forgot needy.'

'That's my favourite.'

'Go,' she said, pulling away from him gently. 'Go now, you smooth-talking architect, before I drag you back to that hotel bed and make sure you don't get to your very annoying meeting at all.'

The air between them expands and relaxes. She lets out a breath she didn't know she'd been holding.

'What will you do?'

She watches him collect up his belongings: keys, wallet, jacket, phone. 'Go and look at some art, probably.'

'I'll text you the moment we're through. I'll come and meet you.' He blows a kiss. 'And then we can continue this pinning-to-the-bed discussion.'

He's halfway up the road when he turns and lifts a hand. '*À bientôt*, Mrs Halston!'

Her smile lasts until he disappears from view.


The concierge had warned her that the queue for the Louvre would be hours long at this time, so she heads to the Musée d'Orsay instead. David had told her the architecture of the building was almost as impressive as the art it housed. But even at ten o'clock in the morning the queue here stretches backwards and forwards around the front of the building like a coiled snake. The sun is fierce already, and she has forgotten to bring a hat.

'Oh, great,' she mutters to herself, as she takes her place at the back. She wonders whether she will even make it into the building before David has finished his meeting.

'It shouldn't take too long. They shift people through pretty quickly.' The man in front of her turns and nods towards the front of the queue. 'They do free entry sometimes. Now that's a queue.' He wears a crisp linen jacket and the air of the independently wealthy.

When he smiles at her, she wonders if the fact that she's English is actually writ large all over her. 'I'm not sure all these people will even fit inside.'

'Oh, they will. It's like the Tardis in there.' When she smiles, he holds out a hand. 'Tim Freeland.'

'Liv Worth – Halston. Liv Halston.' The change of name still wrongfoots her.

'Ah. That poster says there's a big Matisse exhibition on. I suspect that's the reason for our queue. Here. Let me put up my umbrella. That will protect you from the worst of the sun.'

He comes over for the tennis every year, he tells her, as they shuffle forwards a few paces at a time, zigzagging their way towards the front of the queue. And then fills his non-tennis time with a few of his favourite places. He much prefers this gallery to the Louvre, which is too full of tourists to see the paintings. He half smiles as he says this, apparently aware of the irony.

He is tall and tanned with dark blond hair, which is swept back in a way she imagines it has been since his teens. The way he talks about his life suggests freedom from financial concerns. His reference to children and the lack of a wedding ring suggest some distant divorce.

He is attentive and charming. They discuss restaurants in Paris, tennis, the unpredictability of Parisian taxi drivers. It is a relief to have a conversation that is not loaded with unspoken resentment or littered with traps. By the time they reach the front of the queue she is oddly cheerful.

'Well, you made the time pass wonderfully quickly.' Tim Freeland folds up his umbrella and holds out his hand. 'It was lovely to meet you, Olivia Halston. And I'd recommend the Impressionists on the top floor. You should get the best views now, before the crowds get too unbearable.'

He smiles at her, his eyes crinkling, and then he is gone, striding off into the cavernous interior of the museum as if he is already sure where he is headed. And Liv, who knows that even if you *are* on your honeymoon you're allowed to feel cheered by twenty minutes' conversation with an attentive, handsome man, who may or may not have been flirting with you, walks with a slightly perkier stride towards the lifts.

She takes her time, walks slowly along the Impressionists, studying each painting carefully. She has time to kill, after all. She is slightly ashamed to calculate she has not set foot in a gallery since finishing her degree two years previously. She decides, on reflection, that she loves the Monets and the Morisots, and dislikes the Renoirs. Or perhaps they have just been overused on chocolate boxes and it's hard to disassociate the two things.

She sits down, and then she stands up again. She wishes David was here. It's odd to stand in front of the paintings and have nobody to discuss them with. She finds herself looking surreptitiously at other people who might be alone, checking them for signs of freakishness. She wonders whether to call Jasmine, just to talk to someone, but realizes this will signal publicly the failure of her honeymoon. Who calls anyone from their honeymoon, after all? She feels briefly cross with David again and has silently to argue herself out of it.

The gallery fills steadily around her; a group of school-children is led past by a theatrically engaged museum attendant. They stop in front of *Le Déjeuner sur l'herbe*, and he motions to them to sit down as he speaks. 'Look!' he exclaims in French. 'They placed wet paint on wet paint – the first artists to do so! – so that they could move the colours like this . . .' He gesticulates wildly. The children are rapt. A cluster of adults stops to listen too.

'And this painting caused a huge scandal when it was shown! Enormous! Why was the lady wearing no clothes, and the gentlemen were dressed? Why do you think, young sir?'

She loves the fact that eight-year-old French children are expected to debate public nudity. She loves the respect with which the attendant addresses them. Again, she wishes David were here because she knows he would have felt like this too.

It is several minutes before she realizes how many

people have poured into the series of rooms and that it has now become stiflingly crowded. She keeps hearing English and American accents. For some reason they annoy her. She finds herself irritated suddenly by small things.

Keen to escape, Liv ducks away, through one, two rooms, past a series of landscapes, until she reaches the less popular artists, where the visitors are sparse. She slows now, trying to give these lesser artists the same attention she gave the big names, although there is not much that draws the eye. She is about to look for the way out when she finds herself in front of a small oil painting, and there, almost despite herself, she stops. A red-haired woman stands beside a table, laden with the remains of a meal, wearing a white dress that may be some kind of undergarment; Liv can't tell. Her body is half turned away from view, but the side of her face is unobscured. Her gaze slides towards the artist but will not meet it. Her shoulders are hunched forward with displeasure, or tension.

The title of the painting reads: '*Wife, out of sorts*'.

She gazes at it, taking in the exquisite limpid quality of the woman's eye, the points of colour on her cheeks, the way her body seems to suggest barely suppressed rage, and yet a kind of defeat too. And Liv thinks suddenly: *Oh, God. That's me.*

Once this thought has popped into her head it will not be dislodged. She wants to look away but she cannot. She feels almost winded, as if she has been punched.

The painting is so strangely intimate, so unsettling. I'm twenty-three years old, she thinks. And I have married a man who has already put me firmly in the background of his life. I'm going to be that sad, quietly furious woman in the kitchen whom nobody notices, desperate for his attention, sulking when she doesn't get it. Doing things alone and 'making the best of it'.

She sees future trips with David: herself, flicking through guidebooks of local attractions, trying not to show her disappointment when, yet again, there is some important work thing he cannot miss. *I'm going to end up like my mother. She left it too late to remember who she actually was before she became a wife.*

*Wifey.*

The Musée d'Orsay is suddenly too crowded, too noisy. She finds herself pushing her way downstairs, going the wrong way through the advancing crowds, muttering apologies as she meets the resistance of shoulders, elbows, bags. She slips sideways down a flight of stairs, and weaves her way along a corridor, but instead of heading towards the exit, she finds herself beside a grand dining room, where a queue has started to build for tables. Where are the bloody exits? The place is suddenly ridiculously full of people. Liv fights her way through the art-deco section – the huge pieces of organic furniture grotesque, overly flamboyant, and realizes she is at the wrong end. She lets out a great sob of something she can't quite articulate.

'Are you all right?'

She spins round. Tim Freeland is staring at her, a brochure in his hand. She wipes briskly at her face, tries to smile. 'I – I can't find my way out.'

His eyes travel over her face – *is she actually crying?* – and she's mortified. 'I'm sorry. I just – I really need to get out of here.'

'The crowds,' he says quietly. 'They can be a bit much at this time of year. Come on.' He touches her elbow, and steers her along the length of the museum, keeping to the darker rooms at the edges where fewer people seem to congregate. Within minutes they are down a flight of stairs and exiting on to the bright concourse outside, where the queue to enter has grown even longer.

They stop a short distance away. Liv pulls her breathing back under control. 'I'm so sorry,' she says, looking back. 'I don't think you'll be able to get back in.'

He shakes his head. 'I was done for the day. When you reach the stage where you can't see anything for the backs of people's heads, it's probably time to leave anyway.'

They stand there for a moment on the bright, wide pavement. The traffic crawls along the side of the river, a moped weaving noisily in and out of the stationary cars. The sun casts the buildings in the blue-white light that seems peculiar to the city.

'Would you like a coffee? I think it might be a good idea if you sat down for a few minutes.'

'Oh – I can't. I'm meant to be meeting –' She looks down at her phone. There are no messages. She stares at it, taking this in. Digesting the fact that it is now almost an hour later than when he'd said he'd be through. 'Um . . . can you give me a minute?'

She turns away, dials David's number, squinting as she peers at the traffic crawling along the quai Voltaire. It goes straight to voicemail. She wonders, fleetingly, what to say to him. And then she decides not to say anything at all.

She closes her phone and turns back to Tim Freeland. 'Actually, I'd love a coffee. Thank you.'

*'Un café, et une grande crème.'* Even when she employs her best French accent the waiters invariably answer her in English. After the morning's various humiliations it is a minor enough embarrassment. She drinks a coffee, orders a second, breathes in the warm city air and deflects any further attention from herself.

'You ask a lot of questions,' Tim Freeland says, at one point. 'Either you're a journalist, or you've been to a very good finishing school.'

'Or I'm an expert in industrial espionage. And I've heard all about your new widget.'

He laughs. 'Ah . . . unfortunately I'm a widget-free zone. I'm retired.'

'Really? You don't look old enough.'

'I'm not old enough. I sold my business nine months ago. I'm still trying to work out what to do with my time.'

The way he says this suggests he is not particularly

worried about this at all. Why would you be, she thinks, if you could spend your days wandering your favourite cities, taking in art or offering random strangers coffee?

'So where do you live?'

'Oh . . . all over the place. I do a couple of months here in the early summer. I have a place in London. I spend some time in South America too – my ex-wife lives in Buenos Aires with my two eldest children.'

'That sounds complicated.'

'When you're as old as I am, life is invariably complicated.' He smiles, as if he is well used to complication. 'For a while I was one of those rather daft men who found it impossible to fall in love without getting married.'

'How gentlemanly.'

'Hardly. Who was it who said, "Every time I fall in love I lose a house"?' He stirs his coffee. 'Actually, it's all fairly civil, as these things go. I have two ex-wives, both of whom are pretty wonderful women. It's just rather a shame I never worked that out while I was with them.'

He speaks softly, his cadences measured and his words careful, a man who is used to being heard. She gazes at him, at his tanned hands, his immaculate shirt cuffs, and imagines a serviced apartment in the first arrondissement, a housekeeper, an upmarket restaurant where the proprietor knows his name. Tim Freeland is not her type, and at least twenty-five years older than she is, but she wonders, briefly, what it would be like to be with a man like him. She wonders whether, to a casual onlooker, they look like husband and wife.

'What do you do, Olivia?' He has called her Olivia since she introduced herself. From anyone else it might sound like an affectation, but from him it sounds like old-fashioned courtesy.

She is hauled from her reverie, blushes a little when she acknowledges what she has been thinking. 'I . . . I'm sort of between jobs at the moment. I finished my degree and did a bit of office work, a bit of waitressing. The usual middle-class-girl stuff. I suppose I haven't quite worked out what to do either.' She fiddles with her hair.

'Plenty of time for that. Children?' He looks meaningfully at her wedding ring.

'Oh. No. Not for ages.' She laughs awkwardly. She can barely look after herself; the idea of having some mewling infant dependent on her is unthinkable. She can feel him studying her.

'Quite right. Plenty of time for all that.' He doesn't take his eyes from her face. 'If you don't mind me saying, you're very young to be married. In this day and age, I mean.'

She doesn't know what to say to this, so she takes a sip of her coffee.

'I know I shouldn't ask a woman her age, but what are you – twenty-three? Twenty-four?'

'Not bad. Twenty-three.'

He nods. 'You have good bones. I should imagine

you'll look twenty-three for a decade. No, don't blush. I'm just stating a fact . . . Childhood sweetheart?'

'No – more of a whirlwind romance.' She looks up from her coffee. 'Actually, I'm – I'm just married.'

'Just married?' His eyes open just a fraction wider. The question is there within them. 'You're on *honeymoon*?' He says it without drama, but his expression is so bemused, his sudden pity so inadequately disguised, that she can't bear it. She sees *Wife, out of sorts*, turning away defeatedly, a lifetime of other people's faint embarrassment. *Oh, you're married? Your husband is where?*

What has she done?

'I'm so sorry,' she says, her head down, gathering up her things from the table. 'I have to go now.'

'Olivia. Please don't rush off. I'm –'

Blood is thumping in her ears. 'No. Really. I probably shouldn't be here anyway. It was very nice to meet you. Thank you so much for the coffee. And . . . you know . . .'

She does not look at him. She raises a smile, throws it somewhere in his direction, and then she flees, half walking, half running, along the Seine back towards Notre Dame.

# 4

The Marché Monge was packed with shoppers, despite the cool winds and miserable spit of rain. I walked half a step behind Mimi Einsbacher, who made her way around the stalls with a determined sway to her hips and had kept up a constant commentary from the moment we entered the market.

'Oh, you must buy some of these. Édouard does love Spanish peaches. Look, they're so perfectly ripe.'

'Have you cooked him langoustines? Oh! How that man can eat langoustines . . .'

'Cabbage? Red onions? Are you sure? Those ingredients are very . . . rustic. You know, I do believe he might enjoy something a little more sophisticated. He is a great gourmand, Édouard, you know. Why, once we went to Le Petit Fils and he ate the entire *dégustation* menu of fourteen courses. Can you imagine? I thought he was going to burst by the time the *petits fours* arrived. But he was so happy . . .' She shook her head, as if lost in a reverie. 'He is a man of such appetites . . .'

I picked up a bunch of carrots, and inspected them closely, trying to look as if I was interested in them.

Somewhere at the back of my head a distant thumping pulse had started up and I detected the beginnings of a headache.

Mimi Einsbacher stopped in front of a stall stacked with meat products. She exchanged a few words with the stallholder before picking up a small jar and holding it up to the light. She gave me a sideways look, from under her hat. 'Oh, you do not wish to hear such remembrances . . . Sophia. I must suggest the *foie gras*, though. A lovely treat for Édouard. If you are a little . . . light on housekeeping, I would be delighted to purchase it as a small gift for him. As an old friend. I know how erratic he can be with these things.'

'We are quite capable of supporting ourselves, thank you.' I took the jar from her hand and popped it into my basket, handing the stallholder his money. Half of our remaining food budget, I noted, with mute fury.

She slowed her pace so that I had no choice but to walk alongside her. 'So . . . Gagnaire tells me that Édouard has painted nothing for weeks. Rather a pity.'

*Why should you talk to Édouard's dealer?* I wanted to ask, but I let it pass. 'We are only just married. He has been . . . distracted.'

'He is a great talent. He should not lose focus.'

'Édouard says he will paint when he is ready.'

It was as if she hadn't heard me. Mimi had headed over to the patisserie stall, and was gazing at a *tarte framboise*. '*Framboises!* At this time of year! I cannot imagine what the world is coming to.'

Please do not offer to buy this for Édouard too, I said silently. I barely have enough money left for bread. But Mimi had other things on her mind. She bought a small baguette, waited while the stallholder wrapped it in paper, then turned halfway towards me, lowering her voice.

'You cannot imagine how surprised we all were to hear he had married. A man like Édouard.' She placed the baguette carefully through the handle of her basket. 'So I wondered . . . are congratulations in order?'

I looked at her, at her bright, blank smile. And then saw she was gazing pointedly at my waist. 'No!'

It took me several minutes to grasp how she had insulted me.

I wanted to say to her: *Édouard begged me to marry him. It was he who insisted on it. He could not bear the thought of any other man even looking at me. He could not bear the possibility that they would see in me what he saw.*

But I did not want to give her anything of us at all. Faced with her smiling enmity, I wanted to keep every part of Édouard's and my marriage to myself, where she could not puncture it or skew it or make it resemble something it did not. I felt my face flush with colour.

She stood, staring at me. 'Oh you mustn't be sensitive, Sophia.'

'Sophie. My name is Sophie.'

She turned away. 'Of course. Sophie. But my question cannot be entirely unexpected. It is only natural that those who have known Édouard longest will feel a little proprietorial towards him. After all, we know so little about you . . . other than . . . You are a shop girl, yes?'

'I was. Until I married him.'

'And, of course, then you had to leave your . . . shop. What a pity. How you must miss your shop friends. I know only too well how comforting it is to be immersed in one's own social circle, among one's own kind.'

'I'm quite happy in Édouard's circle.'

'I'm sure you are. Although it can be so terribly difficult to make proper friends when everybody else has known each other for years. So hard to penetrate those shared amusements, all that history.' She smiled. 'Still, I'm sure you're doing quite well.'

'Édouard and I are happiest alone.'

'Of course. But you cannot imagine he will want to stay that way for long, Sophia. He is, after all, the most gregarious of creatures. A man like Édouard needs to be allowed the utmost freedom.'

I was struggling to keep my composure. 'You speak as if I have become his gaoler. I have never wanted Édouard to do other than what pleased him.'

'Oh, I'm sure you haven't. And I'm sure you are quite aware of your good fortune in marrying someone like him. I just thought it politic to offer some advice.'

When I did not reply, she added, 'Perhaps you believe me to be terribly presumptuous, advising you on your own husband. But you know that Édouard does not follow the rules of the bourgeoisie, so I felt that I might also be allowed to step outside the constraints of normal conversation.'

'I'm sure I am most grateful, Madame.' I wondered whether I could just turn and leave her then, invent some forgotten appointment. Surely I had endured this for long enough.

She lowered her voice, took a step away from the stall and gestured for me to do the same. 'Well, then, if we are speaking frankly, I feel it my duty to advise you on another front. Woman to woman, if you will. As you will be aware, Édouard is a man of great . . . appetites.' She looked meaningfully at me. 'I'm sure he is delighted to be married now, but as he begins painting other women again, you must be prepared to . . . allow him certain freedoms.'

'I'm sorry?'

'You wish me to spell it out, Sophia?'

'Sophie.' My jaw had become tight. 'My name is Sophie. And, yes, please do spell it out, Madame.'

'I'm so sorry if this is indelicate.' She smiled prettily. 'But . . . you must know that you are not the first of Édouard's models he . . . has had relations with.'

'I don't understand.'

She looked at me as if I were stupid. 'The women on his canvases . . . There is a reason Édouard gets the images he does, of such delicacy and power, the reason he is able to portray such . . . intimacy.'

I think I knew then what she was about to say, but I stood there and let the words fall around me, like the blades of little guillotines.

'Édouard is a man of swift and unpredictable passions.

When he tires of the novelty of being married, Sophia, he will return to his old ways. If you are a sensible girl, and I'm sure you are, given your . . . shall we say *practical*? . . . background, I would advise you to look the other way. A man like that cannot be confined. It is against his artistic spirit.'

I swallowed. 'Madame, I have prevailed upon your time long enough. I'm afraid we must part company here. Thank you for your . . . advice.'

I turned and walked away, her words ringing in my ears, my knuckles white with the effort of not hitting something. I was halfway to rue Soufflot before I discovered I had left the bag that contained the onions, cabbage and cheese sitting on the ground by the stall.

Édouard was out when I returned. It was no great surprise: he and his dealer would generally retreat to a nearby bar and conduct their business over glasses of *pastis*, or if it grew late, perhaps even absinthe. I dropped the basket with my purse and the jar of *foie gras* in the kitchen area and walked through to the washstand, where I splashed my flushed cheeks with cold water. The girl who gazed back at me from the looking-glass was a sombre creature, her mouth set in a thin line of anger, her pale cheeks lit with colour. I tried to smile, to make myself the woman Édouard saw, but she wouldn't come. I could see only this thin, watchful woman, whose happiness felt suddenly as if it were built on shifting sands.

I poured myself a glass of sweet wine, and drank it swiftly. And then I had another. I had never in my life drunk in the daytime before. Having grown up around my father and his excesses, I had had little appetite for drink until I met Édouard.

As I sat there in the silence I kept hearing her words: *He will return to his old ways. The women on his canvases . . . there is a reason Édouard gets the images he does . . .*

And then I hurled the glass at the wall, my cry of anguish carrying over the sound of the splintering glass.

I cannot say how long I lay on our bed, lost in silent misery. I did not want to get up. My home, Édouard's studio, no longer felt like our little haven. I felt as if it had been invaded by the ghosts of his past liaisons, was coloured with their talk, their looks, their kisses.

You must not think like this, I scolded myself. But my mind careered around like a runaway horse, headed in new and terrible directions, and I could not rein it in.

It had begun to grow dark, and outside I could hear the man who lit the streetlamps singing softly under his breath. It was a sound I used to find comforting. I got up, vaguely planning to clear up the broken glass before Édouard returned. But instead I found myself walking towards his canvases, which were stacked along the far wall. I hesitated in front of them, then began to pull them out, gazing at each one. There was Laure Le Comte, the *fille de rue*, wearing a green serge dress, another of her naked, leaning against a pillar like a Greek statue, her breasts small and upright like halves of

Spanish peaches; Emmeline, the English girl from the Bar Brun, her bare legs twisted under her on the chair, her arm trailing along its back. There was an unnamed dark-haired woman, her corkscrew curls cascading over her bare shoulder as she reclined upon a *chaise-longue*, her eyes drooping as if from sleep. Had he lain with her too? Had her slightly parted lips, painted so lovingly, been awaiting his? How could I have thought him immune to that silky, exposed flesh, those artfully crumpled petticoats?

*Oh, God, I had been such a fool. Such a provincial fool.*

And there, finally, was Mimi Einsbacher, leaning towards a looking-glass, the curve of her bare back perfectly outlined by the unforgiving corset below it, the slope of her shoulder a pale invitation. It was lovingly drawn, his charcoal line a flowing, sympathetic thing. And it was unfinished. What had he done after he had drawn this far? Had he walked up behind her, placed those great hands on her shoulders and lowered his lips to the place where her shoulder met her neck? The place that always made me shiver with longing? Had he laid her gently on that bed – our bed – murmured soft words and pushed her skirts up until she –

I balled my fists in my eyes. I felt unhinged, a madwoman. I had never even noticed these paintings before. Now each one felt like a silent betrayal, a threat to my future happiness. Had he lain with them all? How long before he did it again?

I sat staring at them, hating each one and yet unable

to tear away my eyes, inventing whole lives of secrets and pleasures and betrayals and whispered nothings for each of them, until the skies outside were as black as my thoughts.

I heard him before I saw him, whistling as he came up the stairs.

'Wife!' he cried, as he opened the door. 'Why are you sitting in the dark?'

He dropped his great coat on the bed and made his way around the studio, lighting the acetylene lamps, the candles that were lodged in empty wine bottles, wedging his cigarette into the corner of his mouth as he adjusted the drapes. And then he walked up to me and wrapped his arms around me, squinting in the half-light better to see my face.

'It is only five o'clock. I was not expecting you yet,' I felt as if I had woken from a dream.

'So soon after we are married? I couldn't leave you for long. Besides, I missed you. Jules Gagnaire is no substitute for your charms.' He pulled my face gently to his and tenderly kissed my ear. He smelled of cigarette smoke and *pastis*. 'I cannot bear to be away from you, my little shop girl.'

'Don't call me that.'

I stood up and walked away from him, through to the kitchen area. I felt his gaze, faintly bemused, after me. In truth I didn't know what I was doing. The bottle of sweet wine was long empty. 'You must be hungry.'

'I'm always hungry.'

*He is a man of great appetites.*

'I . . . left my bag at the market.'

'Hah! 'Tis of little importance. I, too, was barely conscious for most of the morning. It was a fine night, last night, wasn't it?' He chuckled, lost in reminiscence.

I didn't answer. I fetched two plates and two knives, and the remnants of that morning's bread. Then I stared at the jar of *foie gras*. I had nothing much else to give him.

'I had the most excellent meeting with Gagnaire. He says the Galerie Berthoud in the sixteenth wishes to exhibit those early landscapes. The work I did in Cazouls? He says he has a buyer for the two larger ones already.' I heard him uncork a bottle of wine, the clink of two glasses as he placed them on the table.

'I also told him of our new system for collecting my money. He was most impressed when I told him of last night's efforts. Now I have both him and you working alongside me, *chérie*, I'm sure we will live in the grand style.'

'I'm glad to hear it.' I said, and placed the bread basket in front of him.

I don't know what had happened to me. I couldn't look at him. I sat down opposite and proffered the *foie gras* and some butter. I cut an orange into quarters and put two pieces on his plate.

'*Foie gras!*' he unscrewed the lid. 'How you do spoil me, my love.' He broke off a piece of bread and smeared it with a slice of the pale pink pâté. I watched him eat it, his eyes on mine, and just for a moment I wished desperately that he had never liked *foie gras*, that he hated it. But he blew me a kiss and smacked his lips with delighted relish. 'What a life we lead, you and I, eh?'

'I did not choose the *foie gras*, Édouard. Mimi Einsbacher selected it for you.'

'Mimi, eh?' His eyes rested on mine for a moment. 'Well . . . she's a good judge of food.'

'And other things?'

'Mmm?'

'What else is Mimi good at?'

My food lay untouched on my plate. I could not eat. I had never liked *foie gras* anyway, the bitter knowledge of that forced feeding, those geese gorged until their very organs were swollen. The pain that could be caused by too much of what you loved.

Édouard put his knife on his plate. He looked at me. 'What is the matter, Sophie?'

I could not answer him.

'You seem out of sorts.'

'Out of sorts.'

'Is this because of what I told you before? I told you, my darling, it was before I met you. I have never lied to you.'

'And will you lie with her again?'

'What?'

'When you are bored with the novelty of your marriage? Will you revert to your old ways?'

'What is this?'

'Oh, eat your food, Édouard. Devour your beloved *foie gras*.'

He stared at me for the longest time. When he spoke, his voice was soft. 'What have I done to deserve this? Have I ever given you the slightest reason to doubt me? Have I ever shown you anything but utter devotion?'

'That is not the point.'

'Well, what is the point?'

'How did you get them to look at you like that?' My voice lifted.

'Who?'

'Those women. The Mimis and the Laures. The bar girls and the street girls and every wretched girl who seems to pass by our door. How did you get them to pose for you like that?'

Édouard was dumbstruck. When he spoke, his mouth set in an unfamiliar line. 'The same way I got you to pose for me. I asked them.'

'And afterwards? Did you do to them what you did to me?'

Édouard looked down at his plate before he answered. 'If I remember correctly, Sophie, it was you who seduced me that first time. Or does that not suit your newly remembered version of events?'

'This is meant to make me feel better? That I was the only one of your models you didn't try to make love to?'

His voice exploded into the quiet studio. 'What is wrong, Sophie? Why do you wish to torture yourself like this? We are happy, you and I. You know I have not so much as looked at another woman since we met!'

I began to applaud, each sharp clap breaking into the silent studio. 'Well done, Édouard! You have remained faithful all the way to our honeymoon! Oh, how admirable!'

'For God's sake!' He stood up at the table. 'Where is my wife? My happy, glowing, loving wife? And who is this woman I get in her place? This suspicious misery? This pinch-faced accuser?'

'Oh, so *that* is how you truly see me?'

'Well, is this whom you have become, now we are actually married?'

We stared at each other. The silence expanded, filled the room. Outside a child burst into noisy tears and a mother's voice could be heard, scolding and comforting.

Édouard ran a hand over his face. He took a deep breath and stared out of the window, then turned back to me. 'You know that is not how I see you. You know I – Oh, Sophie, I don't understand the genesis of this fury. I don't understand what I've done to deserve such . . .'

'Well, why don't you ask them?' I thrust my hand out towards his canvases. My voice emerged as a sob. 'For what can a provincial shop girl like me hope to understand about your life, after all?'

'Oh, you're impossible,' he said, and threw down his napkin.

'It's being married to you that is the impossibility. And I'm starting to wonder why you ever bothered.'

'Well, Sophie, you are not alone in that at least.' My husband fixed me with a look, whipped his coat off our bed, then turned and walked out of the door.

# 5

When he calls, she is on the bridge. She cannot say how long she has sat there. Its wire sides are almost obscured with padlocks on which people have inscribed their initials, and all along it tourists stoop, reading them on the little pieces of metal, scrawled in permanent pen or engraved by those with forethought. Some take pictures of each other, pointing to the padlocks they think are particularly beautiful, or have just placed there themselves.

She remembers David telling her about this place before they came here, about how lovers would secure the padlocks and throw the keys into the Seine as a mark of their enduring love, and of how when the padlocks were painstakingly removed by the city authorities they simply reappeared within days, engraved with everlasting love, the initials of lovers who, two years on, might still be together or might by now have moved to different continents rather than breathe the same air. He had told her how the riverbed under the bridge had to be dredged regularly, harvesting the rusting mass of keys.

Now she sits on the bench, trying not to look at them

too closely, beyond the simple spectacle of them, their shimmering surfaces. She does not want to think about what they mean.

'Meet me at the Pont des Arts,' she had said to him. Nothing more.

Perhaps there was something in her voice.

'I'll be twenty minutes,' he'd said.

She sees him coming from the Musée du Louvre, his blue shirt becoming more vivid as he gets closer. He is wearing khaki-coloured trousers and she thinks, with a pang, how much she loves the sight of him. How familiar his shape is to her, even after such a short time. She looks at his soft, ruffled hair, and the planes of his face, and the way his walk always has a touch of impatience, as if he's keen to get to the next thing. And then she sees that over his shoulder he has the leather bag in which he carries his plans.

*What have I done?*

He doesn't smile as he approaches, even though it's clear he has seen her. He walks up to her, slowing his pace, then drops his bag and sits down beside her.

They are silent for some minutes, watching the tourist boats glide past.

And finally Liv says, 'I can't do this.'

She looks down the route of the Seine, squinting at the people who, even now, are stooping to examine the padlocks.

'I think we've made the most awful mistake. *I've* made a mistake.'

'A mistake?'

'I know I'm impulsive. I see now we should have slowed things down. We should have . . . got to know each other a little better. So I've been thinking. It's not like we had a big wedding, or anything. It's not like all our friends even know. We can just . . . We can just pretend like it didn't happen. We're both young.'

'What are you talking about, Liv?'

She looks at him. 'David – it all became clear as you walked towards me. You brought your plans with you.'

The smallest flinch. But she sees it.

'You knew you were going to meet the Goldsteins. You packed your bag of plans and you brought it on your honeymoon.'

He looks down at his feet. 'I didn't know. I hoped.'

'And that's supposed to make it better?'

They are silent again. David leans forward, clasping his hands together above his knees. Then he looks sideways at her, his face troubled. 'I love you, Liv. Don't you love me any more?'

'Yes. So much. But I can't . . . I can't do this. I can't be the woman this makes me.'

He shakes his head. 'I don't understand. This is crazy. I was only gone for a couple of hours.'

'It's not about the couple of hours. This was our honeymoon. It's a template for how we're going to be.'

'How is a honeymoon ever a template for a marriage? Most people go and lie on a beach for two weeks, for

Christ's sake. You think that's how the rest of their lives is going to run?'

'Don't twist my words! You know what I mean. This is meant to be the one time you –'

'It's just this building –'

'Oh, this building. This building. This fucking building. There's always going to be a building, isn't there?'

'No. This is special. They –'

'They want you to meet them again.'

He lets out a breath, and his jaw tightens. 'It's not a meeting as such,' he says. 'It's lunch. Tomorrow. At one of Paris's best restaurants. And you're invited too.'

She would laugh if she wasn't so close to tears. When she finally speaks, her voice is oddly calm. 'I'm sorry, David. I'm not even blaming you for this. It's my own fault. I was so besotted with you that I couldn't see beyond it. I couldn't see that being married to someone who was so consumed by his work would make me . . .' Her voice thickens.

'Make you what? I still love *you*, Liv. I don't understand.'

She rubs her eyes. 'I'm not explaining myself very well. Look . . . come with me. I want to show you something.'

It's a short walk back to the Musée d'Orsay. The queue has died down and they move forward in silence for the ten minutes it takes to gain entry. She is acutely conscious of him beside her, of the new awkwardness between them. A little part of her still cannot believe that this is how her honeymoon is ending.

She summons the lift, confident of where she is headed this time, and David follows. They walk through the rooms of Impressionists on the top floor, dodging the clumps of people who stand and stare. Another school party sits in front of *Le Déjeuner sur l'herbe* and the same enthusiastic attendant talks them through the scandal of the naked woman. She thinks how ironic it is that she now has her husband here, where she had wanted him this morning, and it is too late. It is all too late.

And eventually there they are, in front of the little picture.

She looks at it, and he steps forward.

'"*Wife, out of sorts*",' he reads. '"By Édouard Lefèvre".' He studies it for a moment, then turns to her, waiting for an explanation.

'So . . . I saw it this morning . . . this miserable, neglected wife. And it just hit me. That's not how I want to be. I felt suddenly as if the whole of our marriage was going to be like this – me wanting your attention, and you not being able to give it. And it scared me.'

'Our marriage isn't going to be like that.'

'I don't want to be a wife who feels ignored, even on her honeymoon.'

'I wasn't ignoring you, Liv –'

'But you made me feel unimportant, and on the one occasion I might have reasonably expected you to just enjoy us being together, to just want to be with me.' Her voice lifts, becomes impassioned. 'I wanted to stroll around the little bars of Paris and sit down and drink glasses of wine for no reason, my hand in yours. I wanted to hear about who you were before we met, and what you wanted. I wanted to tell you all the things I'd planned for our life together. I wanted to have lots of sex. *Lots* of sex. I didn't want to walk around galleries alone and have coffee with men I don't even know – just to kill time.'

She can't help but be a tiny bit gratified by his sharp sideways look.

'And when I saw this painting it all made sense to me. This is me, David. This is how I will be. This is what's going to happen. Because, even now, you can't see that there's anything wrong in spending two days – *three* days – of a five-day honeymoon pitching for work to a couple of rich businessmen.'

She swallows. And her voice breaks. 'I'm sorry. I . . . I can't be this woman. I just – can't. It's who my mother was and it terrifies me.' She wipes her eyes, ducking her head to avoid the curious glances of people passing.

David stares at the painting. He doesn't speak for several minutes. And then he turns to her, his face drawn. 'OK, I get it.' He runs a hand through his hair. 'And you're right. About all of it. I've – I've been unbelievably stupid. And selfish. I'm sorry.'

They fall silent as a German couple pauses in front of the painting, exchanging a few words before moving on. 'But . . . but you're wrong about this painting.'

She looks up at him.

'She's not ignored. She's not symptomatic of a failing relationship.' He moves a step closer, gently takes her by the arm as he gestures. 'Look at how he's painted her, Liv. He doesn't want her to be angry. He's still looking at her. Look at the tenderness of his brushstrokes, the way he's coloured her skin there. He adores her. He can't bear that she's angry. He can't stop looking at her even when she's furious with him.' He takes a breath. 'He's there, and he's not going away, no matter how much he's enraged her.'

Her eyes have filled with tears. 'What are you saying?'

'I don't believe this painting should mean the end of our marriage.' He reaches out, takes her hand and holds it until her fingers relax around his. 'Because I look at it and I see the opposite from you. Yes, something's gone wrong. Yes, she's unhappy right then, in that moment. But when I look at her, at them, at this, Liv, I just see a picture full of love.'

# 6

*1912*

A thin rain had started as I began walking the streets around the Latin Quarter shortly after midnight. Now, hours later, it had soaked my felt hat so that the drops seeped down the back of my collar, but I barely felt them, so steeped was I in my misery.

Some part of me had wanted to wait for Édouard to return, but I could not sit in our home, not with those women, with the prospect of my husband's future infidelities hanging over me. I kept seeing the hurt in his eyes, hearing the rage in his voice. *Who is this pinch-faced accuser?* He no longer saw me as the best of myself, and who could blame him? He had seen me as I truly knew myself to be: plain, provincial, an invisible shop girl. He had been trapped into marriage by a fit of jealousy, his fleeting conviction that he needed to secure my love. Now he was regretting his haste. And I had made him conscious of it.

I wondered briefly if I should simply pack my case and leave. But every time that thought flickered through my feverish mind, the answer came back immediately: I loved him. The thought of life without him was unbearable. How could I return to St Péronne and live the life of a spinster, knowing what I knew of how love could feel? How could I bear the thought that he lived, somewhere, miles away from me? Even when he left the room I felt his absence like an aching limb. My physical need for him still overwhelmed me. And I could hardly return home a matter of weeks after our wedding.

But there was the problem: I would always be provincial. I could not share my husband, as the Parisiennes apparently did, turning a blind eye to their indiscretions. How could I live with Édouard and face the possibility of him returning home smelling of another woman's scent? Even if I could not be sure of his faithlessness, how could I walk into our home and see Mimi Einsbacher, or any of these women, naked on our bed as she posed for him? What was I supposed to do? Simply disappear into a back room? Go for a walk? Sit and watch over them? He would hate me. He would see me as the gaoler that Mimi Einsbacher already considered me.

I understood now that I had not thought at all about what marriage would mean for us. I could not see further than his voice, his hands, his kisses. I could not see further than my own vanity – dazzled as I was by the reflection of me I had seen in his paintings, and in his eyes.

And now his magic dust had blown away, and I was left – a wife: this pinch-faced accuser. And I did not like this version of myself.

I walked the length of Paris, along the rue de Rivoli,

up to avenue Foch and down the backstreets of Invalides, ignoring the curious glances of the men, the catcalls of the drunks, my feet growing sore on the cobbles, my face turned away from passers-by so they did not see the tears that brimmed in my eyes. I grieved for the marriage I had already lost. I grieved for the Édouard who had seen only the best in me. I missed our intense happiness together, the sense that we had been impenetrable, immune to the rest of the world. How could we have come to this so soon? I walked, so lost in my thoughts that I barely noticed it had begun to grow light.

'Madame Lefèvre?'

I turned as a woman stepped out of the shadows. When she stood under the guttering streetlight, I saw it was the girl to whom Édouard had introduced me on the night of the fight in the Bar Tripoli – I struggled to recall her name: Lisette? Laure?

'It is no hour for a lady to be out here, Madame,' she said, glancing back up the street. I had no answer for her. I wasn't sure I could actually speak. I recalled one of the girls at La Femme Marché nudging me as he approached: *He consorts with the street girls of Pigalle.*

'I had no idea of the hour.' I glanced up at the clock. A quarter to five. I had been walking the whole night.

Her face was in shadow, but I felt her studying me. 'Are you quite well?'

'I'm fine. Thank you.'

She kept looking at me. Then she took a step forwards and touched my elbow lightly. 'I'm not sure this is a good place for a married woman to walk alone. Would you like to join me for a drink? I know a warm bar not far from here.'

When I hesitated she released my arm, took the smallest of steps backwards. 'Of course, if you have other plans I quite understand.'

'No. It is kind of you to ask. I would relish an excuse to get out of the cold. I . . . I don't think I'd noticed how chilled I am until just now.'

We walked in silence down two narrow streets, turning towards a window lit from within. A Chinese man stepped back from a heavy door to let us in, and she exchanged a quiet word with him. The bar was indeed warm and the windows fugged with steam, a handful of men still drinking. Carriage drivers, mostly, she told me, as she shepherded me towards the back. Laure Le Comte ordered something at the bar and I took a seat at a table at the rear. I peeled my damp cape from my shoulders. The little room was noisy and cheerful; the men had gathered around a card game that was going on in the corner. I could see my face in the mirror that ran along the wall, pale and damp, my hair plastered to my head. Why would he love only me? I wondered, then tried to push away the thought.

An elderly waiter arrived with a tray, and Laure handed me a small goblet of cognac. Now we were sitting there, I could think of nothing to say to her.

'It's good we came inside when we did,' she said, glancing towards the doorway. The rain had started up properly now, running down the pavements in woven rivers, gurgling in the gutters.

'I think so.'

'Is Monsieur Lefèvre at home?'

She had used the formal version of his name, even though she had known him longer than I had.

'I have no idea.' I took a sip of my drink. It slid down my throat like fire. And then suddenly I began to talk. Perhaps it was desperation. Perhaps it was the knowledge that a woman such as Laure had seen so many kinds of bad behaviour that she could not be shocked by anything I had to tell her. Perhaps I simply wanted to see her reaction. I was unsure whether, after all, she, too, was among those women I now had to view as a threat.

'I found myself in an ill temper. I thought it better . . . to walk.'

She nodded, and allowed a small smile. Her hair, I noted, was pulled into a neat twist at her collar, more like a schoolteacher than a woman of the night. 'I have never been married. But I can imagine that it changes one's life beyond all recognition.'

'It is hard to adjust. I had thought myself well suited to it. Now . . . I'm not sure I have the right temperament for its challenges.' Even as I spoke I was surprised at myself. I was not the kind of woman given to confidences. The only person I had ever confided in was my sister, and in her absence, I had only really wanted to talk to Édouard.

'You are finding Édouard . . . challenging?'

I saw now that she was older than I had first thought: clever application of rouge and lipstick had given her a bloom of youth. But there was something about her that made you want to keep talking; a suggestion that what you told her would go no further. I wondered absently what she had done that evening, what other secrets she heard each day.

'Yes. No. Not Édouard exactly.' I could not explain. 'I don't know. I'm – sorry. I should not have burdened you with my thoughts.'

She ordered a second cognac for me. And then she sat and sipped her own, as if considering how much to say. Finally, she leaned forwards and spoke softly. 'It will be no surprise to you, Madame, that I think myself something of an expert on the psyche of the married gentleman.'

I found myself blushing slightly.

'I know nothing of what brought you here this evening, and I believe nobody outside can speak with any authority on what happens within the confines of a marriage. But I can tell you this: Édouard adores you. I can say so with some confidence, having seen many men; and a few, too, who were on honeymoon.'

I looked up now, and she raised a wry eyebrow. 'Yes, on their honeymoons. Before he met you I might confidently have wagered Édouard Lefèvre would never marry. That he would have been perfectly comfortable continuing to lead the life he had. And then he met you.

And with no coquettishness, or guile, you won his heart, his head, his very imagination. Do not underestimate what he feels for you, Madame.'

'And the other women. I'm meant to ignore them?'

'Other women?'

'I have been told . . . Édouard is not the kind of man to give himself over happily to . . . exclusivity.'

Laure looked at me steadily. 'And what poisonous creature told you this?' My face must have given me away. 'Whatever seed this counsellor has planted, Madame, it seems to have been expertly done.'

She took another sip of cognac. 'I will tell you something, Madame, and I hope you will not take offence because it comes well meant.' She leaned forward, over the table. 'Yes, I did not believe Édouard was the kind of man who would marry either. But when I saw you both that evening outside the Bar Tripoli, and I saw how he looked at you, his pride in you, the way he placed his hand so tenderly upon your back, the way he looks at you for approval with almost everything he says or does, I knew that you were most perfectly matched. And I saw he was happy. So happy.'

I sat very still, listening.

'And I will admit that on our meeting I felt shame, a rare emotion for me. Because in the past months, several times when I modelled for Édouard, or even when I saw him, perhaps on his way home from some bar or restaurant, I offered myself to him for free. I have always been terribly fond of him, you see. And on every occasion since he first saw you, he declined with an unusual delicacy, but without hesitation.'

Outside, the rain had stopped abruptly. A man held his hand out of the doorway, and said something to his friend that made them both laugh.

Laure's voice was a low murmur: 'The greatest risk to your marriage, if I may be so frank, is not your husband. It is that the words of this so-called counsellor turn you into the very thing you – and your husband – dread.'

Laure finished her drink. She pulled her shawl around her shoulders and stood. She checked her appearance in the mirror, straightened a lock of hair, then glanced at the window. '*Et voilà* – the rain has stopped. I think today might be a fine one. Go home to your husband, Madame. Rejoice in your good fortune. Be the woman he adores.'

She gave me a brief smile. 'And in future choose your counsellors most carefully.'

With a word to the proprietor, she made her way out of the bar into the damp blue light of the early dawn. I sat there, digesting what she had told me, feeling exhaustion finally seep into my bones, along with something else: a deep, deep relief.

I called the elderly waiter over to pay the bill. He informed me with a shrug that Madame Laure had already settled it, and went back to polishing his glasses.

The apartment was so quiet when I made my way up the stairs that I guessed Édouard must be asleep. He was a constant source of noise when at home, singing or whistling or playing his gramophone so loudly that the neighbours would thump on the walls in irritation. The sparrows chattered in the ivy that covered our walls, and the distant sound of horses' hoofs on the cobbles spoke of a slowly waking city, but the little apartment at the top of 21a rue Soufflot was utterly silent.

I tried not to think about where he might have been, or in what frame of mind. I took off my shoes and hurried up the last of the stairs, my feet muffled on the wooden steps, wanting already to climb into bed beside him and wrap myself around him. I would tell him how sorry I was, how I adored him, how I had been a fool. I would be the woman he had married.

My mind hummed with my need for him. I opened the apartment door quietly, already imagining him lying in a tangle in our sheets and coverlet, his arm rising sleepily to lift them and allow me in. But when I looked, already peeling my coat from my shoulders, our bed was empty.

I hesitated, stepped past the sleeping area and into the main studio. I felt oddly nervous suddenly, unsure of my reception. 'Édouard?' I called.

There was no answer.

I walked in. The studio was dimly lit, the candles burning low where I had left them in my hurry to quit the apartment, the long window glowing a cold blue with the early-morning light. The chill in the air suggested that the fire had gone out hours ago. At the end of the room, beside the canvases, Édouard stood in his chemise and loose trousers, his back to me, gazing at a canvas.

I stood in the doorway staring at my husband, at his broad back, his thick dark hair, before he realized I was there. He turned to me and I saw a fleeting wariness in his eyes – *what's coming now?* – and the sight of it bruised me.

I walked towards him, my shoes in my hand. I had imagined hurling myself into his arms all the way back down rue de Babylone. I had thought I would not be able to stop myself. But now, in the still, silent room, something held me back. I stopped a few inches in front of him, my eyes not leaving his, and found myself turning towards the easel.

The woman in the canvas was hunched forwards, her face mute and furious, her dark red hair tied back loosely at her neck as mine had been the previous evening. Her body spoke of tension, a deeply held unhappiness, her refusal to look directly at the artist a silent rebuke. And a sob rose in my throat.

'It's . . . perfect,' I said, when I could speak.

He turned to me and I saw he was exhausted, his eyes red with what might have been lack of sleep or something else altogether. And I wanted to wipe the sadness from his face, to take back my words, to make him happy again. 'Oh, I have been so foolish –' I began. But he was ahead of me, and stepped forward, gathering me to him.

'Don't leave me again, Sophie,' he said softly into my ear, and his voice was thick with emotion.

We did not speak. We clutched each other so tightly, as if it were years that we had been separated, not hours.

His voice, against my skin, was ragged and broken. 'I had to paint you because I couldn't bear that you weren't here and it was the only way I could bring you back.'

'I'm here,' I murmured. I wound my fingers into his hair, bringing my face to his, breathing the air that he breathed. 'I won't leave you again. Ever.'

'I wanted to paint you as you are. But all that would come was this furious, unhappy Sophie. And all I could think was, I am the cause of her unhappiness.'

I shook my head. 'It wasn't you, Édouard. Let us forget this night. Please.'

He reached out a hand and turned the easel away from me. 'Then I won't finish this. I don't even want you to look at it. Oh, Sophie. I'm sorry. I'm so sorry . . .'

I kissed him then. I kissed him and I made sure my kiss told him how I adored him from within my very bones, how my life before him had been a grey, colourless thing, and a future without him terrifying and black. I told him in the kiss that I loved him more than I had ever thought I was capable of loving anyone. My husband. My handsome, complicated, brilliant husband. I couldn't say the words: my feelings were too vast for them.

'Come,' I said finally, and, my fingers entwined in his, I pulled him by the hand to our bed.

Some time later, when the street below was alive with the sounds of late morning, and the fruit-sellers had made their rounds, and the smell of coffee floating up through our open window had become unbearably delicious, I peeled myself away from Édouard and out of our bed, the sweat still cooling on my back, the taste of him still on my lips. I walked across the studio, lit the fire, and when I was done I stood and turned the canvas round. I looked at her properly, at the tenderness in his line, at the intimacy of it, the perfect representation of me, of a moment.

And then I turned to face him. 'You must finish it, you know.'

He propped himself up on one elbow, squinted at me. 'But – you look so unhappy.'

'Perhaps. But it's the truth, Édouard. You always show the truth. It's your great talent.' I stretched, lifting my arms above my head and lowering them again, enjoying the knowledge that his eyes were on me. I shrugged. 'And, in truth, I suppose there was always going to be a day when we were out of sorts with each other. A *lune de miel* cannot last for ever.'

'Yes, it can,' he said, waiting as I padded across the bare floor back to him. He pulled me into bed and looked at me steadily from across the pillow, a rueful smile upon his face. 'It can last as long as we wish it. And, as the master of this house, I decree that every day of our marriage must be a honeymoon.'

'I find myself utterly bent to my husband's will.' I sighed, nestling into him. 'We have tried it, and found that being disagreeable and out of sorts didn't suit us. I, too, must declare the rest of our marriage to be honey-moon only.'

We lay there in companionable silence, my leg thrown over his, the warm skin of his belly against mine, his arm heavy over my ribs where he held me to him. I wasn't sure I had ever been so content. I breathed in the scent of my husband, felt the rise and fall of his chest, and finally tiredness began to overtake me. I began to doze off, drifting to somewhere warm and pleasurable, perhaps made more so for where I had been. And then he spoke.

'Sophie,' he murmured. 'While we are being so frank – I feel I need to tell you something.'

I opened one eye.

'And I hope your feelings will not be too injured by it.'

'What is it?' My voice was a whisper, my heart braced to stop.

He hesitated for a moment, and took my hand in his. 'I know you bought it for me as a treat. But I really do not like to eat *foie gras*. I never have. I was just trying to be agreea—'

But he did not get to finish his sentence. Because I had already stopped his mouth with my own.

# 7

'I can't believe you're ringing me from your honeymoon.'

'Yes, well, David's downstairs sorting something out in the lobby. I just thought today would be even more perfect if I could squeeze in a two-minute chat.'

Jasmine puts her hand over the receiver. 'I'm going to take this in the Ladies so Besley can't see me. Hang on.' The sound of a door closing, then hurried footsteps. I could almost see the cramped office above the stationer's, the heavy traffic crawling its way up Finchley Road, and smell the lead tang of fuel hanging in the sticky summer air. 'Go on. Tell me everything. In about twenty seconds. Are you walking like John Wayne yet? And are you having the best time ever?'

I gazed around my hotel room, at the rumpled bed David had just vacated, at the suitcase that I had begun packing half-heartedly on the floor. 'It's . . . been a bit weird. Getting used to actually being married. But I'm really happy.'

'Ugh! I'm so envious. I went on a date with Shaun Jeffries last night. Remember him? Fi's brother? With the awful nails? I honestly have no idea why I said yes. He droned on and on about himself. I was apparently meant to be impressed by the fact that he had a maisonette in Friern Barnet.'

'It's a very nice area. Up and coming.'

'And the maisonette itself has a lot of potential.'

I started to giggle. 'It's important to get on the ladder.'

'Especially at our age. You can't go wrong with bricks and mortar.'

'He's got a pension. Go on. Tell me he's got a pension.'

'He has so totally got a pension. And it's index-linked. And he wore grey shoes and he insisted on splitting the bill and he ordered the cheapest bottle of wine in the restaurant "because it all tastes the same after the first glass". Oh, Worthing, I wish you were home already. I so badly need a drink. Dating is crap. You have totally done the right thing.'

I lay back on the bed and gazed up at the ceiling, which was white and as crisply ornate as a wedding cake. 'What? Even though I'm ridiculously impulsive and my impulses are not to be trusted?'

'Yes! I wish I was more impulsive. I would have married Andrew when he asked me and I'd probably be living in Spain now instead of stuck here in this office wondering whether I can sneak off at twenty to five to get my car tax sorted. Anyway – Oh, God, I've got to go. Besley's just walked into the Ladies.' Her voice lifts, changes tone. 'Of course, Mrs Halston. Thank you so much for calling. I'm sure we'll speak soon.'

Liv rings off, just as David returns. He is carrying a box of chocolates from Patrick Roger.

'What's this?'

'Supper. They're bringing up some champagne to go with it.'

She cackles with delight, pulls the wrapper off the beautiful pale turquoise box, pops one into her mouth and closes her eyes. 'Oh, my God, these are amazing. What with these and tomorrow's posh lunch I'm going to go home the size of a house.'

'I cancelled the lunch.'

Liv looks up. 'But I said I –'

David shrugs. 'No. You were right. No more work. Some things should be sacred.'

She pops another chocolate into her mouth, holds the box towards him. 'Oh, David . . . I'm starting to think I overreacted.' The afternoon, with its feverish pitch of emotion, seems so long ago. She feels as if they have been married a lifetime since.

He pulls his shirt over his head. 'You didn't. You had every right to expect my full attention on our honeymoon. I'm sorry. I guess – I guess I've got to learn to remember there are two of us now, not just me.'

And there he is again. The man she had fallen in love with. *My husband*. She is suddenly almost incandescent with lust.

He sits down beside her, and she slides over to him while he keeps talking. 'You want to hear the irony? I rang the Goldsteins from downstairs and I took a deep breath and I explained that I was very sorry but I couldn't take any more time out this week, as this was actually my honeymoon.'

'And?'

'And they were absolutely furious with me.'

The next chocolate stops halfway to her lips. Her heart sinks. 'Oh, God – I'm sorry.'

'Yup, properly furious. They asked me what on earth I thought I was doing, leaving my new wife alone to discuss business matters. "This is no bloody way to start a marriage," I quote.' He gives her a sideways grin.

'I always liked the sound of those Goldsteins,' she says, popping the chocolate into his mouth.

'They said it was a one-off, a time of our lives that I'd never get back.'

'I think I might even love them.'

'You're going to love them even more in a minute.' He stands and walks over to the French windows on to the balcony, throwing them open. The evening sun streams into the little room, while below them the sounds of the rue des Francs Bourgeois, teeming with tourists and lazy shoppers, fills the room. He pulls off his shoes and socks and his trousers and sits down on the bed, turning to her. 'They said they felt partly responsible for dragging me away. So, they've offered us the use of their suite in the Royal Monceau from tomorrow, to make it up to you. Room service, bath the size of an ocean liner, champagne on tap, absolutely no reason to leave the room whatsoever. For two nights. The reason I was downstairs so long was that I've taken a husbandly liberty and changed our return tickets. What do you say?'

He looks at Liv, and even now there is a hint of uncertainty in his gaze. 'Obviously it would involve spending a further forty-eight hours with a man who is, according to our friendly local billionaires, a bloody stupid idiot.'

She regards him steadily. 'Bloody stupid idiots are my absolute favourite kind of husband.'

'I was so hoping you'd say that.'

They fall backwards on to the pillows and lie there side by side, their fingers entwined.

She gazes through the window at the still-bright City of Lights, and finds she is smiling. She is married. She is in Paris. Tomorrow she is going to disappear into a queen-sized bed with the man she loves and probably not come out for two days. This is probably as good as life gets.

But she hopes not.

'I'll get it right, Mrs Halston,' he murmurs, turning towards her and lifting her fingers to his lips. 'It might take me a while, the whole marriage thing, but I will get it right eventually.' He has two freckles on his nose. She has never noticed them before. They are the most beautiful freckles she has ever seen.

'That's OK, Mr Halston,' she says, and reaches back to place the chocolates carefully on the bedside table, out of harm's way. 'We've got all the time in the world.'

Last Year's Coat

The lining of the coat has gone completely. Evie holds it up and runs her finger along the ripped seam, wondering if there is any way she can pull the fine edges of frayed fabric together. She turns it over, looking at the thinned wool, the slight sheen on the elbows, and realizes there is little point.

She knows exactly what she would buy in its place. She sees it in the window of the shop twice a day as she walks past, slowing her stride a little just to gaze at it. Midnight blue, with a silvery lamb's-wool collar; classic enough to last several years but just different enough not to look like every other chain-store coat. It is beautiful.

And it costs £185.

Evie puts her head down and walks past.

Not that long ago, Evie would have bought the coat. She would have held it up in her lunch hour, modelled it in front of the girls in Marketing, carried it home in its expensive bag, its weight banging satisfyingly against her legs.

But some time ago, without apparently applying, they seem to have become official members of the Squeezed Middle. Pete's hours were abruptly cut by thirty per cent.

The weekly grocery bill went up by fifteen per cent. Fuel is so expensive that they sold her car, and she now walks the two miles to work. Heating, a luxury, comes on for an hour in the morning and two at night. The mortgage that had seemed so manageable now hangs over them like a great albatross. She sits at the kitchen table in the evenings poring over columns of figures, warning her teenage daughters against unnecessary expenditure like her own mother had warned her about Bad Men.

'C'mon, love. Let's go to bed.' Pete's hands land gently on her shoulders.

'I'm doing the accounts.'

'Then let's go and huddle together for bodily warmth. I'm only thinking of our heating bill,' he adds solemnly. 'Honest. I won't enjoy it at all.'

Her smile is weak, a reflexive thing. He puts his arms around her. 'Come on, lovely. We'll be fine. We've got through worse.'

She knows he is right. At least they both have work. They have friends who paint on brittle smiles, bat away enquiries about new jobs with a vague, 'Oh . . . got a few things in the pipeline.' Two have sold their houses and downsized, citing 'family reasons'. She finds that many of them move away and fail to keep in touch, as if the shame of not continuing up the ladder is just too much.

'How's your dad?'

'Not bad.' Every evening after work, Pete travels the short journey to his father's house in order to take him a hot meal. 'The car's not right, though.'

'Don't say that!' she wails.

'I know. I think the starter motor is going. Look,' he says, registering her expression. 'Don't panic. I'll pop it into Mike's, see if he can give us a good price.'

She does not mention the coat.

The girls in Marketing do not fret about starter motors or heating bills. They still disappear at lunchtime, returning to show off their purchases with the steel-eyed acquisitiveness of a hunter returning with a trophy hide. They arrive on Monday mornings bearing tales of city breaks in Paris and Lisbon, eat out weekly at the pizza restaurant (Evie insists that, really, she's quite happy with her cheese sandwiches). She tries not to feel resentful. Two of them don't have children; Felicity has a husband who earns three times what she does. I have Pete and the girls, Evie tells herself firmly, and we are all healthy, and we have a roof over our heads, and that is an awful lot more than most people have. But sometimes when she hears them talking about Barcelona or showing off yet another pair of shoes, her jaw clenches so hard she fears for her tooth enamel.

'I need a new coat,' she tells Pete finally. It bursts out of her, anguished, like someone admitting an infidelity.

'You've got loads of coats, surely.'

'Nope. I've had this one four years. Then there's just my mackintosh and that black one I got off eBay, where the sleeve fell apart.'

Pete shrugs. 'So? You need a coat, go buy a coat.'

'But the only one I like is expensive.'

'How expensive?'

She tells him and watches him blanch. Pete thinks that spending more than six quid on a haircut is a sign of insanity. The downside of her running the family's accounts for their entire married life is that his cost thermostat is still set somewhere in the mid-eighties.

'Is that a . . . designer coat?'

'No. Just a good wool coat.'

He is silent. 'There's Kate's school trip. And my starter motor.'

'I know. It's OK. I'm not going to buy it.'

The next morning she crosses the road when she walks to work, just so she cannot see it. But the coat has lodged itself firmly in her mind's eye. She sees it every time she catches her fingers in her ripped lining. She sees it when Felicity returns from lunch with a new coat (red, silk lining) of her own. It feels somehow symbolic of everything that has gone wrong with their lives.

'We'll get you a coat,' says Pete on Saturday when he watches her remove her arm from its sleeve with excessive care. 'I'm sure we can find one you like.'

They stop in front of the shop window, and she looks at him mutely. He squeezes her arm. They walk on through several more shops and finally reach Get the Look, a store her daughters like; it is full of 'fun' fashion, the shop assistants are all apparently twelve and chew gum, and the music is deafening. Pete normally hates shopping but seems to sense how down she is and has adopted an uncharacteristic cheer. He rifles through the rails, holds up a dark blue coat with a fake-fur collar. 'Look – it's just like that one you like! And it's only' – he peers at the label – 'twenty-nine pounds!'

She allows him to slide it on to her, and she looks at herself in the mirror.

The coat is slightly too tight under the arms. The collar is nice, but she suspects it will look matted, like a geriatric cat, within weeks. The cut seems to stretch and sag in just the wrong places. The wool mix is mostly synthetic.

'You look gorgeous,' Pete says, smiling.

Pete would say she looked gorgeous if she were wearing prison scrubs. She hates this coat. She knows that every time she puts it on, it will feel like a silent rebuke. Forty-three years old and you're wearing a cheap coat from the teenagers' shop.

'I'll think about it,' she says, and puts it back on the hanger.

Lunchtimes have become a kind of torture. Today the girls in Marketing are booking tickets for a group outing, a resurrected boy band last popular fifteen years ago. They are gathered around a computer screen, checking seat positions.

'Fancy it, Evie? Girls' night out? Come on, it'll be a laugh.'

She looks at the ticket prices: £75 each, plus transport.

'Not me.' She smiles. 'I never much liked them the first time around.'

It is a lie, of course. She had adored them. She stomps home, allowing the coat only the briefest glance. She feels childish, mutinous. And then, as she walks up the little driveway, she sees Pete's legs sticking out from under the car.

'What are you doing out here? It's raining.'

'I thought I'd have a go at the car myself. Save a few bob.'

'But you know nothing about cars.'

'I downloaded some stuff off the Internet. And Mike said he'd take a look afterwards, to check that I've done everything right.'

She gazes at him, and her heart sags slightly with love. He always has been resourceful.

'Have you been to your dad's?'

'Yeah. I got the bus.'

Evie stares at her husband's soaked, blackened trousers and sighs. 'I'll make him a casserole so that if you can't get there for a couple of days, he'll still have something to eat.'

'You're a star.' He blows her a kiss with oily fingers.

Perhaps picking up on her subdued mood, the girls are sweet over supper. Pete is preoccupied, gazing at printed diagrams of engine innards. Evie chews on her macaroni cheese and tells herself there are worse things than not being able to afford the coat you really want. She remembers her mother exhorting her to 'think of the starving children in Africa' while she pushed mutinously at the greens on her plate.

'I'll get that twenty-nine-pound coat tomorrow. If it's all right with you.'

'You looked lovely in it.' Pete kisses her head. She can see from his face that he knows how much she hates it. When the girls have left the table, he reaches out a hand and says softly, 'Things will change, you know.' She hopes it is in the way that he means.

Felicity has a new handbag. Evie tries to ignore the distant commotion as it is pulled from its box, birthed from its cotton cover, and held up for the others to admire – the kind of bag that costs a month's salary, the kind you have to go on to a waiting list for the privilege of purchasing. Evie pretends to be absorbed by spreadsheets so that she doesn't have to look. She is embarrassed by the waves of envy that steal over her as she hears the oohs and aahs of admiration. She doesn't even like handbags. She just envies Felicity the financial security that enables her to buy something so expensive without even a pang of anxiety. She thinks twice before paying for a plastic carrier right now.

But it does not stop there. Myra has ordered a new sofa. The girls discuss their forthcoming night out. Felicity sets her bag on top of her desk and makes jokes about loving it more than a baby.

Evie heads for Get the Look at lunchtime. She walks blindly, her head dipped, telling herself it is just a coat. Only a shallow person believed that what you wore said anything about you, surely? She counts her blessings like a mantra on one hand. And then she stops outside the other boutique, halted by the big red sign in the window. SALE. Her heart gives an unexpected lurch.

She is inside, her heart beating, refusing to listen to the little voice in her head.

'The blue wool coat,' she says to the assistant. 'How much is it reduced by?'

'Everything in the window is half price, Madam.'

Ninety pounds. Yes, it's still expensive, but it's half price. Surely that counts for something? 'I'll have the size twelve,' she says before reason can seep in.

The assistant returns from the rails as Evie is pulling her credit card from her bag. It's a beautiful coat, she tells herself. It will last for years. Pete will understand.

'I'm so sorry, Madam. The size twelve has gone. And that was our last one.'

'What?'

'I'm so sorry.'

Evie is deflated. She gazes over at the window and slides her purse back into her bag. She raises a small, defeated smile. 'Never mind. It's probably just as well.' She does not go on to Get the Look. Right now she would rather stick with last year's coat.


'Hey, you.'

She is hanging up her coat when Pete puts his head round the door. She closes her eyes as he kisses her.

'You're wet.'

298

'It's raining.'

'You should have told me. I'd have come and picked you up.'

'Is the car working?'

'For now. Mike said I actually did a good job. How amazing am I?'

'Completely amazing.'

She holds him tightly for a minute, then walks through to the comforting fug of her kitchen. One of the girls has been making cookies, and Evie inhales the leftover scent of baking. This is what matters, she tells herself.

'Oh. And there's something for you on the table.'

Evie glances over and sees the bag. She stares at Pete. 'What's this?'

'Open it.'

She lifts the side of the bag and peers inside. She freezes.

'Don't panic. It's from Dad. For all the meals.'

'What?'

'He says he can't keep accepting your food unless you let him give something back. You know what he's like. I told him about the coat, and you wouldn't believe it – there was only a bloody sale on. We picked it up at lunchtime.'

'Your dad bought me a coat?'

'Don't get all tearful. I picked it out, and he paid for it. He reckoned it was the equivalent of thirty steak pies and twenty of your crumbles. He says it's actually pretty good value, given how much you do for him.'

He and the girls exchange looks. Evie has abruptly started laughing, while simultaneously wiping tears from her eyes.

'Yeah, all right, Mum,' says Letty. 'No need to get emotional. It's only a coat.'

Evie walks to work. She is early; the office is almost empty. Felicity disappears to the Ladies to do her makeup, and Evie hums as she drops the marketing budgets on her desk. As she passes, she sees a statement sticking out from under the designer bag and steps back, checking to see whether it refers to a company account. It has been drilled into them at last week's meeting that no financial information is to be left out overnight. But as she looks more closely, she sees it's personal: a credit-card statement. Evie glimpses the total and blinks.

But it really is five figures.

'Are you coming out?' says Felicity at lunchtime. 'We thought we'd try that Thai place. You can show off your new coat!'

Evie thinks for a minute, then pulls her lunch from her bag. 'Not today,' she says. 'But thanks anyway.'

As they leave, she turns and carefully straightens her coat on the back of her chair, smoothing the collar. And even though she is not massively fond of cheese sandwiches, Evie eats all of hers. And it tastes delicious.

Thirteen Days with John C

She had almost walked straight past it. For the last hundred yards, Miranda had been walking with a kind of absentminded determination, half wondering what to cook that night. She had run out of potatoes.

It was not as if she were diverted by much on this route any more. Every night after she returned home from work, while Frank sat glued to yet another 'unmissable' football match (Croatia versus some African country tonight), she would put on her trainers and walk three-quarters of a mile and back along the footpath that ran beside the common. It stopped her from niggling at Frank, while showing him that she did have a life without him. When he bothered to look up from the television, that is.

So she had almost ignored the distant ringing sound, subconsciously filing it with the car horns, the sirens, the other background noises of the city. But when it sounded shrilly, close by, she'd glanced behind her and, registering that there was nobody else around, slowed and followed the sound down to the bushes. And there it was, half hidden in the long grass – a mobile phone.

Miranda Lewis stood and looked down the empty path in front of her, then picked it up – the same model as her own. In the second it took her to register this, the ringing stopped. She was debating whether to leave it somewhere more visible when a chiming chord announced the arrival of a text message. It was from 'John C'.

She glanced around her, feeling oddly furtive. Then she reasoned – it could be the owner, asking the finder to return it, and after a brief hesitation she clicked on the message and opened it:

**Where U darling?** it read. **Its been 2 days!!!** Miranda stared at it and then, frowning, tucked the phone into her pocket and began to walk. There was no point leaving it in the grass. She would work out what to do when she got home.

Miranda, her best friend, Sherry, liked to remind her, was once a bit of a fox. If anyone else had emphasized the 'once' bit quite as much, Miranda might have been offended, but, as Sherry added, twenty years ago boys had actually genuflected at her feet. Miranda's daughter, Andrea, smirked when Sherry said this, as if the idea of her mother being remotely attractive to anyone were hilarious. But Sherry went on and on about it because Sherry was outraged by Frank's lack of appreciation.

Every time Sherry joined her on the evening walk, she would list Frank's faults, comparing him with her Richard. Richard got sad if Sherry left a room. Richard organized 'us' time every Friday for the two of them. Richard left love notes on her pillow. *That's because you never had kids, you earn more than he does, and Richard had an unsuccessful hair weave*, Miranda thought, although she never said it aloud.

But these last eighteen months, she had begun to hear Sherry's views a little differently. Because, if she allowed herself to think about it honestly, Frank had begun to irritate her. The way he snored. The way he always had to be reminded to empty the kitchen bin, even when it was visibly overflowing. The way he said plaintively, 'There's no milk!' as if the milk fairy had not paid a visit, even though she worked just as many hours as he did. The way his hand would snake across her on a Saturday night, as routine as his washing of the car, but with possibly less affection.

Miranda knew she was lucky to have a marriage that had lasted twenty-one years. She believed there was very little in life that could not be solved by a brisk walk and a dose of fresh air. She had been walking a mile and a half every day for the last nine months.

Back in the kitchen, a mug of tea beside her, she had, after the briefest struggle with her conscience, opened the message again.

**Where U darling? Its been 2 days!!!**

Its awful punctuation and abbreviation were somehow offset by the desperation within. She wondered whether to call John C and explain what had happened, how she'd come across the phone, but there was something in the intimacy of the message that made it feel like an intrusion.

*The owner's phone numbers*, she thought. I'll scroll through, and I'll find her. But there was nothing in the list of names. No clue except for John C. It all felt odd. *I don't want to call him*, she thought suddenly. She felt unbalanced by all this raw emotion, as if someone had intruded into her safe little house, her haven. She would hand the phone in at the police station, she decided, and then she registered another icon: Diary. And there it was: tomorrow's date, with '*Call travel agent*'. Below: '*Hair, Alistair Devonshire 2 p.m.*'.

The hairdresser had been easy to find; the name had sounded familiar, and as she looked it up in the directory, she realized she must have passed it many times. A discreetly expensive salon, off the high street. She would ask the receptionist to ask their two-o'clock booking if she'd lost a phone.

Two things happened that made Miranda falter in her resolve. The first was the fact that, seated on the bus in traffic, she had really very little to do except look at the stored pictures. And there he was, a smiling, dark-haired man, grinning into a mug, his eyes lifted in some intimate moment: John C. She glanced at more messages. Just to see if there were any clues, of course. Nearly all were from him.

Sorry could not call last night. W in foul mood, think looking for clues. Thought of you all night.

Can see you in your dress, my Scarlet Woman. The way it moves against yr skin.

Can you get away Thurs? Have told W am at conference. Dreaming of my lips on your skin.

And then a couple more that made Miranda Lewis, a woman who believed there was little in life that could surprise her, thrust the phone into her bag and pray that no one else could see the flaming of her cheeks.

She was standing in the reception area, her ears filled with the drone of a dozen hair dryers, already regretting her decision to come, when the woman approached her.

'Do you have an appointment?' she said. Her hair, a sleek aubergine colour, stuck up in unlikely tufts, and her eyes expressed her complete lack of interest in Miranda's answer.

'No,' said Miranda. 'Er . . . do you happen to have someone coming in at two o'clock?'

'You're in luck. She cancelled. Kevin can fit you in.' She turned away. 'I'll just get you a gown.'

Miranda was left seated, staring at her own reflection in the mirror; a slightly stunned-looking woman with the beginnings of a double chin and mousy hair that she hadn't had time to tidy since climbing off the bus.

'Hello.'

Miranda started as a young man appeared behind her.

'What can I do for you? Just a trim?'

'Oh. Um. Actually, this has been a bit of a mistake. I only meant to . . .'

At that moment her phone pinged, and with a muffled apology she rummaged in her bag to get it. She pressed TEXT MESSAGE and jumped slightly. The phone she had pulled out was not hers.

Been thinking about last time. You make my blood sing.

'All right, now? I've got to be honest, sweetheart. That's not the best style for you.' He picked up a limp lock of hair.

'Really.' Miranda stared at the message, meant for the person who should have been sitting in this chair. *You make my blood sing.*

'You want to go with something else? Shall we freshen up your look a bit? What do you think?'

Miranda hesitated. 'Yes,' she said, looking up at the woman in the mirror.

To her knowledge she had never made Frank's blood sing. He did occasionally tell her she looked nice, but it always seemed like something he felt he should say than something he really meant. It was actually the Arsenal centre forward who really made Frank's blood sing; quite often he would be down in front of the television thumping the carpet with excitement.

'Shall we go mad, then?' Kevin said, comb raised.

Miranda thought of her daughter, yawning audibly whenever Sherry went on about their teenage double dates. She thought of Frank, failing to even look up from the television when she returned home from work. *Hi, babe*, he would say, holding up a hand in greeting. A hand. As if she were a dog.

'I tell you what,' said Miranda. 'Whatever your two-o'clock appointment was going to have, I'll have.'

Kevin raised an eyebrow. 'Ohh . . . good choice,' he said, seemingly reappraising her. 'This is going to be fun.'

She had not run the footpath that night. She had sat in the kitchen and reread the messages and then jumped guiltily and glanced towards the living room when the next text arrived. Her heart gave a little lurch when she saw the name. She hesitated, then opened it.

Am worried about U. Too long now. Can bear it (just!) if you don't want to do this, but need to know U R OK. XXX.

She stared at the message, hearing its loving concern, its attempt at humour. Then she gazed up at her reflection, at the new, shorter cut with the reddish tint that Kevin had pronounced his best work all week.

Perhaps it was the fact that she didn't look like herself. Perhaps it was because she hated to see anyone suffer, and John C was clearly suffering. Perhaps it was because she had drunk several glasses of wine. But, her fingers trembling slightly, she typed a reply.

Am OK, she typed. Just difficult to talk right now. Then she added: X. She pressed SEND, then sat, her heart thumping, barely breathing until the return message came:

Thank God. Meet me soon, Scarlet Woman. Am blue without you. X.

A little cheesy, but it made her laugh.

After that first evening, it became easier to respond. John C would text her several times a day and she would reply. Sometimes, at work, she would find herself thinking about what she would say and her colleagues would remark upon her sudden blush, or her distractedness and make knowing remarks. She would smile and not disabuse them. Why would she, when John C's next text would arrive not half an hour later, professing his passion, his desperation to see her?

Once she had deliberately left one visible on her desk, knowing that Clare Trevelyan would not be able to stop herself from reading it – or passing on its contents in the smoking room. *Good*, she thought. *Let them wonder.* She liked the idea that she could surprise people occasionally. Let them think she was an object of passion, someone's Scarlet Woman. She developed a glint in her eye and a little bounce in her step, and she swore that the post boy hung around her desk far longer than he used to.

If occasionally it occurred to her that what she was doing was wrong, she buried the thought. It was just a bit of make-believe. John C was happy. Frank was happy. The other woman would probably reach him some other way, and then it would stop. She tried not to think about how much she would miss it, picturing herself doing the things he remembered them doing together.

It was almost two weeks when she realized she could no longer put him off. She'd told him that there was a problem with her phone, that she was waiting for a new one, and suggested that until then they speak only by text. But his messages had become insistent:

Why not Tues? May not have another chance till next week.

The English Gentlemen. A drink at lunchtime. Please!

What U trying to do to me?

It wasn't just that. John C had begun to consume her life. Sherry eyed her suspiciously and remarked how good she looked, how Frank must finally be doing something right, in a way that suggested she thought this unlikely. But John C's messages created an intimacy that Miranda had never felt with any other man. They shared the same sense of humour, could express even in abbreviated form the most complex and naked of emotions. Unable to tell him the truth, she told him her hopes and secret wishes, her dreams of travel to South America.

I'll take U there. I miss yr voice, Scarlet Woman, he told her.

I hear yrs in my dreams, she replied, and blushed at her own audacity.

Finally she had sent him the crucial message:

The English Gentlemen. Thursday. 8 p.m.

She wasn't sure why she had done it. Part of her, the old Miranda, knew that this couldn't continue. That it was a temporary madness. And then there was new Miranda, who, while she might never be able to admit this to herself, had started to think of John C as *her* John. Miranda might not be the phone's original owner, but John C would have to admit that there had been a connection. That the woman he had spent the last thirteen days talking to was someone who stirred him, who made him laugh, who scrambled his thoughts. If nothing else, he had to acknowledge that. Because his messages had changed her; they had made her feel alive again.

Thursday evening found her fussing over her makeup like a teenager on her first date. 'Where are you off to?' said Frank, looking up from the television. He seemed a little taken aback, even though she was wearing a long coat. 'You look nice.' He scrambled up from the sofa. 'I meant to tell you. I like your hair.'

'Oh, that,' she said, blushing slightly. 'Drink with Sherry.'

Wear your blue dress, John C had said. She had bought one specially, low in front with a kick in the skirt.

'Have fun,' Frank said. He turned back to the television and lifted the remote.

Miranda's confidence briefly evaporated at the pub. She had nearly turned back twice on the way there and still could not work out what to say if she saw anyone she knew. Plus, the pub was not the kind of place where they dressed up, she'd seen too late, so she kept her coat on. But then, half a glass in, she changed her mind and shrugged it off. John C's lover would not feel self-conscious drinking alone in a blue dress.

At one point a man came up and offered her a drink. She had startled, and then, realizing that it was not him, had declined. 'I'm waiting for someone,' she said, and enjoyed his regretful look as he walked away.

He was almost fifteen minutes late when she picked up her phone. She would text him. She was just starting her message when she looked up to find a woman standing at her table.

'Hello, Scarlet,' she said.

Miranda blinked at her. A youngish blonde woman, wearing a wool coat. She looked tired, but her eyes were feverish, intense.

'I'm sorry?' she said.

'It's you, isn't it? Scarlet Woman? Gosh, I thought you'd be younger.' There was a sneer in her voice. Miranda put down the phone.

'Oh, I'm sorry. I should have introduced myself. I'm Wendy. Wendy Christian. John's wife?' Miranda's heart stalled.

'You did know he had one, right?' The woman held up a matching mobile phone. 'He mentioned me enough times, I see. Oh, no.' Her voice lifted theatrically. 'Of course, you didn't realize it wasn't him you've been talking to these last two days. I took his phone. It's me. It was all me.'

'Oh, God,' Miranda said quietly. 'Look, there's been –'

'– a mistake? You bet there has. This woman has been sleeping with my husband,' she announced to the pub in a ringing, slightly tremulous voice. 'Now she has decided that this might have been a mistake.' She leaned forward over the table. 'Actually, Scarlet, or whatever you call yourself, it's been my mistake, marrying a man who thinks that having a wife and two small children doesn't mean he can't keep screwing around.'

Miranda felt the sudden silence of the pub, the collective eyes burning into her. Wendy Christian took in her stricken expression. 'You poor fool. Did you think

313

you were the first? Well, Scarlet, you're actually number four. And that's just the ones I know about.'

Miranda's vision had become strangely blurry. She kept waiting for the normal sounds of the pub to resume around her, but the silence, oppressive now, continued. Finally she grabbed her coat and bag and ran past the woman to the door, her cheeks burning, her head down against the accusing stares.

The last thing she heard as the door swung behind her was the sound of a phone ringing.

'That you, babe?' Frank raised a hand as he heard her pass by the doorway of the living room. Miranda was suddenly grateful for the irresistible draw of the television. Her ears echoed with the accusations of that embittered wife. Her hands were still trembling.

'You're home early.'

She took a deep breath, staring at the back of his head over the sofa.

'I decided,' she said, slowly, 'that I didn't really want to go out.'

He glanced behind him. 'Richard will be pleased. He doesn't like Sherry going out, does he? Thinks someone's going to steal her away from him.'

Miranda stood very still. 'Do you?'

'Do I what?'

'Worry that someone will steal me away?' She felt electrified, as if whatever he said would have far greater implications than he knew.

He turned to face her and smiled. 'Course. You were a fox, remember?'

'Were?'

'Come here,' he said. 'Come and give me a cuddle. It's the last five minutes of Uruguay versus Cameroon.' He held out a hand, and, after a moment, she took it.

'Two minutes,' she said. 'There's something I have to do first.'

In the kitchen she reached for the mobile phone. Her fingers, this time, were assured.

Dear John C, she wrote. A ring on the finger is worth two on the phone. You'd do well to learn this. She paused, then added: Foxy.

She pressed SEND, then turned off the phone, stuffing it deep into the kitchen bin. She sighed, kicked off her shoes, and then she made two cups of tea and walked them through to the living room, where Uruguay were just about to take a penalty that would propel Frank to the carpet, pounding the wool with delight. Miranda sat and stared at the television screen, smiling distantly at her husband and trying to ignore the distant but persistent sound, somewhere deep in her mind, of a phone ringing.

# Margot

It wasn't the seven-hour flight delay that would finish her off, thought Em, as she again blocked the bearded man from edging his backside on to her plastic seat. It wasn't even the thought of the impending family Christmas. It was the carol singers. The beaming, sweat-shirted choir who had now been singing their tuneless festive medley for two solid hours.

'How long have you been waiting?'

The American woman's gnarly old hand landed squarely on Em's leg, causing her to jump. Em smiled, the kind of smile you use on strangers in emerald-green jackets and matching turbans who could be anywhere from sixty-five to a hundred and five.

'Since eleven. You?'

'Three hours. I'm bored out of my skin already. And if these asses don't shut up, I'm going to play whack-a-mole with their heads using my duty-free gin.' The American woman coughed emphatically into a purple handkerchief. 'Where are you headed, darling?'

'England. Back to my parents.'

'A family Christmas. How lovely for you.' She grimaced. 'My idea of hell. Let's get a drink.'

It sounded like an order. But what else did she have to do? Em found herself following in the wake of the tiny, brightly dressed old woman, who shooed passengers out of her path imperiously and ordered two double Scotches. 'On the rocks. And none of that Irish crap. I'm Margot,' she rasped, downing hers and tapping the bar for another. 'And now you must tell me why such a pretty girl looks so damn sad. Apart from the fact that Christmas is, obviously, intolerable.'

Em swallowed and tried not to grimace. What the hell? She would never see this woman again. 'Well, I'm going home to tell my family that my husband has left me. That would be my brother and his perfect wife, their three perfect kids, my sister and her fiancé, and my parents. Married thirty-four years.'

'Who was it?'

'Who was what?'

'Don't tell me. His secretary. How drearily predictable.'

Em bristled. Was it so obvious? She hadn't been able to face putting on makeup lately. Even the basics seemed beyond her right now.

'Darling, cheer up. It's not the end of the world. Really. By the time you get to number four it barely even registers. And who wants to be perfect? Ugh.' She cackled, tapping Em's glass. 'Drink up. It's medicinal.'

Em hesitated.

'Oh for goodness sake, you're not going to end up on Skid Row if you cut yourself a bit of slack for one day. It's Christmas! We're in purgatory! Chin chin! Then we'll go.'

'Go where?'

The airport was a hot, heaving mass of choleric passengers overburdened with battered gifts and harassed retail staff, the warbling carol singers' voices omnipresent. Margot's birdlike hand gripped Em's sleeve all the way to Duty Free, where she pulled her to a halt in front of the Chanel concession.

'Stay still.' As the shop assistant looked on, incredulous, Margot pulled a deep red Chanel lipstick from its case and carefully painted Em's lips. 'In times of trouble, paint on a smile,' she said. 'That's what my Mama told me. She'll take it,' she announced. 'Where's your mascara?' The girl, apparently paralysed, reached into a drawer and produced one.

'There,' said Margot, once she had finished. 'Now, perfume.' She spritzed Em with something expensive before handing the opened box to the open-mouthed assistant. 'Sweetheart. You should have more testers, otherwise what else can customers do? Let's go, Emmy darling.'

Em found herself propelled into the luxury goods area. Margot exclaimed at shoes, handbags, diamond necklaces ('More use than alimony!'). Em's head was whoozy from the whisky, and she kept giggling at Margot's emphatic cussing.

'What is *wrong* with these damn people! Like the walking dead! Oh, look, Hermes. Don't you love Hermes?'

'I – I don't know.'

Under the hot lights, Margot pulled scarf after scarf from the display, draping them around Em's neck. 'There! You look fabulous! Better than some slutty New Jersey secretary, huh?' The blue scarf felt divine. Even the assistant broke into a brief smile of approval. Then Em glanced down at the price tag.

'Oh, gosh . . . Actually, I feel a little hot. I think I need to . . .'

Margot rolled her eyes at the assistant. 'And they say British girls hold their drink. Go splash your face, darling. Mind your makeup.'

In the Ladies, Em gazed at her reflection. A little flushed from the alcohol, yes, but the mascara and the red lips had turned her into someone she didn't recognize. She straightened up, smoothing her hair. Then she smiled.

*Better Than Some Slutty New Jersey Secretary.*

When she emerged, Margot was squinting up at the departures screen. 'Heathrow, right? You're up, kiddo. And don't you look better! Are you good? Did we have fun?'

'Yes . . . but . . . I don't even –'

'Strangers on a train. The most fun. Now go, forget that lousy cheating husband, and tell your family you'll be just fine. Because you will. Chin chin!' Margot gripped her arm, coughed, and with a cheery wave, disappeared into the throng.

Em treated herself to a taxi from Heathrow. It felt like something Margot would suggest. She sat and watched the blurred grey streets of West London and wondered if she really did want to leave New York after all. That was the home of the new start, right?

But first things first. She reached into her bag for the new lipstick, and it was then that she saw it – a small bag, marked *Hermes*. She peeled back the tissue and pulled out the blue silk scarf. Nestled alongside it was a note, hastily scrawled on the back of a printed letter: 'Merry Christmas – knock 'em dead, kiddo. Chin chin! Margot.'

The letter bore the address of a Florida oncology clinic.

Em tied the scarf carefully round her neck. She closed her eyes and raised a silent glass to the tiny woman in the green turban.

'Chin chin, Margot,' she whispered. 'Merry Christmas to you, too.'

# The Christmas List

Pink Fritillary. Only David's mother would insist on a perfume nobody has ever heard of. Chrissie has walked the length of the West End, and each department store has told her, 'Oh, no. We don't stock that. Try . . .'

As she pushes her way through the crowds, she begins to wonder if Diana has done it deliberately. Just so she can say with a sigh on Christmas Day, *Oh! David said you were getting me perfume. Still . . . this is . . . nice.* Chrissie will not give her the satisfaction. She trudges down Oxford Street, dodging the harassed shoppers laden with shiny bags, ducking into shops until her shoes rub, her ears filled with the tinny sound of 'Jingle Bells' on an electronic loop. One day, she thinks, she will remember that the twenty-third is no time for last-minute shopping.

In Selfridges another assistant shrugs and looks blank. Chrissie thinks she might cry. Outside, it has begun to rain. She feels the weight of the carrier bags pulling at her shoulders and does something she has never done before. She heads into one of the glossy bars and orders a large glass of wine. She drinks it swiftly, feeling mutinous, and overtips as she leaves, as if she is the kind of woman who does this all the time.

'Right,' she says as she heads for the doors. 'One last

push.' And then she sees it, a rare sight on a wet London street: a taxi with its light on. She dives off the pavement, and it swerves to meet her.

'Uh . . . Liberty, I think.' She hurls her bags on to the back seat and sinks into it gratefully. She has never been in the back of a London taxi without feeling vaguely as if she has been rescued from something.

'You "think"?'

'I need a particular perfume. For my mother-in-law. Liberty is my last hope.'

She can see only his amused eyes in the mirror, the close-cut hair of the back of his head.

'Your husband can't help?'

'He doesn't really do shopping.'

The driver raises an eyebrow. There is a whole world in that raised eyebrow. And then her phone pings:

Did you pick up dollars for my NY trip?

She'd had to go all the way home to fetch her passport, because the bank wouldn't let her without it. It's why she is late now. Yes, she types. She waits a moment, but he does not respond.

'Do you buy presents, then?' she asks the driver.

'Yeah. I love all that. Mind you, this year my daughter's come home to live with us because she's had a baby, so . . . we're being a bit careful with what we spend.'

'Is she on her own?' The wine has made her garrulous. It's one of the reasons David doesn't like her drinking.

'Yeah. She had a bloke, bit older, but he said he didn't

want kids. She fell pregnant, and it turns out he meant it. It's a bit of a squash, and money's tight, but . . .' She can hear the smile in his voice. 'It's lovely.'

*I don't want children*, David had told her, right at the beginning. *I never have.* She had heard the words as if through a muffler. Some part of her had always assumed he would simply change his mind.

'Lucky her. Having you.'

'You have any?'

'No,' she says. 'None.'

The taxi queues patiently in the heaving, wet street. Beside it a shop front blares 'Jingle Bells' at deafening volume. The driver glances up.

'Looking forward to Christmas?'

'Not really. My mother-in-law doesn't like me very much. And she's staying a full ten days. Along with her other son, who speaks in grunts and keeps the remote control in his trouser pocket. I'll probably just hide out in the kitchen most of the time.'

'Doesn't sound like much fun.'

'Sorry. I'm a grinch. Actually, I've had a large white wine. Which means I'm saying what I think.'

'Don't you usually, then? Say what you think?'

'Never. Safer that way.' She tries to mask the words with a cheery smile, but there is a short, painful silence. Get a grip, she scolds herself.

'Tell you what,' he says. 'My wife has a friend who works for Liberty. I'll call home. What's this perfume called?'

She can't help eavesdropping. His voice, on the telephone, is low, intimate. Before he rings off, he laughs at some shared joke. She and David have no shared jokes. Somehow the realization of this makes her feel sadder than anything.

'Forget Liberty. Little perfume shop round the back of Covent Garden, she says. Want me to try it?'

She leans forward. 'Oh, yes, please!'

'She knew the perfume. Says it's lovely. And pricey.' He grins conspiratorially.

'Yup. That sounds like Diana.'

'Well, now you'll be in her good books, won't you? Hold on – I'm going to do a U-ey.'

He lurches across the road, and she laughs as she is thrown to the other side of the seat. He grins. 'I love doing that. One day I'm going to get caught.'

'Do you like your job?' She pushes herself upright.

'Love it. My customers are generally OK . . . I don't stop for everyone, you know. Only people who look all right.'

'I looked "all right", then?' She is still laughing.

'You looked anxious. I hate to see an anxious-looking woman.'

She knows immediately what he means. It's the expression that seems to have taken root on her face these last few years: the furrowed brow, the compressed lips. When did I turn into this woman? she thinks. When my boss left and Ming the Merciless took over. When my husband began spending every night behind a laptop, chatting to people I don't know. When I stopped look-ing at myself in shop windows.'

'I've offended you.'

'No . . . I just wish I weren't. Anxious-looking. I didn't used to be.'

'Maybe you need a holiday.'

'Oh, no. We have to take his mother these days. Which isn't really a holiday. Mind you, he gets loads of business trips to lovely places.'

The driver raises his hand in greeting to another taxi driver. 'Where would you go, then? If you could go anywhere?'

She thinks. 'My best friend, Myra, lives in Barcelona. She has her own restaurant, right in the centre. She's the most amazing chef. I think I'd go there. I haven't seen her for years. We email, but it's not the same. Oh. Excuse me. Phone.' She scrabbles in her bag and gazes at the illuminated screen.

Don't forget the stilton Mum likes from that special cheese shop.

Her heart sinks. She had completely forgotten.

'Everything OK?' the driver says after a pause.

'I forgot the cheese. I was meant to go to a shop in Marylebone.' She can't keep the despair from her voice.

'All the way over there? For cheese?'

'She only likes one particular kind of Stilton.'

'Blimey. She's a tough customer,' he says. 'You want me to turn round? Traffic's not great.'

She sighs. Gathers her bags around her. 'No. I'd

better get the Tube. I've probably already blown my taxi budget. Can you pull over?'

His eyes meet hers. 'Nah. Tell you what, I'll turn the meter off.' And he does.

'You can't do that!'

'Just did. I do it once a year. Every year. You're this year's lucky recipient. Tell you what – we'll do the perfume, then we'll go back via the cheese shop, and I'll drop you at your station afterwards. A little Christmas present . . . ah, don't . . . I was trying to put a smile back on that face.'

Something odd has happened. Her eyes have filled with tears. 'Sorry,' she says, wiping at her face. 'I don't know what's come over me.'

He smiles reassuringly. It makes her want to cry more.

'We'll sort the perfume. That'll make you feel better.'

He is right about the traffic. They sit in queues, lurching into sporadic action along back routes. The whole of London feels grey and wet and ill-tempered. She feels lucky in the snug taxi, one step removed from the awfulness of outside. He talks about his wife, of how he likes to get up with the baby at dawn so his daughter can sleep, just him and the little mite in his arms, gazing up at him. When he stops talking, she has almost forgotten why they have come to a halt. 'I'll wait here. Leave your bags,' he says.

The perfume shop is a gloriously scented haven. 'Pink Fritillary,' she says, observing, as she reads her husband's handwriting, what a delicate scent to put on such a sullen, lumpen woman.

'I'm afraid we're out of the fifty-millilitre,' the woman says, reaching behind her. 'We only have the hundred-millilitre left. And it's the parfum, not the eau de toilette. Is that OK?'

It is twice what she has budgeted. But the thought of Diana's face . . . *Oh!* she would exclaim, the corners of her mouth pulling down towards her jaw. *You got the cheap version! Never mind. I'm sure it's just as good for every day . . .*

'It's fine,' Chrissie says. She'll worry about the expense in January. The shopgirl wraps it in six layers of pink tissue.

'Got it!' Chrissie says as she clambers back into the taxi. 'I got the bloody perfume.'

'There you go!' He makes it sound as if she has achieved something wonderful. 'Right. Marylebone it is.'

They chat, her leaning forward through the hatch. She tells him about the passport and the dollars, and he shakes his head. She tells him how she loved her job until the new supervisor arrived, a man for whom she can apparently do nothing right. She says little of David, feeling disloyal. But she wants to. She wants to tell someone how lonely she is. How she feels she is missing some clue: the late nights, the business trips. How she feels stupid and tired and old.

And then they are at the cheese shop. There is a long queue visible through the big glass window, but the driver doesn't seem to mind. He cheers when she finally emerges with the heavy, stinking wheel. 'You're done!' he says, like she has achieved a miracle, and she can't help cheering, too.

333

And then her phone beeps:

I asked you specifically to get the Waitrose Christmas pudding. You've bought the Marks & Spencer pudding. I have just had to go to Waitrose myself, as you are taking so long, and they have sold out. I have no idea what we are going to do about this.

It is as if she has been winded. Suddenly she sees the four of them around the table, hears David's pointed apology to his family for her 'wrong' Christmas pudding. And something in her gives.

'I can't do it,' she says.

'Can't do what?'

'Christmas. I can't sit there with the cheese and the wrong Christmas pudding and . . . them. I just . . . can't.'

He pulls over. She stares at her bags. 'What am I doing? You say you have nothing, but you have a family you adore. I have a posh Stilton and three people who don't even really like me.'

He turns in his seat. He is younger than she thought. 'So what's keeping you?'

'I'm married!'

'Last time I looked, it was an agreement, not a prison sentence. Why not go to your friend's? Would she be pleased to see you?'

'She'd love it. Even her husband would. They're always asking me to come. They're . . . they're . . . cheerful.'

He lifts his eyebrows. Laughter lines fan out from each eye.

'I can't just . . . go.'

'You have your passport in your bag. You told me.'

Something has ignited in her stomach, a flash of burning brandy on a steamed pudding.

'I could drop you at King's Cross. Get the Piccadilly line to Heathrow, jump on a flight. Seriously. Life is short. Too short to look that anxious.'

She thinks of Christmas freed of Diana's disapproval. Of her husband's unfriendly slab of a back, his claret-soaked snore.

'He'd never forgive me. It would be the end of my marriage.'

The driver grins. 'Well, wouldn't that be a tragedy?'

They stare at each other. 'Do it,' she says suddenly.

'Hold tight.' And with a screech, he does his second U-turn of the day.

The whole way around the back streets, her heart thumps. Bubbles of laughter keep forcing their way out of her chest. Myra's response is quick and unequivocal: YES!! COME!! Chrissie thinks of her supervisor, glaring at his watch when she does not turn up at work after the Christmas break. She thinks of Diana's appalled dis-belief. She thinks of Barcelona and Myra's husband's emphatic bear hugs and their surprised laughter. And then they are at King's Cross station. And the driver is screeching to a halt.

'You really going to do it?'

'I'm really going to do it. Thank you –'

'Jim,' he says. And he reaches through the hatch and shakes her hand.

'Chrissie,' she says. She pulls the shopping bags from the seat. 'Oh. All this stuff . . .'

And then she looks up. 'Here – give the perfume to your wife. And the vouchers. For your daughter.'

'You don't need to –'

'Please. It would make me happy.'

He hesitates, then accepts the bags, shaking his head. 'Thank you. She'll absolutely love it.'

'I don't suppose you want the Stilton, too?'

He grimaces. 'Can't stand the stuff.'

'Nor me.'

They both start to laugh.

'I feel . . . a bit insane, Jim.'

'I think it's called the spirit of Christmas,' he says. 'I'd just go with it.'

She starts to run towards the concourse, her legs flying up like a girl's. Then she pauses, dumps the cheese ceremonially into a bin, and looks up in time to see him, one hand lifted in salute. As she runs through the crowds towards the ticket office and he navigates his way back into the crawling Christmas traffic, they are both still laughing.

# Acknowledgements

Thank you to those who first used these stories: Radio 4, *Woman & Home*, *Stylist*, The Orion Publishing Group, Bragelonne and Penguin Books.

Coming soon – the greatly anticipated third
Lou Clark novel, following the number one
international bestsellers *Me Before You* and *After You*

# jojo
# moyes
## Still Me

**Praise for Jojo Moyes**

'Raw, funny, real and sad, this is storytelling at its best'
*Marie Claire*

'Moyes somehow manages to break your heart
before restoring your faith in love'
*Sunday Express*

**AVAILABLE TO ORDER NOW**

Know, first, who you are; and then adorn yourself
accordingly.

Epictetus

# Chapter One

It was the moustache that reminded me I was no longer in England; a solid, grey millipede firmly obscuring the man's upper lip; a Village People moustache, a cowboy moustache, the miniature head of a broom that meant business. You just didn't get that kind of moustache at home. I couldn't tear my eyes from it.

'Ma'am?'

The only person I had ever seen with a moustache like that at home was Mr Naylor, our maths teacher, and he collected Digestives crumbs in his; we used to count them during algebra.

'Ma'am?'

'Oh. Sorry.'

The man in the uniform motioned me forward with a flick of his stubby finger. He did not look up from his screen. I waited at the booth, long-haul sweat drying gently into my dress. He held up his hand, waggling four fat fingers. This, I grasped after several seconds, was a demand for my passport.

'Name.'

'It's there,' I said.

'Your name, ma'am.'

'Louisa Elizabeth Clark.' I peered over the counter. 'Though I never use the Elizabeth bit. Because my mum realised after they named me that it would make me Lou Lizzy. And if you say that really fast it sounds like lunacy. Though my dad says that's kind of fitting. Not that I'm a lunatic. I mean, you wouldn't want lunatics in your country. Hah!' My voice bounced nervously off the Perspex screen.

The man looked at me for the first time. He had solid shoulders and a gaze that could pin you like a Tazer.

He did not smile. He waited until my own faded.

'Sorry,' I said. 'People in uniform make me nervous.'

I glanced behind me at the immigration hall, at the snaking queue that had doubled back on itself so many times it had become an impenetrable, restless sea of people. 'I think I'm feeling a bit odd from standing in that queue. That is honestly the longest queue I've ever stood in in my life. I'd begun to wonder whether to start my Christmas list.'

'Put your hand on the scanner.'

'Is it always that size?'

'The scanner?' He frowned.

'The queue.'

But he was no longer listening. He was studying something on his screen. I put my fingers on the little pad. And then my phone dinged.

Mum: *HAVE YOU LANDED?*

I went to tap an answer with my free hand but the man turned sharply toward me.

'Ma'am, you are not permitted to use cell phones in this area.'

'It's just my mum. She wants to know if I'm here.' I surreptitiously tried to press the thumbs-up emoji as I slid the phone out of view.

'Reason for travel?'

*WHAT IS THAT?* came Mum's immediate reply. She had taken to texting like a duck to water and could now text faster than she could speak. Which was basically warp speed.

*YOU KNOW MY PHONE DOESN'T DO THE LITTLE PICTURES. IS THAT AN SOS? LOUISA TELL ME YOU'RE OKAY.*

'Reason for travel, ma'am.' The moustache twitched with irritation. He added slowly: 'What are you doing here in the United States?'

'I have a new job.'

'Which is . . .?'

'I'm going to work for a family in New York. Central Park.'

Just briefly, the man's eyebrows might have raised a millimetre. He checked the address on my form, confirming it.

'What kind of job?'

'It's a bit complicated. But I'm sort of a paid companion.'

'A *paid companion.*'

'It's like this – I used to work for this man. I was his companion but also I would give him his meds and take him out and feed him – that's not as weird as it sounds, by the way – he had no use of his hands. It wasn't like something pervy. But the thing is it's hard not to get close to people you look after and Will – the man – was amazing and we . . . well, we fell in love . . .' Too late, I felt the familiar welling of tears. I wiped at my eyes briskly. 'So I think it'll be a bit like that. Except for the love bit. And the feeding.'

I looked up. The immigration officer was staring at me. I tried to smile. 'Actually I don't normally cry talking about jobs. I'm not like a genuine lunatic, despite my name. Hah! But I loved him. And he loved me. And then he . . . well, he chose to end his life. And so this is sort of my attempt to start over.'

I wiped my palms at the tears that were now leaking relentlessly, embarrassingly, from the corners of my eyes. I couldn't seem to stop them. I couldn't seem to stop anything.

'Sorry. Must be the jet lag. It's something like two o'clock in the morning in normal time, right? Plus I don't really talk about him anymore. I mean, I have a new boyfriend. And he's great! He's a paramedic! And hot! That's like winning the boyfriend lottery, right? A hot paramedic?'

I scrabbled around in my handbag for a tissue. When I looked up, the man was holding out a box.

I took one.

'Thank you. So anyway, my friend Nathan – he's from New Zealand – works here and he helped get me this job and I don't really know what it involves yet apart from looking after this rich man's wife who gets depressed. But I've decided this time I'm going to live up to what Will wanted for me, because I didn't get it right before. I just ended up working in an airport.'

I froze. 'Not – uh – that there's anything wrong with working at an airport! I'm sure Immigration is a very important job. *Really* important. But I have a plan. I'm going to do something new every week that I'm here and I'm going to say yes.'

'Say yes?'

'To new things. Will always said I shut myself off from new experiences. So this is my plan.'

The officer studied my paperwork.

'You didn't fill the address section out properly. I need a zip code.'

He pushed the form towards me. I checked the number on the sheet that I had printed out and filled it in with trembling fingers.

I looked to my left, where the queue at my section was growing restive. At the front of the next queue a Chinese family was being questioned by two officials. As the woman protested, they were led into a side room. I felt suddenly very alone.

The immigration officer glanced down the line at the people waiting. And then, abruptly, he stamped my passport.

'Good luck, Louisa Clark,' he said.

I stared at him. 'That's it?'

'That's it.'

I smiled. 'Oh, thank you! That's really kind. I mean, it's quite weird being on the other side of the world by yourself for the first time and now I feel a bit like I just met my first nice new person and –'

'You need to move along now, ma'am.'

'Of course. Sorry.'

I gathered up my belongings and pushed a sweaty frond of hair from my face.

'And, ma'am.'

'Yes?' I turned, wondering what I had got wrong now.

He didn't look up from his screen.

'Be careful what you say yes to.'

Nathan was waiting in Arrivals, as he had promised. I scanned the crowd, feeling self-conscious, secretly convinced that nobody would come, but there he was, his huge hand waving above the shifting bodies around him. He raised his other arm, a smile breaking across his face, and pushed his way through to meet me, picking me up off my feet in a gigantic hug.

'Lou!'

At the sight of him, something in me constricted unexpectedly – something linked to Will and loss and the raw emotion that comes from sitting on a slightly too bumpy flight for seven hours – and I was glad that he held me tight, so that I had a moment to compose myself. 'Welcome to New York, shorty! Not lost your dress sense, I see.'

He held me at arm's length, grinning. I straightened my 1970s tiger-print dress. I had thought it might make me look like Jacqueline Onassis. If Ms Onassis had spilled half her airline coffee on her lap.

'It's so good to see you.'

He swept up my leaden suitcases like they were filled with feathers. 'C'mon. Let's get you back to the house.

The Prius is in for servicing so Mr G lent me his driver's car. Traffic's terrible, but you'll get there in style.'

Mr Gopnik's driver's car was sleek and black and the size of a bus and the doors closed with that emphatic, discreet *thunk* that signalled a six-figure price tag. Nathan shut my cases in the boot and I settled into the passenger seat with a sigh. I checked my phone, answered Mum's fourteen texts with one that told her simply that I was in the car and would call her tomorrow. And then answered Sam's, which told me he missed me, with *Landed xxx*.

'How's the fella?' said Nathan, glancing over at me.

'He's good, thanks.' I added a few more *xxxx*s just to make sure.

'Wasn't too sticky about you heading over here?'

I shrugged. 'He thought I needed to come.'

'We all did. Just took you a while to find your way, is all.'

I put my phone away, sat back in my seat, and gazed out at the unfamiliar names that dotted the highway, Milo's Tire Shop, Richie's Gym, the ambulances and U-Haul trucks, the rundown houses with their peeling paint and wonky stoops, the basketball courts and drivers sipping from oversized plastic cups. Nathan turned on the radio and I listened to someone called Lorenzo talking about a baseball game, and felt, briefly, as if I were in some kind of suspended reality.

'So you've got tomorrow to get straight. Anything you want to do? I thought I might let you sleep in and then drag you out to brunch? You should have the full NY diner experience on your first weekend here.'

'Sounds great.'

'They won't be back from the country club till tomorrow evening. There's been a bit of strife this last week. I'll fill you in when you've had some sleep.'

I stared at him. 'No secrets, right? This isn't going to be –'

'They're not like the Traynors. It's just your average dysfunctional multimillionaire family.'

'Is she nice?'

'She's great. She's . . . a handful. But she's great. He is too.'

That was as good a character reference as you were likely to get from Nathan. He lapsed into silence – Nathan never was big on gossip – and I sat in the smooth, air-conditioned Mercedes GLS and fought the waves of sleep that kept threatening to wash over me. I thought about Sam, now fast asleep several thousand miles away in his railway carriage. I thought of Treena and Thom, tucked up in my little flat in London. And then Nathan's voice cut in.

'There you go.'

I looked up through gritty eyes and there it was across the Brooklyn Bridge – Manhattan – shining like a million jagged shards of light; awe-inspiring, glossy, impossibly condensed and beautiful, a sight that was so familiar from television and films that I couldn't quite accept I was seeing it for real. I shifted upright in my seat, dumbstruck as we sped towards it, the most famous metropolis on the planet.

'Never gets old, that view, eh? Bit grander than Stortfold.'

I don't think it had actually hit me until that point. *My new home.*

'Hey, Ashok. How's it going?' Nathan wheeled my cases through the marble lobby as I stared at the black-and-white tiles and the brass rails and tried not to trip, my footsteps echoing in the cavernous space. It was like the entrance to a grand, slightly faded hotel: the elevator in burnished brass, the floor carpeted in a red and gold livery, the reception a little darker than was comfortable. It smelt of beeswax and polished shoes and money.

'I'm good, man. Who's this?'

'This is Louisa. She'll be working for Mrs G.'

The uniformed porter stepped out from behind his desk and held out a hand for me to shake. He had a wide smile and eyes that looked like they had seen everything.

'Nice to meet you, Ashok.'

'A Brit! I have a cousin in London. Croy-down. You know Croy-down? You anywhere near there? He's a big fella, you know what I'm saying?'

'I don't really know Croydon,' I said. And then when his face fell: 'But I'll look out for him the next time I'm passing through.'

'Louisa. Welcome to The Lavery. You need anything, or you want to know anything, you just let me know. I'm here twenty-four seven.'

'He's not kidding,' said Nathan. 'Sometimes I think he sleeps under that desk.'

'Three kids under five, man,' said Ashok. 'Believe me, being here keeps me sane. Can't say it does the same for my wife, but you know.' He grinned. 'Seriously, Miss Louisa. Anything you need, I'm your man.'

'As in drugs, prostitutes, houses of ill repute?' I whispered as the elevator doors closed around us.

'No. As in theatre tickets, restaurant tables, best place to get your dry cleaning done,' Nathan said. 'This is Fifth Avenue. Jesus. What have you been doing back in London?'

The Gopnik residence comprised seven thousand square feet on the second and third floors of the huge limestone building, a rare duplex in this part of New York, and testament to generations of Gopnik family riches. This, Nathan told me, was one of the oldest co-ops on the Upper East Side. Nobody could buy or sell an apartment here without the approval of a board of residents who were staunchly resistant to change. While the glossy condominiums across the park housed the new money – Russian oligarchs, pop stars, Chinese steel magnates, and tech billionaires – with communal restaurants, gyms, child care and infinity pools, the residents of The Lavery liked things Old School.

These apartments were passed down through generations; their inhabitants learned to tolerate the 1930s plumbing system, fought lengthy and labyrinthine battles for permission to alter anything more extensive than a light switch, and looked away politely from the way that New York was changing around them in the same way one might ignore a beggar with a cardboard sign.

I barely glimpsed the grandeur of the duplex itself, with its parquet floors, elevated ceilings, and floor-to-ceiling damask drapes, as we headed straight to the staff quarters, which were tucked away at the far end of the second floor, down a long narrow corridor that led off from the kitchen – an anomaly left over from a distant age. The newer or refurbished buildings had no staff quarters: housekeepers and nannies would travel in from Queens or New Jersey on the dawn train and return after dark. But the Gopnik family had owned these tiny rooms since the building was first built. They could not be developed or sold, but were tied through deeds to the main residence, and lusted after as storage rooms. It wasn't hard to see why they might naturally be considered storage.

'There you go.' Nathan opened a door and dropped my bags.

My room measured approximately twelve foot by twelve foot. It housed a double bed, a television, a chest of drawers and a closet; a small armchair, uphol-stered in beige fabric, sat in the corner, its sagging seat testament to previous exhausted occupants. A small window may have looked south. Or north. Or east. It was hard to tell, as it was approximately six feet from the blank bricked rear of a building so tall that I could only see the sky if I pressed my face up against the window and craned my neck.

Nathan was next door, alongside a communal kitchen to be shared by me, Nathan and a housekeeper, whose own room was across the corridor.

I gazed around me. On my bed sat a neat pile of five dark-green polo shirts and what looked like black trousers, bearing a cheap Teflon sheen.

'They didn't tell you about the uniform?'

I picked up one of the polo shirts.

'It's just a shirt and trousers. The Gopniks think a uniform makes it simpler. Everyone knows where they stand.'

'If you want to look like a pro golfer.'

I peered into the tiny bathroom, tiled in limescale-encrusted brown marble, which opened off the side of the bedroom. It housed a loo, a small basin that looked like it dated from the 1940s, and a shower. A paper-wrapped soap and a can of cockroach killer sat on the side.

'It's actually pretty generous by Manhattan standards,' Nathan said. 'I know it looks a little tired but Mrs G says we can give it a splosh of paint. A couple of extra lamps and a quick trip to Crate and Barrel and it'll –'

'I love it,' I said. I turned to him, my voice suddenly shaky. 'I'm in New York, Nathan. I'm actually here.'

He patted me on the shoulder. 'Yup. You really are.'

I managed to stay awake just long enough to unpack, eat some takeaway with Nathan (he called it takeout, like an actual American) and flick through some of the 859 channels on my little television, the bulk of which seemed to be on an ever-running loop of American football, adverts for digestive issues, or badly lit crime shows I hadn't heard of, and then I zonked out before waking with a start at 4.45am. For a few discombobulating minutes I was confused by the distant sound of an unfamiliar siren, the low whine of a reversing truck – then I flicked

CHAPTER ONE

on the light switch, realised where I was, and a jolt of excitement whipped through me.

I pulled my laptop from my bag and tapped out a chat message to Sam.

You there? xxx

I waited, but nothing came back. I couldn't remember when he had said he was on duty, and was too befuddled to work out the time difference. I put my laptop down and tried briefly to get back to sleep (Treena said when I didn't sleep enough I looked like a sad horse). But the unfamiliar sounds of the city were a siren call, and at six I finally climbed out of bed and showered, trying to ignore the rust in the sputtering water that exploded out of the shower head. I dressed (denim pinafore sundress and a vintage turquoise short-sleeved blouse bearing a picture of the Statue of Liberty) and went in search of coffee.

I padded along the corridor, trying to remember the location of the staff kitchen that Nathan had shown me the previous evening. I opened a door and a woman turned and stared at me. She was middle-aged and stocky around the middle, with her hair set in neat dark waves, like a 1930s movie star. Her eyes were beautiful and dark but her mouth dragged down at the edges, as if in permanent disapproval.

'Um . . . good morning!'

She kept staring at me.

'I – I'm Louisa? The new girl? Mrs Gopnik's . . . assistant?'

'She is not Mrs Gopnik.'

The woman left this statement hanging in the air.

'You must be . . . ' I racked my jet-lagged brain but no name was forthcoming. *Oh, come on*, I willed myself. 'I'm so sorry. My brain is like porridge this morning. Jet lag.'

'My name is Ilaria.'

'Ilaria. Of course, that's it. Sorry.' I stuck out my hand. She didn't take it.

'I know who you are.'

'Um . . . can you show me where Nathan keeps his milk? I just wanted to get a coffee.'

'Nathan doesn't drink milk.'

'Really? He used to.'

'You think I lie to you?'

'No. That's not what I was s—'

She stepped to the left and gestured towards a wall cupboard that was half the size of the others and ever so slightly out of reach. 'That is your cupboard.'

Then she opened the fridge door to replace her juice and I noticed the full two-litre bottle of milk on her shelf. She closed it again and gazed at me implacably.

'Mr Gopnik will be home at six-thirty this evening. Dress in uniform to meet him.' And she headed off back down the corridor, her slippers slapping against the soles of her feet.

'Lovely to meet you! I'm sure we'll be seeing loads of each other!' I called after her.

I stared at the fridge for a moment, and then decided it probably wasn't too early to go out for milk. This was the city that never slept, after all.

\*

New York might be awake, but The Lavery was cloaked in a silence so dense it suggested communal doses of Zopiclone. I walked along the corridor, closing the front door softly behind me and checking eight times that I had remembered both my purse and keys. I had planned to use the service lift, but figured the early hour and the sleeping residents gave me licence to look a little closer at where I had ended up.

As I tiptoed along, the plush carpet muffling my steps, from inside one of the doors a dog started to bark – a yappy, outraged protest – and an elderly voice shouted something muffled that I couldn't make out. I hurried past, not wanting to be responsible for waking up the other residents, and instead of making my way down the main stairs, headed downstairs in the service lift.

There was nobody in the lobby so I let myself out on to the street and stepped straight into a clamour of noise and light so overwhelming that I had to stand still for a moment just to stay upright. In front of me the green oasis of Central Park stretched on. On my left, the side streets were already busy – enormous men in overalls unloaded crates from an open-sided van, watched by a cop with arms like sides of ham crossed over his chest. A road sweeper hummed industriously. A taxi driver chatted to a man through his open window. I counted off the sights of the Big Apple in my head. Horse-drawn carriages! Yellow taxis! Impossibly tall buildings! As I stared, two weary tourists with children in buggies pushed their way past me clutching Styrofoam coffee cups, still operating perhaps on some distant time zone.

Manhattan stretched in every direction, enormous, sun-tipped, teeming, and glowing.

My jet lag evaporated with the last of the dawn. I took a breath and began to walk, aware that I was grinning but quite unable to stop myself.

I walked eight blocks without seeing a single convenience store. I walked over to Madison Avenue, past huge glass-fronted luxury stores with their doors locked, and, dotted between them, the occasional restaurant, windows darkened like closed eyes, or a gilded hotel whose liveried doorman didn't look at me as I passed.

I walked another five blocks, realising gradually that this wasn't the kind of area where you could just nip to the grocer's. I had pictured New York diners on every corner, staffed by brassy waitresses and men with white pork pie hats, but everything looked huge and glossy and not remotely like a cheese omelette or mug of tea might be waiting behind its doors. Most of the people I passed were tourists like me, or fierce, jogging hard-bodies, sleek in Lycra and oblivious between earphones, stepping nimbly around homeless men who glared from furrowed, lead-stained faces. Finally I stumbled upon a large coffee bar, one of a chain, in which half of New York's early risers seemed to have congregated, bent over their phones in booths or feeding preternaturally cheerful toddlers, with generic easy listening music filtering through speakers on the wall.

I ordered a cappuccino and a muffin, which, before I could say anything, the barista sliced in two, heated, and slathered in butter, all the while never breaking his conversation about a baseball game with the barista next to him.

I paid, sat down with the muffin wrapped in foil, and then took a bite. It was, even without the clawing jet-lag hunger, the most delicious thing I had ever eaten.

I sat in a window seat gazing out at the early morning Manhattan street for half an hour or so, my mouth alternately filled with claggy, buttery muffin or scalded by hot, strong coffee, giving free rein to my ever present internal monologue *('I am drinking New York coffee in a New York coffeehouse!' 'Just been walking along a New York street! Like Meg Ryan! Or Diane Keaton!' 'I am in Actual New York!')* and, briefly, I understood exactly what Will had been trying to explain to me two years previously; for those few minutes, my mouth full of unfamiliar food, my eyes filled with strange sights, I existed only in the moment. I was fully present, my senses alive, my whole being open to receive the new experiences around me. I was in the only place in the world I could possibly be.

And then, apropos of apparently nothing, two women at the next table launched into a fist fight, coffee and bits of pastry flying across two tables, baristas leaping to pull them apart, and so I dusted the crumbs off my dress, closed my bag, and decided it was probably time to return to the peace of The Lavery.

The stunning sequel to *Me Before You*

jojo
moyes
after
you

THE SEQUEL TO
me before you

Also by

# jojo
# moyes

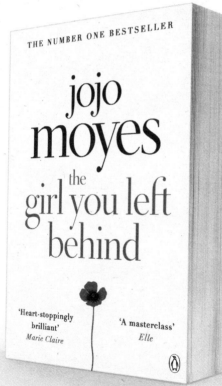

THE NUMBER ONE BESTSELLER

jojo
moyes
the
girl you left
behind

'Heart-stoppingly
brilliant'
*Marie Claire*

'A masterclass'
*Elle*

# He just wanted a decent book to read ...

Not too much to ask, is it? It was in 1935 when Allen Lane, Managing Director of Bodley Head Publishers, stood on a platform at Exeter railway station looking for something good to read on his journey back to London. His choice was limited to popular magazines and poor-quality paperbacks – the same choice faced every day by the vast majority of readers, few of whom could afford hardbacks. Lane's disappointment and subsequent anger at the range of books generally available led him to found a company – and change the world.

*'We believed in the existence in this country of a vast reading public for intelligent books at a low price, and staked everything on it'*
**Sir Allen Lane, 1902–1970, founder of Penguin Books**

The quality paperback had arrived – and not just in bookshops. Lane was adamant that his Penguins should appear in chain stores and tobacconists, and should cost no more than a packet of cigarettes.

Reading habits (and cigarette prices) have changed since 1935, but Penguin still believes in publishing the best books for everybody to enjoy. We still believe that good design costs no more than bad design, and we still believe that quality books published passionately and responsibly make the world a better place.

So wherever you see the little bird – whether it's on a piece of prize-winning literary fiction or a celebrity autobiography, political tour de force or historical masterpiece, a serial-killer thriller, reference book, world classic or a piece of pure escapism – you can bet that it represents the very best that the genre has to offer.

## Whatever you like to read – trust Penguin.